BRI

INVISIBLE DEATH

BRIAN FLYNN was born in 1885 in Leyton, Essex. He won a scholarship to the City Of London School, and from there went into the civil service. In World War I he served as Special Constable on the Home Front, also teaching "Accountancy, Languages, Maths and Elocution to men, women, boys and girls" in the evenings, and acting in his spare time.

It was a seaside family holiday that inspired Brian Flynn to turn his hand to writing in the mid-twenties. Finding most mystery novels of the time "mediocre in the extreme", he decided to compose his own. Edith, the author's wife, encouraged its completion, and after a protracted period finding a publisher, it was eventually released in 1927 by John Hamilton in the UK and Macrae Smith in the U.S. as *The Billiard-Room Mystery*.

The author died in 1958. In all, he wrote and published 57 mysteries, the vast majority featuring the super-sleuth Antony Bathurst.

BRIAN FLYNN

INVISIBLE DEATH

With an introduction by
Steve Barge

DEAN STREET PRESS

INTRODUCTION

"I believe that the primary function of the mystery story is to entertain; to stimulate the imagination and even, at times, to supply humour. But it pleases the connoisseur most when it presents – and reveals – genuine mystery. To reach its full height, it has to offer an intellectual problem for the reader to consider, measure and solve."

THUS WROTE Brian Flynn in the *Crime Book Magazine* in 1948, setting out his ethos on writing detective fiction. At that point in his career, Flynn had published thirty-six mystery novels, beginning with *The Billiard-Room Mystery* in 1927 – he went on, before his death in 1958, to write twenty-one more, three under the pseudonym Charles Wogan. So how is it that the general reading populace – indeed, even some of the most ardent collectors of mystery fiction – were until recently unaware of his existence? The reputation of writers such as John Rhode survived their work being out of print, so what made Flynn and his books vanish so completely?

There are many factors that could have contributed to Flynn's disappearance. For reasons unknown, he was not a member of either The Detection Club or the Crime Writers' Association, two of the best ways for a writer to network with others. As such, his work never appeared in the various collaborations that those groups published. The occasional short story in such a collection can be a way of maintaining awareness of an author's name, but it seems that Brian Flynn wrote no short stories at all, something rare amongst crime writers.

There are a few mentions of him in various studies of the genre over the years. Sutherland Scott, in *Blood in Their Ink* (1953), states that Flynn, who was still writing at the time, "has long been popular". He goes on to praise *The Mystery of the Peacock's Eye* (1928) as containing "one of the ablest pieces of misdirection one could wish to meet". Anyone reading that particular review who feels like picking up the novel – out now from Dean Street Press – should stop reading at that point, as later in the book, Scott proceeds to casually spoil the ending, although as if he assumes that everyone will have read the novel already.

It is a later review, though, that may have done much to end – temporarily, I hope – Flynn's popularity.

"Straight tripe and savorless. It is doubtful, on the evidence, if any of his others would be different."

Thus wrote Jacques Barzun and Wendell Hertig Taylor in their celebrated work, *A Catalog of Crime* (1971). The book was an ambitious attempt to collate and review every crime fiction author, past and present. They presented brief reviews of some titles, a bibliography of some authors and a short biography of others. It is by no means complete – E & M.A. Radford had written thirty-six novels at this point in time but garner no mention – but it might have helped Flynn's reputation if he too had been overlooked. Instead one of the contributors picked up *Conspiracy at Angel* (1947), the thirty-second Anthony Bathurst title. I believe that title has a number of things to enjoy about it, but as a mystery, it doesn't match the quality of the majority of Flynn's output. Dismissing a writer's entire work on the basis of a single volume is questionable, but with the amount of crime writers they were trying to catalogue, one can, just about, understand the decision. But that decision meant that they missed out on a large number of truly entertaining mysteries that fully embrace the spirit of the Golden Age of Detection, and, moreover, many readers using the book as a reference work may have missed out as well.

So who was Brian Flynn? Born in 1885 in Leyton, Essex, Flynn won a scholarship to the City Of London School, and while he went into the civil service (ranking fourth in the whole country on the entrance examination) rather than go to university, the classical education that he received there clearly stayed with him. Protracted bouts of rheumatic fever prevented him fighting in the Great War, but instead he served as a Special Constable on the Home Front – one particular job involved warning the populace about Zeppelin raids armed only with a bicycle, a whistle and a placard reading "TAKE COVER". Flynn worked for the local government while teaching "Accountancy, Languages, Maths and Elocution to men, women, boys and girls" in the evening, and acting as part of the Trevalyan Players in his spare time.

It was a seaside family holiday that inspired him to turn his hand to writing. He asked his librarian to supply him a collection of mystery novels for "deck-chair reading" only to find himself disappointed. In his own words, they were "mediocre in the extreme." There is no record of what those books were, unfortunately, but on arriving home, the following conversation, again in Brian's own words, occurred:

> "ME (unpacking the books): If I couldn't write better stuff than any of these, I'd eat my own hat.
>
> Mrs ME (after the manner of women and particularly after the manner of wives): It's a great pity you don't do a bit more and talk a bit less.
>
> The shaft struck home. I accepted the challenge, laboured like the mountain and produced *The Billiard-Room Mystery*."

"Mrs ME", or Edith as most people referred to her, deserves our gratitude. While there were some delays with that first book, including Edith finding the neglected half-finished manuscript in a drawer where it had been "resting" for six months, and a protracted period finding a publisher, it was eventually released in 1927 by John Hamilton in the UK and Macrae Smith in the U.S. According to Flynn, John Hamilton asked for five more, but in fact they only published five in total, all as part of the Sundial Mystery Library imprint. Starting with *The Five Red Fingers* (1929), Flynn was published by John Long, who would go on to publish all of his remaining novels, bar his single non-series title, *Tragedy At Trinket* (1934). About ten of his early books were reprinted in the US before the war, either by Macrae Smith, Grosset & Dunlap or Mill, and a few titles also appeared in France, Denmark, Germany and Sweden, but the majority of his output only saw print in the United Kingdom. Some titles were reprinted during his lifetime – the John Long Four-Square Thrillers paperback range featured some Flynn titles, for example – but John Long's primary focus was the library market, and some titles had relatively low print runs. Currently, the majority of Flynn's work, in particular that only published in the U.K., is extremely rare – not just expensive, but seemingly non-existent even in the second-hand book market.

In the aforementioned article, Flynn states that the tales of Sherlock Holmes were a primary inspiration for his writing, having read them at a young age. A conversation in *The Billiard-Room Mystery* hints at other influences on his writing style. A character, presumably voicing Flynn's own thoughts, states that he is a fan of "the pre-war Holmes". When pushed further, he states that:

> "Mason's M. Hanaud, Bentley's Trent, Milne's Mr Gillingham and to a lesser extent, Agatha Christie's M. Poirot are all excellent in their way, but oh! – the many dozens that aren't."

He goes on to acknowledge the strengths of Bernard Capes' "Baron" from *The Mystery of The Skeleton Key* and H.C. Bailey's Reggie Fortune, but refuses to accept Chesterton's Father Brown.

> "He's entirely too Chestertonian. He deduces that the dustman was the murderer because of the shape of the piece that had been cut from the apple-pie."

Perhaps this might be the reason that the invitation to join the Detection Club never arrived . . .

Flynn created a sleuth that shared a number of traits with Holmes, but was hardly a carbon-copy. Enter Anthony Bathurst, a polymath and gentleman sleuth, a man of contradictions whose background is never made clear to the reader. He clearly has money, as he has his own rooms in London with a pair of servants on call and went to public school (Uppingham) and university (Oxford). He is a follower of all things that fall under the banner of sport, in particular horse racing and cricket, the latter being a sport that he could, allegedly, have represented England at. He is also a bit of a show-off, littering his speech (at times) with classical quotes, the obscurer the better, provided by the copies of the *Oxford Dictionary of Quotations* and *Brewer's Dictionary of Phrase & Fable* that Flynn kept by his writing desk, although Bathurst generally restrains himself to only doing this with people who would appreciate it or to annoy the local constabulary. He is fond of amateur dramatics (as was Flynn, a well-regarded amateur thespian who appeared in at least one self-penned play, *Blue Murder*), having been a member of OUDS, the Oxford University Dramatic Society. Like Holmes, Bathurst isn't averse to the occasional disguise, and as with Watson and Holmes, sometimes even his close allies don't recognise him. General information about his background is light on the ground. His parents were Irish, but he doesn't have an accent – see *The Spiked Lion* (1933) – and his eyes are grey. We learn in *The Orange Axe* that he doesn't pursue romantic relationships due to a bad experience in his first romance. That doesn't remain the case throughout the series – he falls head over heels in love in *Fear and Trembling*, for example – but in this opening tranche of titles, we don't see Anthony distracted by the fairer sex, not even one who will only entertain gentlemen who can beat her at golf!

Unlike a number of the Holmes' stories, Flynn's Bathurst tales are all fairly clued mysteries, perhaps a nod to his admiration of Christie, but first and foremost, Flynn was out to entertain the reader. The problems posed to Bathurst have a flair about them – the simultaneous murders, miles apart, in *The Case of the Black Twenty-Two* (1928) for example, or the scheme to draw lots to commit masked murder in *The Orange Axe* – and there is a momentum to the narrative. Some mystery writers have trouble with the pace slowing between the reveal of the problem and the reveal of the murderer, but Flynn's books sidestep that, with Bathurst's investigations never seeming to sag. He writes with a wit and intellect that can make even the most prosaic of interviews with suspects enjoyable to read about, and usually provides an action-packed finale before the murderer is finally revealed. Some of those revelations, I think it is fair to say, are surprises that can rank with some of the best in crime fiction.

We are fortunate that we can finally reintroduce Brian Flynn and Anthony Lotherington Bathurst to the many fans of classic crime fiction out there.

Invisible Death (1929)

"My master was murdered, sir, in a way that we couldn't see! Murdered by those perishers just as surely as if they'd cut his bloody throat."

THERE WAS some confusion when researching Brian Flynn as to the correct chronological order of *Invisible Death* and *The Five Red Fingers*. *Invisible Death* was the final book to be published by John Hamilton, whereas *The Five Red Fingers* was the first to be released by John Long, the publisher who Flynn would remain with for the rest of his career (bar the standalone children's title *Tragedy at Trinket*). Possibly due to the switch in publishers, *The Five Red Fingers* was released first (September 1929, as opposed to December 1929) and refers to Flynn as the author of "The Silver Troika", presumably a working title for *Invisible Death*. Thankfully, we have Flynn's habit of referring to earlier adventures in his books to clear up which came first. In *Invisible Death*, Peter Daventry recalls the five previous cases that Bathurst has solved, including the murder of Julius Maitland. Hence, despite the jump from one publisher to another, and back again, *The Five Red Fingers* is the fifth Antony Bathurst mystery and *Invisible Death* is the sixth.

Invisible Death has a fascinating setting, so much so that the casual reader may be confused as to what sort of tale they are reading. After five mystery novels that are very much in the classic style, we open with Anthony Bathurst in Liverpool doing his best to elude a group of four undesirables – "a man with a withered arm or something, a huge, dirty, brown-bearded client, a fat, silky-voiced slug of a man who hisses out his words" and "Mister Beaux Yeux" – as Bathurst tries to reach Swallowcliffe Hall in Lancashire. He has been summoned by Constance Whittaker, a cousin of Diana Prendergast (*The Murders Near Mapleton*), to protect her husband, Major Whittaker, from an unnamed threat. The opening section plays out more like a thriller, as Bathurst enlists Peter Daventry (from *The Case Of The Black Twenty-Two*) to help him elude his pursuers and reach Swallowcliffe Hall in one piece. Daventry seems to have changed somewhat since that first encounter, not just in his speech patterns, but he now seems to be something of a man of action, a crack shot and good in a fight.

After a few close shaves, Bathurst arrives to find the house under siege from the villains, the so-called Silver Troika, but as they attack, the plot suddenly reveals itself to be the murder mystery the the reader would be expecting from Flynn. One of the household suddenly drops dead, despite the Troika – or anyone else – being nowhere near him. When poison is revealed to be the method of execution, Bathurst finds himself asking how the villains can poison from a distance, or whether someone else entirely is to blame . . .

After the locked room of *The Case Of The Black Twenty-Two*, Flynn returned to the "impossible crime" genre once again with this impossible poisoning. The idea of poison introduced by unknown means is not uncommon in the genre, but often it is a case of which of many potential delivery methods was used, or one obvious method that was not in fact the case (such as in *Strong Poison* by Dorothy L Sayers). Here, there seems to have been no way that the fast-acting poison could have been delivered. In more recent times, it has been a problem posed a number of times by historical mystery writer Paul Doherty, such as in *The Nightingale Gallery* but probably the best known example in the genre is *The Red Widow Murders* by Carter Dickson or the Dorothy L. Sayers short story "The Poisoned Dow '08", both of which have use very different methods than here.

Invisible Death met with praise from the reviewers of the time, despite seemingly eluding the attention of the national press. The *Northern Whig* describes it as "an excellent tale of its kind" featuring "a number of fresh ideas and ingenious plots". The *Aberdeen Press and Journal* praises Flynn for using "several red herrings with great skill", while the *Dundee Courier* describes it as an "an eery skeery drama" and a "nightmare sensation", which has "the compulsion of the *Ancient Mariner*".

For unknown reasons, *Invisible Death* was the first of Flynn's titles not to be released in the United States – the first four titles were published by Macrae Smith almost simultaneously with the UK releases, and *The Five Red Fingers* came seven years after the original release, by which time Macrae Smith had published five other titles from later in the range. *Invisible Death*, despite its original setting, was completely overlooked and has, as far as we can ascertain, never been reprinted since that time, an oversight that we are delighted to be able to correct.

Steve Barge

CHAPTER I
MR. BATHURST FEELS THE NEED OF COMPANIONSHIP

IT WAS when Mr. Bathurst realised that no fewer than four gentlemen that day had evinced a most inquisitive and unwholesome interest in his comings and goings that he definitely decided to chance his arm and send for Peter Daventry. For he felt that Peter must be a source of comfort to him. Odds of two to one he had never found completely deterrent—sometimes he had even found them attractive—but odds of three to one—the condition that he had discovered to be in existence at nineteen minutes past eleven that morning—had been sufficiently impressive to give him pause. When the three became four—about half-an-hour later—it was time to pull a man out of the pack and strengthen the back division.

Mr. Bathurst had been in Liverpool almost exactly three hours. As he sat in 'Rigby's' over a 'Guinness' and a most delectably-appetising crab sandwich that a white-habited attendant had brought him and came to the momentous decision recorded above, he thought also that it would be just as well to take at the same time entire stock of the situation. This fourth gentleman to have obtruded himself upon Mr. Bathurst's vision sat at a table in the opposite corner of the bar, ostensibly employed with a glass of spirits and a newspaper. Inasmuch as Mr. Bathurst had noticed him at his heels at the top of Water Street, had encountered him again outside St. George's Hall, had turned suddenly to find him at his elbow as he crossed Lord Street and now found him partaking of refreshment in the same hostelry, he had no doubt whatever as to the soundness and accuracy of his conclusions. The man was not attractive—that is to say, physically. His chief bodily feature was a pair of wolfish, red-lidded eyes, sore and inflamed. He was of middle height. "A decidedly nasty-looking customer," reflected Mr. Bathurst, "in whom, as I sit here, I will apparently show no interest. But all the same a worthy addition to the gallery that I had named for the time being 'The

League of the Dauntless Three'." There was the tall, thin, lithe man whose left coat-sleeve dangled empty, who had met him seemingly accidentally as he had left the Brunswick Dock early that morning and who had asked him the direction to Upper Hill Street; there was the huge, dirty, brown-bearded fellow who had lurked in the shadow of the dock wall while the interview was taking place and whom Mr. Bathurst had observed afterwards from the corner of his eye join the empty-sleeved gentleman a little further up the street; and then there had been the rubicund, fat-faced, sleek-headed gentleman who had ranged alongside him on the platform of Brunswick Dock station on the overhead railway and whom just previously Mr. Bathurst had heard behind him ask for his ticket at the booking-office in a strangely hissing sort of voice. Curiously enough for the same station—Pierhead—that Mr. Bathurst himself had desired.

He called the waiter and ordered another 'Guinness' and another plate of crab sandwiches. Being anchored in 'Rigby's' certainly had its points. After a moment or two's careful reflection, he took a letter from his pocket and proceeded to read it. He knew all the time that the gentleman with the red eyelids was watching him from the other corner. One of his sweeping, comprehensive glances round the bar assured him of the fact. Nevertheless Mr. Bathurst felt that to read the letter in full view of this person with the pretty eyes would matter little. He and his companions in the shadowing business evidently knew as much already as the reading of the letter would convey. Besides, it might give the gentleman food for thought. Anthony Bathurst read again what he had previously read very many times before.

> "Swallowcliffe Hall,
> Buttercross,
> LANCASHIRE.
> August 7th, 1928.

Dear Mr. Bathurst,

My cousin, Diana Prendergast, whom you met at Mapleton some time ago, I believe, advises me that she feels sure that you will help us in our trouble.

I say 'our' because I think to do so will perhaps influence your decision. But my husband, Major Guy Sanderson Whittaker, is in grave danger and appeals to you for help. If you can see your way to answer this appeal, your answer must be as secret as possible, because his enemies must not know that you have joined forces with us. You have a week in which to act. To-day is Tuesday. If you decide to help us, you must be here by next Monday. If you can give us the help which we implore, a car'll meet you at the tram terminus at Aigburth on Monday evening next at nine o'clock. You will recognise it from the fact that the chauffeur will wear a crimson gardenia in his uniform and will accost you with the words, 'There's no moon like the hunter's moon.' To this you will reply, 'But it waxes and wanes.' He will then drive you to Ugford Moor, where you will alight to enter a horse-driven cart that will be awaiting you on the edge of the moor. The driver of this cart will greet you with the phrase, 'There's no star like the Arctic star.' You will reply, 'Then let the She-Bear reign.' He will put you down eventually half a mile from Swallowcliffe Hall. Walk the rest of the way and when you reach the Hall itself ask for 'Diana.' But for God's sake come, Mr. Bathurst! My cousin assures me that you would never be heedless of a cry for help. Come and earn the undying gratitude of

Yours very sincerely,

CONSTANCE V. WHITTAKER."

Beyond assisting Anthony Bathurst to form the opinion that either his lady correspondent or her husband probably had racing interests, the letter had taught him very little. Investigations made subsequently to its receipt had given him the additional information that Major G. S. Whittaker, D.S.O., of the 3rd Northshire Regiment, had served with distinction in France, 1914-1917, had been wounded there twice and had eventually been sent upon a most important diplomatic mission to Petrograd in the autumn of 1917. It seemed to be for this latter service that he had been given the D.S.O. He was now living in retirement at Swallowcliffe Hall, Buttercross, Lancashire. However, after some cogitation, Mr. Bathurst had decided that the lady should not seek his services in vain. He felt that the cry for help at least was genuine, that the distress came from her heart, that once again he was being asked to step into what might very well prove to be very deep waters. The somewhat fantastic precautions that were going to be taken to ensure his safe and secret arrival at Swallowcliffe Hall hinted at something very dark and very sinister. But perhaps Mr. Bathurst found this an added incentive.

On the Thursday following the writing of Mrs. Whittaker's letter, therefore, Anthony had slipped a revolver into his pocket, made certain arrangements, telephoned to a very old friend, heard as a result news that was definitely good and suitable and as a consequence had travelled down equipped to Whelan's Wharf, Northfleet, where he boarded a Dutch-built cement boat. 'The Oarsman' ran between Northfleet and Liverpool and as a friend of the owner Mr. Bathurst was made very welcome by the genial skipper, Captain Hawley. He placed his own cabin at Mr. Bathurst's disposal and generally took him to his heart. Save for a slight bucketing round the Foreland, weather held good and 'The Oarsman' made Liverpool on the Monday morning.

Mr. Bathurst reflected as he glanced across the apartment and finished his last appetising square of crab sandwich that if he wanted Peter Daventry, as he had decided that he most certainly did, he had very little time left in which to get him—that is, if he were to prove of any use. He looked at his wrist-watch and, looking up suddenly from it, met "Red Lids'" eyes fixed fairly and squarely upon him. He determined upon his immediate plan of campaign. He beckoned to the waiter. As the latter approached his table, Mr. Bathurst inquired for an *A.B.C.* The inquiry was made in quiet tones, but the elocution was sufficiently good for the words to travel distinctly across the apartment and for "Red Lids" to hear.

"I want a train for London," remarked Anthony in casual confidence and most competent enunciation. "Thank you."

"Yes, sir. I'll get it for you, sir."

Three minutes later Mr. Bathurst became aware that the two-thirty-five restaurant-car from Euston should land Mr. Daventry (and a few hundred others) at Lime Street by a quarter to seven at night. It was now twenty minutes past twelve. He resolved to take no unnecessary risks. It could be done and it should be done. For the benefit of the matinee idol who was watching him, Mr. Bathurst took his fountain-pen and appeared to jot down the times of a few convenient trains. To the waiter standing at the side of his table he pointed them out with every appearance of solicitude. But the waiter, as he bent to look at the writing, read something entirely different. Mr. Bathurst's inscription read as follows: "I want the following message 'phoned at once. It is most important. Can you do it without exciting undue attention? If you can, say nothing but 'yes', nod your head and don't show the slightest surprise." Underneath was the message and the necessary particulars for its delivery.

Luckily the waiter was intelligent. "Yes, sir," he nodded.

Mr. Bathurst smiled nonchalantly, closed the A.B.C. carelessly, returned it to his new-found ally, leant back in his chair and extended a pound note.

"When you bring me the change, which by the way I shall not require, except of course for the sake of appearances, let me know exactly what happened."

"Thank you, sir." The waiter bowed as he accepted what Mr. Bathurst handed to him. "I will try to be as quick as possible, sir."

"I am sure you will," murmured Anthony, ostentatiously pointing to his wrist-watch with an equally ostentatious and dubious shake of the head.

The waiter vanished with alacrity.

Mr. Bathurst extracted a cigarette from his case and elaborately tapped the end on the back of it.

"God send Daventry's in," he murmured to himself, "for I'm thinking that before long I'll be needing him! Despite all my precautions, I seem to have set a pretty hornet's nest of beauties buzzing round my ears. Ah well, here's luck to a bonny struggle and good hunting!" He drained his 'Guinness' to the last drop and with the same affected coolness that he had shown before, lit the cigarette that he had just previously taken. The gentleman opposite was still watching him. "I hope this waiter Johnny isn't too long, else my patrician friend over there with the inflamed blinkers will smell at least a couple of rats. He will become the vision of suspicion. Getting a note changed shouldn't take too—"

His pessimistic musings were happily cut short by the appearance in the offing of the friendly attendant. The latter proffered a tray upon which were scattered a ten-shilling note and a number of loose coins. Mr. Bathurst made a pretence of picking up some of the coins.

"Well?" he asked under his breath. "What luck?"

"Everything O.K., sir. I got your message through, sir, and the answer is 'all right'. Lime Street, six-forty-five, sir!" The waiter spoke very quietly.

Mr. Bathurst nodded an almost imperceptible acceptance of the situation as it had developed and rose from his seat, obviously about to take his departure.

"Thank you, waiter. That's all right. If you see a gentleman follow me out rather pointedly, get in his way for a moment or two, will you, because I have an idea that he's not a gentleman— at least not what you or I or any thoroughly nice person would call one."

The waiter grinned in appreciation of Mr. Bathurst's sally. The latter made his way out and with his few seconds' start turned sharply to the left.

"What I must keep in front of me," he said to himself, "is the fact that when I meet Peter Daventry at Lime Street at six-forty-five or thereabouts this evening, I must endeavour to be unattended by any one of my four 'musketeers'. They're well-informed, but I don't see how they can possibly be expecting Daventry, so it will be as well for me to keep him up my sleeve as the unknown factor. Advantage number one."

He crossed the road behind an oncoming tram to run on ahead and re-cross it in front of the same vehicle. The shop he found facing him gave him an idea. It was a "Finnis."

"I want a hat and a light raincoat."

"Same sort of hat as you're wearing, sir?"

"On the contrary! An entirely different one! I propose to invest in, say, a fawn 'snap-brim'. The 'bowler' I find a trifle heavy for the time of the year."

Whilst he spoke, Anthony kept a sharp watch on the entrance. As he did so, to his intense surprise and discomfiture a figure passed across the front of the shop. It was the fat-faced man with the voice that hissed! Judging from the somewhat anxious expression on the gentleman's face, he was not aware of Mr. Bathurst's precise whereabouts, for he looked both worried and perturbed.

"So near and yet so far," murmured Mr. Bathurst commiseratingly, as he tried on the first hat.

"I beg your pardon, sir?" queried the assistant.

"That's very nice of you. It does me good to hear you say that. How much did you say this one was? It suits me very well, don't you think? And don't forget I want a coat as well."

Freshly-hatted and newly-habited, Anthony paid his bill and asked another question.

"The best way to Birkenhead, sir? Well, you can please yourself. There are two—and either's aw reet. Take tram to Pierhead and then take ferry over. Or cross t' road a little lower down and take tube railway. There's naught wrong with either."

Mr. Bathurst thanked him and departed. He looked up and down the street. For the moment at least the coast seemed clear. There were no signs of the 'companions'. A tram was passing with destination-indicator showing 'Pierhead'. He boarded it, swinging himself on to the platform with smooth celerity. Temporarily he appeared to have successfully eluded the espionage.

Alighting at the terminus, there was still nothing to indicate that this idea of his was in any way inaccurate. Anthony thereupon decided to survey the entire situation from every angle as dispassionately as possible. He had approximately a matter of five hours to fill up before the arrival of Peter Daventry. The best thing that he could do, he considered, would be to disappear. For the time being, to efface himself temporarily from the busy life of the City of Liverpool.

He adjusted his thinking-cap. If one of the four shadowers had by any unlucky chance seen him board the Pierhead-bound car, he would be certain to have deduced the possibility of Anthony employing the ferry. Mr. Bathurst, as was his wont, came to a sudden decision. He determined to lose himself for a period before burying himself in beautiful Birkenhead. He crossed the road again and, walking hurriedly down the 'Piazza', came to a hairdressing saloon. A hair-cut, shave and shampoo would cut a comfortable and considerable wedge into the better part of three-quarters of an hour. He would play 'possum' in a barber's shop.

The attendant was not unduly garrulous, taking into account his profession, and Mr. Bathurst had reached the supremely dishevelled stage of the wet shampoo when another customer entered and proceeded to occupy the next chair but one to his left. Anthony was just quick enough to repress a start and watch him carefully through the long mirror that faced him. It was the man with the red eye-lids! Things were getting warm again!

CHAPTER II
WHICH MR. DAVENTRY IS DELIGHTED TO SUPPLY

As THE hairdresser wielded the towel and the electric drier, Mr. Bathurst found it very necessary to screw his face up and produce a series of quite tolerable grimaces. During his shave, it did not take him very long to form the opinion that the gentleman who had recently entered the establishment had not yet recognised him, if indeed he had noticed his presence at all. The door was almost directly behind the line of chairs and the pegs upon which hung Mr. Bathurst's hat and coat were on the right—that is to say, in the opposite direction to which "Red Lids" was sitting. He decided that it would be quite possible to give his sore-eyed friend a good view of his back when he vacated his chair and settled his bill during the usual brushing-down process. Then, by the judicious use as cover of his hat and outstretched arm, he might effectively shield his face as he made his exit through the door. Carrying out this idea immediately, he brought off his manoeuvre and made his way into the street.

Walking to the end of the row of shops, he looked round. There was no one in sight to disconcert him, but he realised that the man he had left behind might be at any minute. There was certainly no time to waste. Crossing quickly, Anthony reached the landing-stage.

The Woodside boat was on the point of leaving and he was only just in time to get aboard. He scanned the faces of the crowd, mixed and motley as it was. Holidaymakers, workers and casual sightseers jostled each other indiscriminately and very often, it must be said, discourteously. As far as Mr. Bathurst could judge from his quick tour of inspection, the 'Daffodil', proud in the glory of her illustrious history, was innocent of (1) the man with the empty sleeve, (2) the man with the dirty brown beard, (3) the man with the hissing voice, and (4) Monsieur 'Beaux Yeux'.

Birkenhead reached, Anthony once again was quick to swing himself upon a passing car.

"As far as you go, conductor, wherever it is. But no farther."

"Tranmere, sir."

"That'll do," returned Mr. Bathurst. "I'm just having a look round. What sort of place is it? Worse than Wigan?"

The conductor grinned. "Tha'll see it all in five minutes. Tha'll reckon it better than Wigan." Then he brightened perceptibly. "It's where 'Dixie' Dean came fra'."

After a brief run, the car ascended a steep hill and Mr. Bathurst alighted. Three o'clock! He bought a paper and walked into the recreation ground, one of the first places to which he came. The day was gloriously hot, the sky beautifully cloudless. There were worse things than stretches of green turf! Mr. Bathurst discovered one such stretch and extended his lithe length.

There was certainly one operation he intended to perform before nine o'clock that night and, as François Villon had it, when he preened it in the plumes of the Grand Constable, "there is no time like the now time." Mr. Bathurst, as he lay on the Tranmere turf, overhauled his revolver thoroughly and satisfied himself that it was in complete working order. This performed, he exhausted the interest of the paper and then resolved to scribble a hasty note to Sir Austin Kemble, the Commissioner of Police at Scotland Yard. It would be just as well to let Sir Austin know exactly where he was and where he was likely to be during the next few days or so, besides which he desired to thank him for something. Self-reliance is not rendered any less effective by a due measure of care. He would post the letter on his way back to Birkenhead. Between then and now a little sleep might not be out of place. Who knew what the coming night would bring forth? There were very few people about now and Anthony was absolutely certain that he had not been followed by anybody since he had left the landing-stage at Liverpool. He reflected again that, as he was unaware of what lay in front of him that night at Swallowcliffe Hall, the rest would without doubt prove to be invaluable.

For just over half-an-hour, Mr. Bathurst permitted himself to sleep. At ten minutes to six, he started to stroll quietly back to Birkenhead. Dropping Sir Austin Kemble's letter in the first pillar-box that he passed, Anthony found himself on the Liverpool ferry at thirteen minutes past six and on the Pierhead again at twenty-five minutes past. If they traced him again before the six-forty-five ran into Lime Street, they would be damned lucky!

He arrived at the bookstall with about eleven seconds to spare, picked up his suitcase from the cloak room and two minutes later was holding Peter Daventry's hand in his.

"It's good of you to come, Daventry. No end good of you! I must apologise for troubling you so precipitately, and I do hope I haven't put you to a lot of bother. But the long and the short of the matter is that I need you."

Peter grinned, but nevertheless thrilled at the warmth of old Bathurst's welcome.

"That's all right. Cut out the apologies. I was only too glad to have the chance of blowing along. Life's been unutterably dull since our hectic time at Assynton together, I can assure you. Into what little 'scrum' are we butting now?" He tapped the side of his pocket significantly. "I brought the trusty old revolver in accordance with your message. Tell me, what's really doing? Bowie-knives and buckshot?"

Anthony looked at his wrist-watch.

"It's ten to seven, Daventry. I suggest that first of all we feed. We'll split a bird and a bottle and I can tell you all about it—certainly all that I know, which happens, in this instance unfortunately, to amount to precious little."

He flung a quick glance round the throng that was entering and leaving the station, but saw nothing to excite his apprehension. The taxi-driver listened attentively to what Mr. Bathurst said to him.

"That's all right, sir! I think I know a place that will suit you and your friend. Leave it to me."

Five minutes' driving brought them to a smartly-lighted restaurant. Mr. Bathurst ordered a couple of short ones—a dry Martini for Peter Daventry and his usual 'Clover Club' for himself.

"On second thoughts, I suggest we try the 'table d'hôte.' It will be quicker for one thing. We mustn't be here much longer than an hour."

Peter assented cheerfully.

"Right-o! I'm in your hands of course—and dying to hear what's afoot."

Anthony smiled and shook his head.

"Patience, laddie. I owe you too much for having answered my summons so sportingly to spoil your feed. All in good time. Over the coffee, my boy—that's when you're going to hear the news."

"Oh, don't rot, Bathurst! The boot's on the other foot, I can assure you. Coming down here hasn't troubled me a flick. I'm your man any old time—you know that well enough."

"You're a good fellow, Daventry. Excellent turnip soup this—made with cream, I fancy."

Peter grunted evasively, and it must be confessed with some measure of disappointment, but he knew his Bathurst well enough to realise that his natural curiosity as to the position in which he found himself at the moment would remain unsatisfied until the precise moment during the coffee that Anthony would in his wisdom select.

The latter turned the immediate conversation to cricket. After a time they reached the inevitable.

"What do you think of the team for Australia, Daventry? Strong enough for the job, do you think?"

"Weak in bowling, Bathurst, I'm afraid. Tate's finished, Larwood's a doubtful quantity—may break down at any minute—Geary may or may not go—it depends on his arm, no doubt, wants more power to his elbow—and Freeman and Jack White won't be suited by the wickets 'down under'. I should certainly have included—"

"So should I, Daventry"—Anthony grinned somewhat satirically—"though I haven't the least idea whom you were about to name. But I've noticed, if you will allow me to say so, that the men the English side *don't* take out are always the men who *should* have gone—they are always the men who would 'have turned the scale' and 'been better suited by the Australian climate and conditions.' Those are the correct Press expressions, I believe. All the same, I'm glad Chapman's skippering. Particularly so. The old place is getting spot-light, you see, with that and Jimmy Richardson's place-kicking last season."

Peter's eyebrows went up a trifle.

"The old place?" he questioned.

"I remember him at Uppingham. Had you forgotten! I suppose that sort of thing always makes a difference. Although of course he went up to Cambridge. Richardson followed me to Oxford."

"Of course! I had forgotten the Uppingham connection for the time being. Naturally—naturally."

Peter pushed the plate that had recently held a rather delicious *pêche melba* away from him.

"Black or white coffee, sir?" questioned the waiter.

"Oh, white, please."

"Black for me," said Mr. Bathurst. "Cigarette, Daventry?"

"Thanks. And as the waiter Johnny has just breathed the magic word coffee, I'm all attention, Bathurst. In fact, I'm fairly bubbling with curiosity."

Anthony exhaled a stream of smoke from his nostrils, smiled at Mr. Daventry's enthusiasm, and handed his *vis-à-vis* the letter of Constance V. Whittaker.

Peter wrinkled his brows as he read it. The smile that had played about his lips as he took it disappeared completely. Something like doubt or apprehension came into his eyes to vanish again as they began to dance with excitement. This was the goods right enough! He looked across the table to see Anthony rubbing his hands—the old sign that came back to him so vividly and which he knew so well. By Jove, it was good hunting with old Bathurst at your side!

"Deuced queer business," he said, "but it sounds as though it might turn out interesting. But tell me, what about me? Where do I come in on this? Why did you—?"

Anthony cut him summarily.

"Listen, Daventry. You're only on the fringe of the affair so far. But in that—you're no different from me. So am I! For I said just now that I'd tell you all I knew, which wasn't much. But from some points of view it's quite enough with which to be going on. Most decidedly! Lean over—I'm going to talk very quietly."

Peter listened with solemn attention to Mr. Bathurst's recital, from his embarkation at Whelan's Wharf, Northfleet, in the county of Kent, on 'The Oarsman' to his sojourn that same afternoon in the park at Tranmere. At the finish of the narrative, Peter's eyes jazzed with the emotions of a still greater excitement. The restaurant orchestra struck up the haunting notes of 'Ramona', but even this seductive musical allurement passed unnoticed by Mr. Daventry. Even memories of Gracie could not lure him from the Elysian!

"By Jove, how perfectly priceless, Bathurst! I wouldn't have missed this for all the wealth of the Indies. Little Peter's bag is already labelled 'Swallowcliffe'. This has got the Stuart screens and the jolly old black pearls left at the post without an earthly—whacked to the fragment of a frazzle. But tell me more of the 'Four-Just-Behind'. I can't remember all you said. Describe them to me again. What were the 'signs of the four'?"

Anthony smiled again at Peter's enthusiastic reception of his information. He proceeded to identify again descriptively his society of the morning and afternoon.

"There is a man with a withered arm or something, a huge, dirty, brown-bearded client, a fat, silky-voiced slug of a man who hisses out his words, and finally we have the gentleman who trailed me into 'Rigby's' and afterwards into the barber's. Monsieur Beaux Yeux I've christened him."

Peter grinned at the sally.

"Monsieur Beaucaire? More likely Sweeney Todd's great-grandson. The barber's chair was his spiritual home, I should say." He stopped suddenly as a new idea struck him. Then he turned quickly to Anthony. "What puzzles me about the whole thing is this, Bathurst. How have these pretty little dears got on to you? For instance, how the hell did they know you had come by water, on the sprightly old 'Oarsman'? Who gave 'em second sight as regards that? They certainly *must* have known to have been waiting at the dock for you. You say they got on to you there, don't you?"

"Just outside, Daventry, that's all—only just outside. I don't suppose I was twenty yards away from the dock gates when the first encounter materialised. Rather startling, wasn't it? I confess, Daventry, that the same point puzzles me, and from some angles continues to puzzle me. Although, of course, if you come to think of it, there are two quite possible and reasonable explanations of the matter."

Peter looked at him questioningly. "Two?"

"I think so. There is the possibility that there may be treachery going on within the precincts of Swallowcliffe Hall, Buttercross, in the domicile of the fear-ridden major with the dominating wife, or there is the distinct chance that—"

Mr. Bathurst stopped to take another cigarette from his case. He tapped it carefully.

"What?" demanded his companion.

"I think we'll leave the somewhat engrossing question of the second possibility, for the moment at least, Daventry. We mustn't forget what I've told you before. It is fatal to yield to the temptation of theorising without sufficient data. It's never a paying proposition." He knocked the ash from the end of the cigarette. "It's time we were getting a move on, Daventry. Remember we have to be at the Aigburth tram terminus by nine o'clock to meet our friend with the crimson gardenia. Provided, of course, you have no desire to return to the comparative tranquillity of Cornhill now you know what the going's like. I feel that it is incumbent upon me to inform you that I consider, without any doubt at all, that you will be running into very great danger."

His eyes twinkled as he watched the light in Mr. Daventry's eyes. Peter thrust his hand across the table with theatrical fervour.

"Sing me to sleep, Bathurst, your hand in mine! Tell me some more of these poisonous swine, but don't—oh, don't—for the love of Mike, suggest P. Daventry goes on strike. Put it there, Bathurst! When I hit your 'slug' man, I'll give you 'tens' you'll hear him squelch."

Anthony laughed at Peter's careless irresponsibility.

"Mind he doesn't hit you first, laddie. For when he does, I'll wager it will be from behind. I don't suppose his school motto is either 'Manners makyth man' or 'Floreat Etona'. You'll find he won't be overburdened by scruples of any kind. Keep your eyes skinned, as our cousins across the Atlantic say, and biff him good and plenty at the first tee. Thank you, waiter. Yes, quite good, thank you! You go first, Daventry. We shall know a bit more in a matter of half-an-hour or so."

They emerged from the restaurant and walked on until an Aigburth car overtook them.

"I'm travelling on the City Corporation's car tonight purposely," whispered Anthony to his companion. "It will prevent any jiggery-pokery before we reach the rendezvous."

Ten minutes to nine—and the Aigburth terminus. It was just beginning to get dark. The sky was now overcast. A few people boarded the car for its return journey, but Anthony was speedily able to satisfy himself that none of the four was in the immediate vicinity. The contents of Mrs. Whittaker's letter might possibly, after all, not be known to them. Their information might be merely general, and not particular. Unless—! Mr. Bathurst made another rapid survey of the situation as it appeared to him, and came to the decision to take a chance. In life, he always averred, it was necessary and inevitable at times to take one's risks. Progress, development, adventure—not one of them is born and nurtured of the ways of contentment and safety. Mere possession must be always static and glorious acquisition just as definitely ecstatic. Mr. Bathurst would take his risks. He certainly would take one now. A church clock struck nine away in the distance, and as it did so Anthony caught Peter Daventry by the arm.

"Our man, I fancy," he whispered. The dazzling headlights of a car shone down the road. "But be careful, Daventry. Have your revolver handy, because you never can tell. Watch carefully and be guided by me." Peter grinned back at him appreciatively.

"No, as you said, you can never 'B. Shaw'. Not bad that, on the spur of the moment. 'Every day in every way I'm getting better and better.' Look out, Bathurst, the car's stopping."

As Daventry spoke, the car stopped, manoeuvred for a second or two, and swung round. Then it drove very slowly towards the two figures standing, carefully expectant, at the side of the road. Peter's right hand went to the butt of his revolver that reposed in the right-hand pocket of his coat. The feel of it gave him a comfortable confidence. The chauffeur, with one hand on the steering-wheel, leant slowly and carefully forward. It was obvious that careful handling of the situation was not going to be on one side only. He peered into the faces of the two men who watched him. The car was empty. Anthony flung a rapid and comprehensively vigilant glance around the immediate environment. There was nothing to arouse apprehension. Everything seemed quiet. He made a sign to Peter Daventry and stepped briskly forward. He could see the crimson gardenia in the chauffeur's coat. So far, so good!

"Yes?" said Mr. Bathurst. "Are you looking for me?"

The man addressed leant forward still further and his words came low and distinct.

"There's no moon like the hunter's moon."

Anthony regarded him with grave interest before he replied:

"But it waxes and wanes."

The man touched his cap.

"Jump in, gentlemen, and, if you don't mind, you'll travel with the interior of the car in darkness."

"I have an idea that it will be safer myself," replied Mr. Bathurst.

CHAPTER III
COPPINGER THE CARRIER

BUT HE DID not take advantage of the invitation immediately. Mr. Bathurst craned his neck forward and as he did so, Peter Daventry watched him curiously and anxiously, for Mr. Daventry prided himself upon being ready to meet an emergency. But evidently Anthony was satisfied with what he saw, for he said very quietly:

"All right, chauffeur, get away with her."

Stepping back quickly away from the front of the car, he motioned to Peter to open the door and enter. Anthony stepped in behind him at once and slammed the door.

The car ran for a few yards at a moderate pace and then, gathering speed, dashed off into the rapidly-descending darkness. As it did so, Anthony drew back from the window on his side. Peter took his cigarette case from his pocket and appeared to be on the point of lighting up.

"Cigarette, Bathurst?" He found Anthony's hand holding his wrist.

"Don't smoke, Daventry. I'd rather you didn't, if you don't mind. I'm not altogether—" He broke off and shrugged his shoulders expressively.

Peter replaced his case with mock submissiveness.

"Sorry, Bathurst, I'd forgotten your four friends for the moment. But surely you don't think—you don't fear—"

Anthony cut into him before he could finish his sentence.

"I'm not altogether sure of things, Daventry. That's all I mean—nothing more and nothing less. And when I'm in the condition of not feeling sure, I make a point of considering all the chances and all the possibilities. You see, until you come up against probabilities, which you will admit we haven't up to the moment, it's the possibilities that you must examine." He laughed, but there was a tinge of grimness in his tone as he spoke. "That's all, Daventry. All the same, I don't like the look of one or two things in connection with this case at all."

Peter peered out into the night before he glanced at his watch.

"Where are we? It's a quarter past nine. Any idea of the country round about?"

"Not a lot, but we're apparently *en route* for Ugford Moor, wherever that may be. The map at which I looked didn't show it, so I presume it can't be so very big. But Buttercross is about forty-three miles from Aigburth—across country. I satisfied myself on that point. I'm going to 'check up' on that when we get there. What are we doing now, would you say? Thirty-five?"

Peter looked out again and cocked his head knowingly as he considered the question Anthony had put to him.

"Forty, easy, if I'm any judge," he responded, "and I shouldn't be surprised at a shade over."

"You aren't far out, laddie. If then, as I imagine, our cart journey is at the most going to be a matter of five miles, we ought to be hopping out of this car somewhere in the region of ten o'clock. But I shall know exactly how far we have travelled when we do get out."

"How?" Peter wrinkled his brows.

"I took a squint at the mileage indicator before we took our luxurious seats. I intended doing that, whatever happened. That's what I was doing when you fell a-wondering. I shall take another look when we alight. There's not a lot in it, but it will help to satisfy me more." Peter grunted.

"Rain wouldn't surprise me," he muttered engagingly. "Look at the clouds."

"Tut-tut, Daventry! And in Lancashire too? You surprise me."

Anthony grinned at Peter's look of comic dismay. But before Daventry could contribute a reply, Anthony spoke again, but this time very much more quietly.

"Have you noticed the car behind? How far away is it? Look out of the window at the back. Don't show yourself too much either, if you can help it."

Peter looked cautiously.

"Not more than a quarter of a mile. Overtaking us too, I should say if I were asked. It's moving, I can tell you, and we're not loitering."

"Come away then and get into the corner, although it may be nothing, of course. My little crowd of internationals don't know you, as far as I can judge, that is, and if only because of that you're going to be valuable to me. Never throw an early advantage away, old son, if you can avoid it."

As he spoke a great car flashed by with an amazing burst of speed. Mr. Bathurst's head drooped somnolently under his right arm as it passed and Mr. Daventry was almost invisible as he huddled formlessly into his corner. But Anthony as usual had slept with at least one eye open.

"I thought so, Daventry," he announced very quietly.

"I am moderately confident that the gentleman who favoured our car with a glance of much more than ordinary interest wore a coat the left sleeve of which was empty. I slipped them in Liverpool for a time, no doubt, but they are evidently on my track again."

"What will they do?"

Once again Mr. Bathurst shrugged his shoulders with rare eloquence.

"How can I tell you? What do I know? But they're making for Swallowcliffe Hall, unless I'm mistaken, and the driver's trodden on the juice. There's no doubt that they'll make it before we do. Then there may be trouble. Still, to a certain extent I'm prepared for that. I was when I first set out."

Peter could not fail to detect the earnestness in his voice or miss the light of resolute purpose in his eyes. Once again he was impressed by the sense of absolute physical and mental

fitness that always seemed to radiate from Anthony Lotherington Bathurst in no matter what circumstances he found himself.
Trained to a hair, hard as a bag of nails and without an ounce of
superfluous flesh, Mr. Bathurst was an eminently useful man in
most places.

"There's one thing," Peter thought and decided to himself,
"whoever these poisonous blighters are that are trailing old
Bathurst and me, we'll give 'em a decent little sprint for their
money. I may not be able to keep up with old A.L.B. when it
comes to mental gymnastics, but should it come to a rough
house when thick ears are being handed out with graceful gener-
osity, well, then little Peter will run up to form and will be also,
as the tipsters say in perfidious unison, 'bang on the premises.'
Or certainly, 'there or thereabouts'."

He found himself rubbing his hands in the way that he had
seen Anthony do many times in the past. Glancing at Bathurst,
he saw him take another look at his wrist-watch.

"A quarter to ten, Daventry! We've been travelling forty-one
minutes, and, I fancy, in a generally north-easterly direction.
That darkish patch, I should say, is Ugford Moor." As he spoke,
he pointed away in the distance.

Peter Daventry poked his head out of the window. He could
just see a dark grey-looking expanse of moor that rolled away
and away until it lost itself against the sky-line.

"If so, it's pretty extensive, Bathurst. Rather different from
what you prepared me for—seems to me that you ought to have
found that place on any map—on any decent map."

"H'm! I'm inclined to agree with you. I shall have to think
about it. It's our place right enough. He's stopping."

The pace of the car was now slowing down considerably and
before long the driver ran it to a clump of bushes that skirted
the road and stopped. A path across the dark grey moorland
could now be plainly seen. Peter noticed that Anthony was
listening intently.

"What is it?" he whispered. "What can you hear?"

"Horses' hoofs—or hooves, as the precisians say. Our cart, I
fancy, Daventry, for the second stage of our journey."

As he spoke, Peter was surprised to see him open the door instantly and alight. The flash of his torch played on the chauffeur for the fraction of a moment. Peter followed him out of the car. Just as suddenly the car, having dropped its passengers, darted forward again.

"Good-night, sir," came from the chauffeur. Without looking round or waiting for a reply from Anthony, he accelerated and, still keeping to the road, was quickly lost to view.

"Thirty-nine and a half miles, Daventry, and I shall know our driver again—anywhere. Dark face, longish nose, thick, bushy eyebrows and the left-hand canine tooth a trifle longer than all his other front teeth. Good business! Now we'll wait for the village cart."

He paced up and down. The moon was struggling hard to break through the bank of clouds that hid it.

Peter Daventry's prediction might not come true after all. The cart, or rather the horse that was drawing it, dropped to a walk. As it approached, Mr. Bathurst was able to see that it was a covered van, the kind of van employed in most English villages to convey goods from the 'general' shop. Once more he brought his torch into play. The name of the owner was plainly discernible under the light of the torch. Anthony could read it quite easily: "Frederick Coppinger, Carrier and General Merchant, Holmedale, Buttercross." The driver reined his horse to a standstill and bent down from his seat to the two men who stood in the path and barred his further way.

"I give you good-evening, gentlemen," he said, taking his pipe from his mouth, "although I was only expecting one of you." He paused and twirled the lash of his whip carelessly but deftly round the handle. "There's no star like the Arctic star."

Came Anthony's prompt reply:

"Then let the She-Bear reign."

"Jump up, sir, and your pal too. I reckon I'm satisfied."

Anthony swung himself into the seat beside Coppinger—if this were Coppinger and he supposed it was—and Peter climbed into the back of the cart.

"All aboard?" queried the man. "Come up, my gal."

The mare answered the summons and broke into a quick trot. As the man spoke, Anthony eyed him keenly, and it must be confessed with a strong measure of curiosity. He saw at the side of him a dark, clean-shaven man with a heavy cast of countenance, apparently in the early thirties. His face was saturnine, almost morosely phlegmatic. Two black, brooding eyes were perhaps the most distinctive feature that his face held. His swarthy hair hung a trifle untidily over his forehead and showed dark on his cheeks and chin, although Anthony saw that it was not very long since the man had shaved. For at least five minutes the cart travelled in comparative silence. The moon had at last triumphed for a time at least over the beleaguering clouds that had beset it and was now shedding its white brilliance over the dark grey moorland.

"Lovely moon now," remarked Mr. Bathurst.

"Yes," answered the driver.

Anthony continued his lunar conversation.

"Perhaps not so fine as we may expect it to be next month. The hunter's moon can be very wonderful."

The only answer was a grunted assent—at least Mr. Bathurst took it to be an assent, although it may have been entirely non-committal. Certainly the man betrayed no particular interest in the superlative quality of the hunter's moon and his face showed no sign of change. Another five minutes passed when Anthony thought he would essay another question.

"This is Ugford Moor, I suppose, that we're crossing?"

The driver touched the mare lightly on her heaving quarters with a dexterous flick of his whip.

"Some call it so. Others don't. More often out this way they call it 'The Knype.' 'The Knype's' the old name—all the old 'uns round about here call it that."

"That explains why I couldn't find Ugford Moor on my map. But I remember seeing 'The Knype' marked now you mention the name. It didn't occur to me to connect the two. I suppose you're an old inhabitant of these parts?"

"Been here longer than I've wanted to be. Three minutes 'ud be a long time in these parts. I shouldn't call 'em alloorin'. Steady, gal!"

The mare had now settled down to a good, even trot and the air around was so quiet and still that Anthony could hear Peter Daventry breathing behind him. The only noise, apart from the occasional flick of the driver's whip, was the 'clop-clop' of the mare's feet. The driver seemed to have neither the desire nor the inclination for speech or conversation of any kind.

Anthony began to feel that the real business of the adventure was drawing very close to him. They couldn't—in any circumstances—be very far now from their destination of Swallowcliffe Hall. The letter from Mrs. Whittaker had stated that there would be a walk of half-an-hour's duration after the cart had put him down. He was positive that they couldn't be far away now from the commencement of that walk. In this conjecture he was right, for suddenly the driver of the van pointed with his whip to a belt of trees in front and just away to the right.

"Little Knype Wood," he announced laconically, as he made the more even ground again. "You get out there, make your way through the woody plantation, and you'll come out by the side of Swallowcliffe Hall itself. You can't miss your way—there's a clear way right through. The path is well-trodden. Here we are!"

"Thank you," said Mr. Bathurst. "Which way is Buttercross from here?"

"The other side of the Hall, out beyond Holmedale, where my place is."

"I see. Thank you. Take this, driver, will you?"

The man addressed looked sourly at the Treasury note that Anthony held out to him and shook his head somewhat churlishly.

"No thank you, sir. I've already been well paid for to-night's work. So there's no call for you to give me any more." He climbed quickly back to his seat in the front of the cart and took the reins again in his hands. Then he leant forward with a very definite intentness and spoke in a low, tense voice. "If I hadn't been, I wouldn't have done what I have done. I wouldn't have meddled in this business for any mortal thing you could have offered me. No, not by a long chalk. I'd have tackled anything first." His face was white and working as he spoke and his body seemed to shiver a little in apprehension.

Mr. Bathurst made no reply. He watched him touch the mare with his whip and drive away again into the darkness.

CHAPTER IV
GETTING TO GRIPS

"H'M!" said Peter. "Comfortin' and consolin', what? Don't think we've altogether arrived for a tea-party. What do you think yourself?"

Anthony's reply was to the point.

"Revolver all right, Daventry?"

"Absolutely."

"Right! Good! We'll get along then—through Little Knype Wood and then to Swallowcliffe Hall. Fit?"

"Never fitter, Bathurst. Lead the way."

The path through the wood that their late companion had mentioned was easy to find, as he had stated, and they struck into it almost immediately. It was very dark with the moon almost completely obscured by the clouds that had now in their turn triumphed over her. A light breeze had sprung up and the soughing of it through the branches of the trees produced a feeling in the mind of Peter Daventry that Little Knype Wood was not very far from being the eeriest place that it had been his misfortune to encounter. He himself was not far off feeling depressed. He flung a quick glance at Anthony as he walked beside him. That gentleman seemed engrossed in thought. His long, devastating stride was so relentless that it took Peter all his time to keep up with him.

Anthony, for a time, seemed disinclined to conversation and it appeared to Peter, more than once, that as he walked, he was listening. Two or three times, as Anthony shifted his suitcase from one hand to the other, Peter could have sworn that he was listening either to or for something.

Suddenly Mr. Bathurst broke the silence.

"I'm very much afraid, Daventry, that our visit to Swallowcliffe Hall may be attended with some difficulty."

Peter grinned with definite appreciation. This was something he could better understand.

"Danger, you mean, don't you, old son?"

Anthony shook his head.

"Possibly I expressed myself carelessly. Danger there certainly will be, but difficulty is the word that I chose purposely. What I meant exactly was this. It seems to me that our entrance into Major Whittaker's domain may be contested. I'm thinking of that carload that has gone on ahead. I'm inclined to think that there may be gentlemen in front somewhere between here and there, sufficiently interested in our coming to be quite unenthusiastic about it. This lack of enthusiasm may be translated into active resistance."

Peter patted his pocket.

"Ah well, two can play at that game—and more than two if necessary. In that case it's little Peter for the picnic, with two spoons and his bib on."

But the lines of Mr. Bathurst's face were set and the ridge of his jaw showed firmly. He ignored Mr. Daventry's little pleasantry and shook his head again doubtfully.

"As I said in the car just now, I don't like the look of one or two things, Daventry, still less now that I have thought over them more. What chance will you or shall I have if these devils—"

He broke off abruptly and gripped Peter's arm. The latter halted as Anthony had done.

"Listen! S-sh! I'll swear I heard—"

He glanced round with renewed anxiety in all directions. Peter's eyes followed his, but could see nothing beyond trees, bushes and shrubs. Mr. Bathurst took out his penknife, stuck the largest blade in the ground and silently and carefully lay down beside it. Peter watched him curiously as he lay there listening, for he thought that his face seemed strained and unusually anxious. Eventually Anthony rose and replaced his knife. Then he motioned to Peter to leave the path and stand beneath a big tree.

"Daventry," he said, "I'm afraid that there are people in this wood now who don't love us. Execrable taste on their part, no doubt, nevertheless there it is. What we've got to consider is what's to be done about it. Where I'm tied up for the moment is in not knowing the geography of Little Knype Wood. I haven't the foggiest notion of the lie of the land. What's it like when we emerge, for instance? The country I mean!"

Peter nodded sagely and pursed his lips.

"What did our late friend, the grandson of Nimshi, say?"

"That we came out by the side of Swallowcliffe Hall itself. That may mean anything, though. It's beautifully vague and entirely unsatisfying."

"What's your main point?" queried Peter.

"Just this, Daventry. Is there likely to be any cover between, say the edge of Little Knype Wood and the Hall itself? If the only way out be along this path, over which constant watch can so easily be kept—well, you must see what I mean. We shall probably emerge on to a road of some sort, I imagine."

Mr. Bathurst shrugged his shoulders as he made the statement. Peter nodded with the strangely assured acquiescence of inferior understanding.

"You mean that if these Comrades of the Cloth are merely moderately competent, it's long odds against you and me—"

"Seeing the inside of Swallowcliffe Hall in a hurry. You've said it." Mr. Bathurst finished his sentence for him.

"H'm! I'm beginning to take hold. What's our best plan do you think then?"

"I've been thinking that over for some time, Daventry. Ever since we entered this confounded place, to be truthful." He paused and looked at Peter somewhat doubtfully.

"Have you come to any conclusion? What's the old brain-box saying?"

"Well, I hardly like putting the suggestion forward, from some points of view, that is, but on the whole I think it will be the best course for us to adopt. I'm not altogether enamoured of the idea, but I think we had better part company for the time being—separate before we go any farther." He paused again, but before Peter could say anything went on with his point: "I'm sorry, Daventry, to have to recommend such a plan, but you see I must remember this. One of us *must* get through to the Whittakers, by hook or by crook, that's certain. I haven't come so far to fail them now. Perhaps the luck will hold and we both shall. Here's hoping. But anyhow it's pretty evident to me that dividing our forces should double our chances—two we've then against one. In fact, I think that one of us, under my new plan, is almost bound to bring it off."

Peter nodded wholeheartedly.

"Should be a stone ginger," he remarked jocularly. "Peter Daventry should certainly be supported each way. I can confidently assert that he was never fitter in his life, will find the course to his liking and his extra burst of speed should be more than a match for—"

"Exactly," intervened Anthony. "Now what about making other arrangements? What had we best do?"

"Bathurst commands—Daventry obeys. Command!"

"Well, this is how I see things. They know me—at least pretty well. I don't think that they know you at all. I'm clinging to the hope that I slipped them for a time by going to Birkenhead and Tranmere and that they didn't hit my trail again until that car whizzed past us on the way out from Aigburth. If that's as I surmise, they've never seen you, Daventry at all. You're a card that I've still up my sleeve. That was one of the reasons why I sent for you. You may, in fact, turn out to be my ace."

Peter broke in irrepressibly. He found the idea exhilarating.

"I'm your man! I've got you! Gang of crooks play the deuce—Anthony Bathurst plays the ace—permit me to introduce you to—"

"Pursuing my argument then, Daventry, I'm going to ask you to attempt to make Swallowcliffe Hall by the main route. There seems to me a chance that you may get through comparatively easily, if you keep your head. If you make the Hall, don't forget to ask for Diana. If you ask for the wrong lady—Mary Ann, for example—you may have difficulty in establishing identity and be denied admittance, despite your undeniable charm of manner. Now for myself. This is what I purpose doing. I'm going to leave this path and strike off in another direction in the hope that I may be able to elude the attentions of these gentlemen and get through that way. Fit?"

Peter Daventry nodded. His light-heartedness for the moment had deserted him and he began to sense more and more the grim reality of the venture in which he had engaged.

"Just a minute, Bathurst, before you go. Have you a revolver with you? Because if not, hadn't you better—"

Anthony smiled. He saw where Peter was heading.

"That's very sporting of you, old man, but I shouldn't ask you to bring something which I hadn't brought myself. Don't worry about me. I remember when we were staging the final scene at Assynton in that strange case of the 'Black Twenty-two'—"

He seized Peter by the arm and dragged him away into the darkness, swiftly and silently. The action was so amazingly sudden that Daventry lost himself temporarily in bewilderment.

"What the—"

"S-sh!" whispered Anthony. "Not a sound. Look!"

Peter did as directed. Coming towards the tree they had just left and from the direction where they supposed Swallowcliffe Hall to lie were two men. The stealthy nature of their approach was far too obvious to be missed. They were certainly not in Little Knype for exercise. Peter felt his arm gripped even more tightly and held his breath. The first man was huge and wore an untidy brown beard. In different circumstances Mr. Daventry would have murmured ecstatically: "Beaver". The other was fat and ponderous. Peter could just hear him speaking.

"So," he heard him say, "so! It is surprising! I suppose you are quite sure of what you say, my dear Verensky. Our birds are here somewhere, eh? There is no doubt?"

He then broke into a foreign tongue which Peter was unable to place. Daventry turned inquiring eyes to Anthony Bathurst, but Anthony placed a peremptory finger on his lips. The two men were peering carefully to either side of the path-track. Suddenly the bearded man whipped something from his pocket like a flash. Bending forward just as quickly, he fired into a dark patch not six yards from where Anthony and Peter were crouching. The silence that followed was broken only by the echoes of the shot. Peter, his heart beating rapidly, watched, but Mr. Bathurst made no sign. With a hoarse laugh "Brown Beard" turned to "The Slug" by his side and muttered an exclamation. "The Slug" listened with his head cocked to one side and then moved his fat, sleek head as though in agreement with whatever it was Verensky had said. To Peter's undisguised relief, they moved on. As he pushed his revolver back into his pocket, Anthony touched him lightly on the shoulder.

"Now's our time, Daventry," he whispered. "There are two less in front, anyway! Good-bye, good luck and good hunting."

As Peter turned to signify his assent, Mr. Bathurst, suitcase in hand and obviously in no mood for further conversation, slipped noiselessly away into the dark shadows of the lesser known fastnesses of Little Knype Wood. It was now up to Peter Daventry. With the most incredible foolishness, however, that gentleman struck a match and lit a cigarette. The Daventrys also evidently had wills of their own.

CHAPTER V
MR. BATHURST BREAKS
THE CORDON

FIVE MINUTES after he had left Peter Daventry in the recesses of Little Knype Wood, Mr. Bathurst decided to take stern measures. He had been considering the whole question very carefully for some little time now and the very recent encounter with Verensky and the man whom he had nicknamed "The Slug" had caused him to make up his mind summarily. There was no possible doubt now that these men, whoever they might be, meant business and in all probability would be without scruples and would stick at nothing. There was Mrs. Whittaker's letter with its cry for help, there was the sinister reference to current events of Frederick Coppinger, the carrier, and above all, from the point of view, that is, of value towards his own personal opinions, there were these four men whom he continued to meet in and about the affair—men, so far, who had resisted his attempts to shake them off! Charming customers, all of them!

"Verensky!" he muttered to himself. "I fancied it was Russian that M. Slug was talking. That gives me an idea! I'm afraid there's nothing else for it. After all, it might have been worse. Thank God it's August and not January."

Plunging into a thicket, Mr. Bathurst opened his suitcase. Ten minutes afterwards he emerged therefrom and the enterprising young gentleman who found Mr. Bathurst's suitcase two days later may well be excused the delight with which he took it home to his mother. That lady—birthplace, Wigan—with true Palatine extravagance offered to purchase it from him, the price being hot-pot for supper two evenings in succession. The offer, it may be said, was accepted and the suitcase changed hands, but only half the purchase price was ever paid. Heredity and tradition can never be entirely ignored.

It was now Anthony's firm intention to get away to the west a trifle, for, from his memory of the map that he had previously examined, this plan would bring him out on the Buttercross side of Swallowcliffe Hall and by a detour would enable him to work back to it. It was vitally essential to his plan now that he should be neither seen within the wood nor leaving it. It was also now impossible for him, if he ever did get clear of Little Knype, to ask any questions as to the whereabouts of his intended destination. It was imperative therefore that he should know his bearings as well as possible when he got into the open again.

Suddenly he stopped dead in his tracks, pulses racing and every nerve tingling and alert. Another revolver shot, followed by yet another, had rung out startlingly on to the stillness of the night. Anthony listened attentively for any reply. There was none for a moment or so. Then Bathurst's blood ran cold in his veins. A third revolver shot rang through the wood and in reply as it were a horrible wailing cry was wafted across to him—the most horrible sound that Anthony had ever heard. It seemed to him like the scream of some poor creature in the throes of an agonising pain. It stopped and then came again—more wailing and more blood-curdlingly horrible! Then just as suddenly it stopped and there was nothing that disturbed the almost appalling silence that followed. Instinctively Mr. Bathurst's fingers sought the butt of his revolver. But they only rested there for the fraction of a moment. After all, it was his duty to press forward. He pulled himself together and looked at his watch. It was just on eleven o'clock. He pushed on, feeling certain that before long, if he continued to keep this direction, he must reach the edge of Little Knype. Once there and once cognisant of the character of the country on the edge of the plantation, he would complete his plans, for until he knew more he felt that he could do nothing. To make his way now was by no means difficult, although care had to be taken to avoid injury to his eyes and face from overhanging branches and brambles. Slowly but surely he came through to find himself behind a line of fine trees that skirted at brief intervals a lonely-looking road.

He was about to leave the shadows of Little Knype when a movement well away to the right attracted his attention. Keeping well in the background of the trees, Anthony watched the spot where he thought the movement had been, with the utmost care. He was right. There was a man standing against one of the trees that lined the road. It was the shadow that he had thrown on to the road that had attracted Mr. Bathurst's attention.

It did not take Anthony very long to come to an opinion. This must be the road that commanded the entrance to the Whittakers' house and the man whom he could see represented the limit of the surveillance on this, the Buttercross side. He looked at the time again. It was now nearly half-past eleven. Had Peter Daventry got through, he wondered? Or had that excruciating cry meant—Anthony thrust the dreadful possibility away from him. He decided that there was only one thing for it—to make certain of getting into Swallowcliffe Hall that night. On no account must the watcher by the tree observe him leave the cover of the wood and make the light stretch of road. If that happened, the game was up. Four or five to one are impossible odds against which to contend. He would crawl as far as possible away from the watcher in the shadow of the trees until the fringe of forestry ended and then make the road, trusting to good fortune not to be seen. If he could but make the road, he knew he would be all right.

Unfortunately there was but a little distance to traverse and Anthony had to wait a considerable time for the man's back to be turned towards him before he would essay the risky business of taking to the road. But his luck held. The light was uncertain now and he had to take a risk. It came off. The watcher, hearing Mr. Bathurst's approaching footsteps ringing down the middle of the road, turned inquiringly to the oncoming figure. But Anthony had no fears now. Only one thing could undo him. If this man happened to be "Red Lids", it might be touch and go. But Mr. Bathurst, from what he had seen from his coign of vantage, was moderately confident that it was not his faithful companion of the morning. For one thing, he was of the opinion that the man in front was too tall. He was right. When he came near, he could see that it was the tall, lithe man whose left coat-sleeve dangled empty. As he was now, he did not fear recognition by this man. Only the rankest of bad luck could let him down now.

Anthony plodded down the road and, as he passed his unsuspecting adversary, shifted the burden on his shoulder with the uplifting ease of the practised hand. The man that watched, eyed him carelessly as he walked by, but, not seeming to desire to show himself too much, slunk back into the shadow of the tree. Exultation pounded its message into Mr. Bathurst's heart. Unless his calculations were hopelessly wrong, Swallowcliffe Hall itself could not be far away. At any rate, he would keep to the road and see what happened. The only imminent danger that menaced him, as far as he could see, was a face-to-face encounter with "Red Lids" himself and he intended to do all in his power to avoid this. The only thing that troubled him was the possibility that the main path through Little Knype that came out, he believed, almost opposite to Swallowcliffe Hall might have been left to the vigilance of the gentleman just mentioned. Considering that he could account for the where-abouts of the other three Captains of Chivalry, this possibility that he was considering looked suspiciously like a probability. But he took heart. He remembered that some time had elapsed since Verensky and "The Slug" had passed Daventry and him in Little Knype and it was quite feasible that they had returned by now. If this were so, they might be guarding the Little Knype path and "Red Lids" might be otherwise engaged. As far as he could reasonably gauge, twenty minutes or so should bring him very near to the central theatre of operations. The question was how many of the members of the Friendly Society was he likely to meet on the way?

The road seemed clear. Nocturnal pedestrianism was evidently unpopular in these parts. Ten minutes' sharp walking brought him to a sudden turn in the road and what he saw, as he negotiated the bend, afforded him considerable pleasure. There on his left stood what was undoubtedly Swallowcliffe Hall. He could see its chimneys silhouetted against the sky. He slowed his pace down as he approached, for he realised that he must avoid all semblance of hurry. He could see now that a high wall ran right round the Hall. At an estimate he put it at about ten feet high, and all round the top were steel spikes eminently busi-ness-like in appearance. Each of these spikes looked to be about eighteen inches in length. Mr. Bathurst's eyes travelled to the other side of the road. As he had surmised, the main path from Little Knype lost itself in an open clearing about two hundred yards farther down. As he looked, his heart went to his mouth. By all the power of poisonous luck, there was "Red Lids" with another man whom he couldn't remember having seen before!

As Mr. Bathurst came into sight, one of the two—he couldn't be sure which—gave a low whistle, and the twain lurched forward towards him. When they realised that Anthony would reach the iron gates of the Hall before they would, they broke into a run. Mr. Bathurst, unperturbed and making the most of his slight start, rang the bell twice decisively, put his burden on the ground, took from it a parcel and a big sheet of paper and calmly awaited events. A feeling of thankfulness pervaded him that his peaked cap came well over his face. The man with "Red Lids" had by this time come abreast and flooded him with light from a powerful electric hand torch. Anthony, keeping his face well averted, gave him a familiar nod well in keeping with the uniform of His Majesty's Postal Service. At the sight of the mail-bag on the ground and the familiar trappings, the man with the torch seemed satisfied and passed on. "Red Lids", by a stroke of luck, slunk back as the gates opened. A man in a dress-coat, double-breasted dress waistcoat and striped trousers stood in the opening.

"Yes. What is it, postman?" he inquired.

"Special parcel for Major Whittaker. Very important. I shall want his signature on this sheet, please."

Anthony could now see that the man that moved in front of him walked with a stiff right leg. It showed the fact unmistakably as he bent down to inspect the paper as it was held out to him. Anthony pointed out the particular line for signature. The man's face brightened at what he saw.

"Come this way—quickly, please."

Anthony slipped quickly between iron gates, which swung to behind him with a resounding clang. Following the stiff-legged man up the drive, he speedily reached the main entrance. A light was burning in the porch, which diffused a pale yellow glow over the adjacent surroundings. A lady—charming, tall, slim and beautifully dressed—stood near the heavy door as the man with Anthony opened it. She had her hand to her face in an attitude of harassed emotion.

"What is it, Neville?" she queried, and it was easy to detect the weariness and anxiety in her tone. "Who is it? Who's that man there? For God's sake, Neville, be careful what you're doing! Who is—"

Anthony removed his peaked cap.

"Call me 'Diana,' madam," he remarked pleasantly. "I hope that I come in time."

The lady shrank back with her hand to her breast, but in her grey eyes there shone the light of intense relief. Mr. Bathurst had kept his appointment!

CHAPTER VI
SWALLOWCLIFFE HALL

ALTHOUGH, as has been said, intense relief was manifest in the lady's eyes, nevertheless she lifted her eyebrows with more than a suggestion of questioning.

"You will pardon the costume, madam," said Anthony in explanation, "but needs must when Satan steers. I doubt whether I could have answered your appeal in person, had I not decided to travel the last stages of my journey here 'incognito'. I am Anthony Bathurst."

The lady held out a friendly hand.

"I am Constance Whittaker. Thank you—oh, thank you for coming, Mr. Bathurst! My husband and I had almost abandoned hope of your arrival. Richardson was back ages ago, it seems. But come into the—Neville, tell the Major that Mr. Bathurst is here. Don't wait. At once, please."

The man addressed bowed.

"Yes, madam. I will tell the master what you say at once."

He withdrew, stiff-legged and stiff-backed. The lady saw Anthony's eyes as they followed him.

"That's Neville, Mr. Bathurst. He was my husband's batman in France and after he had lost his leg went with him when Major Whittaker went to Russia in 1917. He is devoted to my husband and after the Armistice wouldn't hear of being separated from him. Everyone tells me they would be lost without each other."

Anthony nodded in sympathetic understanding and then with an eloquently humorous gesture indicated his attire.

"I am fully aware, Mrs. Whittaker, that clothes may or may not make the man, but I should be eternally—"

Mrs. Whittaker broke in upon him with a low, musical laugh.

"Forgive me my seeming negligence, Mr. Bathurst. I had forgotten. My mind was so intent upon the fact that you had come. You would like to change, but I doubt if I can help you much—my husband is a much smaller man than you. I'm afraid a dress-suit of his would—" She measured Anthony's frame and shook her head in grave doubt.

Anthony smiled at her despondency. Then he tapped the mail-bag that lay at his feet.

"Don't trouble about that, Mrs. Whittaker. I harbour no sartorial designs upon the Major. My ordinary costume is in here. I'm afraid I didn't trouble to bring 'dress', but when I was forced to change some hour or so ago in the recesses of Little Knype Wood, I used one of His Majesty's mail-bags as a suit-case. Something of the kind had become very necessary. By the way—"

Mrs. Whittaker interrupted him, her eyes full of fear.

"You were forced to change in Little Knype? Is it as bad as that then? You were in danger? Are they here already?"

"I don't know whom you mean by 'they', Mrs. Whittaker, but I have certainly had a little trouble with four or five 'lewd fellows of the baser sort.' In fact, I have been hard put to it to shake off their attentions."

Her eyes betrayed more apprehensions.

"My husband will tell you. I had better say nothing for the present. It will be better for you to hear all the facts from him. But, oh, Mr. Bathurst, I am afraid, I am afraid!"

"Before I go to my room and change, Mrs. Whittaker, am I the first messenger labelled of Artemis? To arrive here to-night, I mean."

"The first messenger—of Artemis?" She repeated his question before she saw his meaning. "Why? Why should you expect another? Nobody else knows the—"

"I was accompanied by a friend, that is all, Mrs. Whittaker. But we had to separate in Little Knype. Things were getting just a trifle too hot for us. Each took his chance. I am to understand, then, that Mr. Daventry has not arrived?"

She shook her head.

"Nobody has come but you."

As she spoke, the faithful Neville appeared again.

"The master wishes—"

"Show Mr. Bathurst to his room, Neville. I will go to Major Whittaker."

Anthony picked up his Santa Claus equipment and followed Neville up the stairs, conscious of being an anachronism.

"I will come for you in a quarter-of-an-hour, sir," said Neville.

The bedroom into which he was shown was altogether delightful and quite away from the commonplace. It had evidently been planned round a suite of lacquer furniture, the ground of which was an exquisite turquoise with each panel banded in Madonna. The figures were mostly green and scarlet. But withal it was a modern suite—a modern suite at its best. The bed was on Queen Anne lines—happily so, he considered, after a second's meditation. For Queen Anne stuff blends more felicitously with lacquering than almost any other design. The mirror hung on the wall above the dressing-table and there were wardrobe and chest of drawers, besides a table, two chairs and box-ottoman. The carpet was a close-cover 'pile' of Madonna blue. The figured furniture precluded any idea of a patterned bedspread or even patterned curtains. They were, however, of shot artificial silk, a shaded sea-green to sea-blue. This took up the prevailing note of turquoise and sustained it against the Madonna. Mrs. Whittaker was a person of taste, concluded Mr. Bathurst.

He changed quickly, washed and waited for the stiff-legged batman. Where was Peter Daventry, he wondered? What creature out of Hell had been responsible for that dreadful cry that had frozen his blood an hour ago in Little Knype? Had Peter—" He heard the unmistakable gait of the butler, or whatever he was, approaching his bedroom door. His eye caught the bedroom windows and he walked towards them to make sure that he was right in his surmise. They were protected by iron bars. Neville's voice in the doorway jerked him away from their contemplation.

"Major Whittaker would like to see you at once, sir. He will see you in the dining-room. There is supper laid for you in there. Mrs. Whittaker presumes that you have already dined?"

"Thank you, Neville."

He made a quick descent of the stairs. As he entered the dining-room, Major Whittaker rose to greet him. Anthony saw before him a man of middle height of about forty-five years of age. He was fair and inclined to have that full floridity that goes with a certain type of fairness. He wore a slight 'military' moustache, but his eyes were nondescript. His hair was cut very short and his neck was red. Highish cheek-bones with the skin drawn, it seemed, tightly across them, gave him a 'tigerish' appearance. His eyes, face and mouth looked to Anthony 'feline', as though he could be definitely cruel, should the occasion occur to him to warrant it. And there was something else in his face as well as cruelty. There was fear! Anthony decided not to judge him too hazily or too harshly. He had caught him at a bad time, no doubt, and after all there must be some quality in the man's character to have inspired the batman's affection as Mrs. Whittaker had described.

She came forward with the Major.

"This is Mr. Bathurst, Guy. My husband, Mr. Bathurst—Major Whittaker."

Anthony bowed. The Major extended a cordial hand.

"It's damned good of you to come. I'm very sure that lots of men wouldn't have done. For I'm afraid you've run your head into a nest of hornets."

He laughed nonchalantly as he spoke, but Anthony was confident that the nonchalance was affected. Major Whittaker waved him to the table.

"But you'd better feed, my dear chap. We're safe till to-morrow at any rate."

Mrs. Whittaker flinched at the suggestion contained in the words, but rose to the occasion as hostess.

"No doubt you have dined, Mr. Bathurst. But you look like a hungry man. I'm good enough judge of character to assert that. I've met your kind before." She smiled with a kind of whimsical challenge. "There is a cold game-pie over there on the sideboard, or if you prefer it a tongue on cut. Help yourself to salad. If neither appeal, there is a chicken *vol-au-vent*."

As he ate, Anthony took stock of the room.

"I won't worry you with my story till you've fed."

The Major made the statement with an air of graciousness and with perhaps a slight touch of condescension. Nevertheless Mr. Bathurst was pleased to accept the situation as it was presented to him.

Like the bedroom into which he had been conducted, the room in which he now sat was most distinctive in its setting. He could not remember ever having seen a room quite like it before. It seemed to be floored with a composition that resembled stone of a rich golden tone. The windows were closed with wooden shutters covered on the inside with Italian damask. The dining-table, as far as Anthony could judge sitting as he was, was genuine old Italian adorned at either end with a green-tubbed orange tree. The leaves and blossom of the trees were of shell and the fruit filled with electric light. The chairs were undoubtedly old Italian with two extremely fascinating high-back seats covered in old Genoese velvet placed at the head and foot of the table. To the left of the fireplace, part of what Anthony put down as having been an old Italian altar-piece had been made up into a piece of furniture that stood against the wall. The ceiling of the room was beamed and the walls had been stippled. The general effect was altogether charming.

"I'm all attention," said Anthony at length.

He rose from his seat at the table and took the chair that the Major indicated. Mrs. Whittaker pressed the bell. A maid entered after a brief interval.

"Clear away, Fothergill, and then go to bed. We shan't want you any more to-night. Has Colonel Fane gone to bed, do you know?"

"Yes, madam. The Colonel and Mrs. Fane went up when Neville called the master from the lounge. Miss Pennington went shortly afterwards."

"Very well, Fothergill. Be as quick as you can, please."

As he looked at her, Anthony was caught by a curious expression on the maid's face. Sulky would have been the epithet he would by choice have applied to it. As he glanced in her direction, he detected distinct signs of uneasiness. He determined that something had happened, probably recently at that, to have put her out of temper with the world generally.

Major Whittaker pushed over the cigars.

"You will smoke, Bathurst, of course? I can recommend these."

Anthony accepted the invitation. The cigar was good, like everything else that he had so far encountered. Not only was Major Whittaker well supplied with the good things of this world, but his wife knew how to use them to the best advantage. That fact emerged very clearly to Mr. Bathurst from the medley of his first impressions, and he reflected that the two things did not always go together.

The Major's voice broke in upon his musings.

"I am going to tell you first of all, Mr. Bathurst, that the letter which has brought you here was sent to you without my knowledge. Mrs. Whittaker acted upon her own initiative. She sent the letter to you and told me of what she had done afterwards. I will be candid. I have never believed in being otherwise—but I was not too pleased." He broke off and laid his hand on his wife's arm. "I told you so, Connie, at the time, so you won't mind me repeating it to Mr. Bathurst here. It is as well that he should understand the position."

Mrs. Whittaker shook her head and the Major turned again to Anthony.

"And with no disrespect to you, Mr. Bathurst, either. Don't think for a moment that I under-rate your ability to help me or depreciate anything that you've done in the past. I know enough both of you and of your reputation to do neither. Certainly Mrs. Whittaker's cousin, Di Prendergast, never seems tired of singing your praises. You ran across her down at Mapleton, some time ago, if you remember. No, I didn't feel that way about it a bit. It's hard to explain to you perhaps. But I'm a soldier—it goes against the grain with me to have to ask for help. I think that sums up the situation as well as anything. Seems like squealing. If my medicine's there, I suppose it's my job to gulp it down—unpleasant or otherwise. That's all there is to it." He laughed nervously and jerkily and the hand that held his cigar trembled a little.

Anthony nodded understandingly.

"I see your point perfectly, Major Whittaker. But there are times when the best and strongest of us needs assistance, when to ask for help implies no weakness on our part at all. No man can bowl both ends at once, for instance. And judging from what I have met since I came to Lancashire, things are shaping up to be pretty warm before very long. Please command me, and please tell me all."

The Major coughed and the cough was as 'nervy' as his laugh had been.

"My wife had told me of your difficulties in getting through to us and of the ingenuity that enabled you to surmount them. It is a very comforting thought to me now that you have come that that ingenuity will be employed upon my behalf and against my enemies, for I assure you, Mr. Bathurst, that we shall need all of it, for they are clever, cunning, ruthless and implacable. There will be no question of mercy. If they get me, I'm worth no more than a kid in the mouth of a man-eater." His tones were light, but affectedly light and there was unmistakable fear awake now in his eyes.

Anthony glanced across at Mrs. Whittaker. The fear had travelled to her. She watched her husband with lips half-parted and cheeks drained of every vestige of colour. What was the danger overhanging these Whittakers and this Swallowcliffe Hall in which they lived?

"Yes, Mr. Bathurst," proceeded the Major, "they'll crush me as mercilessly as I should tread on a beetle. But you'll be wanting the facts, as you said."

Anthony closed his eyes, drew up his knees and clasped them with his two hands. This was one of his favourite attitudes for complete concentration, which condition is as much the result of mental habit as it is of mental endowment.

"In the early autumn of 1917—September, I think, to be exact—I was recuperating from a nasty wound in the abdomen, down at Shoreham in Sussex. I got it at Monchy in the April, but I pulled round all right and stayed a couple of months or so at Shoreham. Colonel Fane's sister lives there. She has a very charming house, and when Nick Fane knew of my trouble and of my being in dock, he fixed things up for me to go down there to stay. I puddled about down there for nine or ten weeks."

"One moment." Mr. Bathurst put his first question. "Colonel Fane? The same Colonel Fane to whom I heard Mrs. Whittaker refer just now?"

"The same. One of my oldest pals, although to look at him you'd take him for years my senior. We were at Sandhurst together. He, with his wife and niece, is staying with us now. Nick Fane knows something of my danger. The two ladies with him don't. We haven't told them. But Nick has offered to lend me a hand if it should be needed. But I will go back to the autumn of 1917. While I was stopping with Mrs. Pennington—that's Nick's sister—I was sent for to go up to the War Office. Well, to cut a long story short and much to my surprise, half-a-dozen of the biggest noises they could lay their hands on interviewed me, burbled pleasantly for quite a lengthy spell about my military record and eventually came down to brass tacks. I was to be given quite a special mission. My destination was Petrograd and I was to be entrusted with a most delicate piece of work. It appeared that our people had got wind of the coming military revolution which you will remember took place in the November of 1917. Things in the other theatres of war were so ticklish about this time that the Russian outlook, from the point of view of the Allies, was desperately important. At this time—I've no doubt you know, but I will refresh your memory—the Russian administration was in the hands of a Republican Cabinet that had been set up in the previous May by Alexander Kerensky. But he had failed to establish a settled government. Things were still moderately chaotic. Anyhow there was a tremendous amount of secret plotting going on to undermine as much as possible the cause of the Allies. No man was sure of his next-door neighbour. More than one starosta was concerned in it. Many powerful societies were formed and carried on for this one specific purpose. Believe me, Mr. Bathurst, the propaganda work of the Central

Powers had a very healthy rival, from the standpoint of ruthless efficiency, in what is now known as the *Rosta*. One of these societies was proving very troublesome—it stuck at nothing. Its favourite afternoon pastime was murder, and its favourite evening occupation was the same, only a trifle more so. It was removing many of England's best friends—people whose influence was badly needed to weigh down the scales in our favour. My job was to smash it! I did! I can assert that without fear of contradiction. With the help of many brave fellows, several of whom gave their lives, we removed these rat-faced excrescences one by one. Not by murder, Mr. Bathurst. We tried them and executed them. We administered justice, that was all. But the assassination of the Tsar and his family in the following July caused such an upheaval that half-a-dozen or so of the ringleaders—men that we wanted very badly—slipped through our hands. One of these was the gentleman they called the President, a product of one of their universities, who speaks three or four languages like a native, English included. He was a pleasant customer to look at, I can tell you. His lips had been cut away by a Tartar acquaintance in Kazan, I believe, some years previously. He had cherished designs, so I have been informed, upon the seventh commandment in such a particular direction as to cause the Tartar a certain amount of domestic disturbance."

Anthony raised a hand.

"Pardon me a moment, but before you go any farther, Major, why were you selected by the Powers-that-be for this Russian mission? Have you any idea? Did they tell you? It would help me to know."

"I had a first-rate knowledge of Russian. My mother had a Russian connection. One of her closest school-friends came from St. Petersburg, as it was in her time, and she had been desperately keen always on me learning the language. That was the chief qualification, no doubt. All the other chaps in the job with me had the same. That fact must have had a great deal to do with our selection. That and a reputation for seeing a thing through, taking two hands to a job always."

"Thank you, Major, I understand. Go on, please!"

"Well, eventually I was recalled. The Big Ones thought we had done enough. Russia was hopeless for years as an effective ally. That was obvious to anybody. I came home and they chucked me a D.S.O., because I had been in charge of the business, I suppose. I retired, went for a trip round the world that lasted a few years, and eventually came up here. Married in 'twenty-six and settled down. But I've always had a feeling in my heart of hearts that I hadn't finished with my Petrograd friends—more than a feeling, a downright certainty." He shrugged his shoulders. "I can't tell you exactly why, but there it is. It's been in my bones ever since I put a bullet through the last one I—er—executed. And now, Mr. Bathurst, I know it. I'll show you something."

Anthony stopped him again.

"Before you proceed, Major—have you appealed for help to the British Government?"

"It would be useless, Mr. Bathurst. Work of that nature is always undertaken by us on that understanding. We worked unofficially—it was our pigeon, and, if necessary, it would have been our funeral. That's always a *sine qua non*, as it were. I can't appeal to the Government or to the Police."

"I see. But still, I should have thought—"

Anthony paused for a moment and left the sentence unfinished. "What were you going to show me?" he eventually said.

Major Whittaker walked over to a table and pulled open a drawer. From it he took nine sheets of paper.

"These are what tell me of my danger. When I heard that you had arrived, I brought them in here. Read the first."

Anthony took it. It was in English, dated August fifth.

> "Put what we have come for on the tennis-court at midnight. We will give you until the 13th. If you have not obeyed by then, we shall administer Justice. The Servants of the Silver Troika. Eight Days!"

He looked at the other sheets. They were dated daily from the sixth to the thirteenth. They read respectively "seven days", "six days", and so on, down to the most recent, which simply stated "to-morrow". Anthony raised his eyebrows.

"The Silver Troika?"

"The name of the society that I helped to dismember."

Major Whittaker went deathly white as he answered Mr. Bathurst's laconic question. "They're all round me, Bathurst. What you have told me concerning your journey strengthens my opinion. They're everywhere—I feel it—I know it. I'm caught like a rat in a trap."

"Not yet, Major. Pull yourself together." Anthony tapped the message dated August 5th. "Please tell me this, Major. I don't think you have done yet. What do the 'Servants of the Silver Troika' mean by the phrase, 'what we have come for'? What are you to put on the tennis-court at midnight? It would interest me to know."

As he looked up to point his question, Major Whittaker went even whiter than he had gone a few moments before. Mr. Bathurst was quick to notice the fact.

CHAPTER VII
WHERE IS MR. DAVENTRY?

THE MAJOR moistened his lips before he replied and Anthony noticed that Mrs. Whittaker was also watching him intently. When at length his reply did come, his voice was distinctly hoarse and showed signs of strain.

"The official documents, papers, and minute-book of the Society of the Silver Troika, Mr. Bathurst, containing the inner-most secrets of the association. I carried them away with me when I left Petrograd at the end of 1918. They incriminated some of the greatest and most influential names in Russia. But I burned the whole lot soon after I settled down here. That's where I'm helpless. I can do nothing."

"Tell them so," returned Anthony with prompt decision. "See what happens then. Tell them all their papers are destroyed. They must realise then that you are telling the truth. No man would wilfully endanger his life out of sheer, obstinate perversity—"

"The Major has done so, Mr. Bathurst. He has told them. That was my advice when he first informed me about things. I advised him to do that and he did it. Didn't you, Guy?"

"What Mrs. Whittaker says is perfectly true. I put an attaché case on the tennis-court at midnight on the sixth of August. In it was a letter in which I declared to them the truth of what had happened. I swore that all the papers were burned."

"Was it removed?" Mr. Bathurst's question came—rapid and resolute.

"The letter was. The same night, Neville—that's my servant who let you in to-night—kept watch on the courts. It was removed, moreover, within half-an-hour of being put there. The case was left behind. Two men removed it. He was just able to catch a glimpse of their features. One had a great gap where his mouth should have been; the other had a withered arm. I remembered them at once from Neville's description. One was the President, the other was a man named Loronoff."

Mr. Bathurst pulled at his upper lip with his fingers. "I take it you would also recognise the name Verensky? Its owner sports a dirty brown beard."

"My God!" said Whittaker. "Is he here too? If he is, then Schmidt will have—Tell me, Mr. Bathurst, have you run across a fat porpoise of a man—"

"Who hisses when he speaks?" Anthony completed the sentence for him and proceeded to embellish it. "Most assuredly. I have applied to him the sobriquet of 'The Slug'. What about him?"

"He's the cruellest devil of them all," replied the Major. "We almost had him in our clutches once in the early part of 1918, but, owing to a leakage of information somewhere, he slipped through the meshes of the net. He's Schmidt—half German, half Slav."

"I see. Now tell me this. Why do you imagine they persist in their demands notwithstanding the fact that you have told them the papers are destroyed? Why should they? What can they gain?"

"They mean to kill me if they can, Mr. Bathurst. They will revenge themselves upon me for all that I have done to them.

They're after me, now they know they can't get the papers. But I'll give the murdering devils a run for their money even yet."

"How is it you haven't been troubled before, then? There seems to have been a long break between their activities. Where have they been all this time?"

Major Whittaker shrugged his shoulders again.

"I can't answer that with any degree of certainty. Russia was disrupted so completely and for so long. Anything may have happened. The process of dilaceration was long and tedious. They may have been trailing me for years, unable to strike the trail until now."

"Yes, I suppose that's quite possible," conceded Mr. Bathurst, "although I should have thought it hardly likely." He thought for a moment or two. "This tennis-court to which reference is made in the first of the threatening messages—is it visible to passers-by? Can it be seen easily from the road, for example?"

"Not easily. There is a wall all the way round it. But the grounds of the Hall are fairly extensive and anyone scaling the wall could see the court fairly comfortably. But the wall would have to be climbed."

"When the two emissaries carried away the letter from the attaché case that you put there, they presumably scaled the wall, then, and made their way across to the tennis-court?"

"Presumably. Neville didn't actually see them do that. He said they seemed to appear from nowhere and creep towards the court. But there's no doubt that that's what they did do."

"Where was Neville concealed?"

"In the tennis pavilion, right close to the courts themselves."

"Was he armed?"

"You bet he was, Mr. Bathurst. He likes to be on the safe side, does Herbert. He's met gentlemen of their kidney before."

"This man, Neville, Major Whittaker—tell me about him. I understand from Mrs. Whittaker that he was your batman in France and afterwards. Am I right?"

"That is so, Mr. Bathurst."

"The question may sound unnecessary, in view of all the facts, but I can't afford to take any chances. You realise that,

Major Whittaker, I am sure. Do you regard Neville as absolutely to be trusted? Believe me, I have a particular reason for asking."

The Major nodded his head decisively and with unmistakable sincerity.

"Absolutely, Mr. Bathurst. I trust him implicitly. You need have no qualms on that score. Neville's one man in ten thousand."

"H'm! That's all right then. He travelled with you to Russia doubtless? Was he with you there all the time?"

"He has never left me since coming to me in France. I don't think he ever will—or ever want to, come to that."

Mrs. Whittaker broke in impulsively.

"If it will help you, Mr. Bathurst—help you to feel more satisfied, I mean—I can vouch for what my husband says. Neville, I should say, is thoroughly devoted to him. He would go through fire and water for the Major."

"Thank you, Mrs. Whittaker. Corroborative evidence such as you have just given must always be helpful. It strengthens weak spots and supports belief." Anthony turned to the Major again. "You say that they have given you until the thirteenth—that's to-day. When do you imagine that the amnesty period will actually terminate? It's a difficult question to answer, I quite appreciate, but you know their methods—I don't."

Major Whittaker set his lips together with a grim determination.

"I haven't the least doubt that I am in danger *now*, as I sit here. But both the front of the Hall and the back are well guarded. You've noticed the windows, no doubt?"

Anthony nodded.

"Do you anticipate an early attack? Please speak very frankly."

Major Whittaker's face was lined with apprehension as he replied to Mr. Bathurst's question.

"Well, let me put it like this. It's a quarter to one now. Without a doubt they watched the tennis-courts at midnight to-night. They may have expected that the papers would be there."

Anthony intervened immediately.

"Your pardon, Major, for just one minute. Do you think that they could have nursed an expectation of that kind, in the light of what you had previously told them—that all the papers were burned?"

"I see your point perfectly, Mr. Bathurst. There is just this possibility, however. They may have thought that I was putting up a bluff until the expiration of the given period, simply trying to gain time."

"I see. Please proceed."

"Well, what I was going to say was this. It was not until midnight that they could have been definitely certain that I wasn't parting—see what I mean? Therefore, I presume that it may take some time for them to get their attacking machinery in order." He shrugged his shoulders. "I may be wrong, I admit, but that's just how I figure things out. I shall expect the fun to start to-morrow—Tuesday, the fourteenth of August. I don't *think* that we need reasonably anticipate trouble before then."

"Old Lammas Day, I fancy," reflected Mr. Bathurst. "H'm! That gives me a little time to look round the position. Now tell me some more, Major. What is the personnel of your household? Include everybody, please."

"Colonel Fane is staying here, as I told you, and Mrs. Fane, his wife. Also his niece, Enid Pennington. Then there are a Miss Whittingham, my secretary—I do a great deal of political work— Neville, Richardson, my chauffeur, Fothergill and Appleton, the two maids, and a Mrs. Chamberlain, the cook. She's a widow. Her husband was one of my men—he was blown up at Hulluch, poor devil. Not a trace of him ever found."

"All the servants reasonably old?"

"Old? I don't quite—"

"Old in your employ, Major. There is none a recent importation, for example?"

"None, Mr. Bathurst."

"Good! So that, with you and me, we can count on five men?"

"That's so. There are Fane, Richardson, Neville, you and I."

"Against us," continued Mr. Bathurst, "there are the President, Verensky, Schmidt and I think you mentioned another name just now—Loronoff, wasn't it? But there is at least one other. There is a singularly unpleasant gentleman who suffers rather acutely from inflamed eyes."

"Krakar!" burst in the Major. "Krakar! A fiend in human form if ever there was one, a devil from the depths of Hell. The whole of the inner circle of the Silver Troika has surrounded me. There's not a doubt about it."

"Five of them, of whom we know," said Mr. Bathurst, "but of course they may have others with them. We must make allowances for that possibility. If they haven't—and it's just a possible contingency that they haven't—it's a case of level pegging. The sides are on an equality." Mr. Bathurst spoke with some degree of satisfaction. "There is this to be said. It might have been worse—in fact, it might have been a great deal worse."

Mrs. Whittaker rose from her chair and walked towards him.

"What are you going to do, Mr. Bathurst? Save him! Save him if you can!"

"I will do my best, Mrs. Whittaker. Please be assured of that. Why not send for the Police in the morning?"

The lady looked at him and then back to her husband. The Major disclaimed the idea somewhat peremptorily.

"No, no! I can't do that. The Government of the country cannot protect me. I cannot claim its protection. I am aware of it now just as fully as I was when I took on the job in the first instance. If my salvation is to be found, I must find the way to it myself. To do anything else would be contrary to the traditions of the service to which I had the honour to belong and to which I like to think I still belong."

"Very well. I am in your hands. But before I come to any decision regarding the disposition of our forces, I feel that I must tell you something—something about which I am to a certain extent troubled. As I told you just now, Mrs. Whittaker, I did not come here alone."

The Major became more anxious-looking than ever and a puzzled look appeared on his face.

"Tell me what you mean, Mr. Bathurst."

"When I realised the strength of the little nest into which I had strayed, I enlisted the services of a friend. You need have no fear, Major, on the score of his discretion. I will vouch for that. Also his courage and resourcefulness are equally beyond reproach. But as events transpired, we were forced to separate in Little Knype Wood. It was a question of policy on our part to do so. It gave us two chances against one, you see, of getting through to help you. I am here, Major Whittaker, but my friend is not. If he is not here, where is he?"

"You mean you are afraid, Mr. Bathurst? You mean that he may have been—" Major Whittaker broke off abruptly. There was fear in his eyes.

Anthony made an eloquent gesture with his hands.

"I do not say that I am afraid, Major. I simply say, where is Peter Daventry?"

The Major made no reply. Mr. Bathurst went on:

"I am not concerned so much with the fact that his presence here might give us an ascendancy numerically. I am more inclined to blame myself for having implicated him in the affair. I keep saying to myself, where is Peter Daventry?" He paced the room backwards and forwards, two or three times. "I am sorry now that we separated. On the other hand, if we had not, I might never have succeeded in breaking through to you." He stood by the left of the fireplace, looking carefully into the heavy piece of furniture by its side. Suddenly he threw up his head and there were confidence and determination in his grey eyes. "Go to bed, Major. I think with you that we are safe from attack until to-morrow. Sufficient for to-night shall be this evil. At any rate, I am going to chance it. But take a precaution and have Neville with you in your bedroom. Tell him to keep his eyes open all night. He hasn't got very long to go before the dawn. The sun rises at a quarter to five. Good-night, Mrs. Whittaker! Good-night, Major! I can find my way to my room. And keep a stout heart. We may match the cunning of these devils yet."

When he got to his bedroom, he walked across to the window. Besides the iron bars which he had noticed before, he now saw that there was a shutter on either side. Apparently the room was at the back of the house. Anthony looked through the bars. The position of the bedroom was as he thought. The marking of the tennis-court could be plainly seen under the light of the moon.

Suddenly he detected a shadow as it fell across the stretch of grass. Mr. Bathurst watched it carefully. It ceased moving. Anthony felt his nerves tingling as he strained his eyes to obtain a better vision. A man was standing there on the courts in the moonlight. Mr. Bathurst was unable to see who it was. Suddenly the man seemed to raise his arm as though in a movement of execration. Then he turned and ran swiftly out of sight.

Chapter VIII
THE MORNING OF AUGUST THE FOURTEENTH

As ANTHONY descended the flight of stairs on his way to the breakfast-room, he looked at his watch. It showed but a few minutes past eight. He had awakened at half-past seven and had bathed, shaved and dressed within a matter of thirty-three minutes.

As he turned the corner by the stairs, he passed one of the maids. It was the maid whom he had seen in the dining-room the night before—Fothergill. Once again he was struck by the expression on her face. Unless Mr. Bathurst was very much mistaken, the girl had been crying. Her eyes were heavy and there were, he thought, distinct traces of tears—and recent tears at that. He found Neville in the breakfast-room. Anthony thought he looked a trifle out of temper.

"Where is the Major, Neville?" he asked him.

"He will be down in one moment, sir. Everything is quite satisfactory, sir, and so far there is nothing to report. The Major told me what you suggested last night. I did all that you said. Nothing of any consequence occurred in the night."

As he spoke, a big, burly man entered, two ladies following him. His silvery-white hair, white moustache, florid cheeks and sharp, piercing eyes gave him *dans la toute ensemble* a most distinguished appearance.

"Your pardon, sir." He approached Anthony with hand outstretched and a pleasant smile of greeting. "But I've no doubt that you are Mr. Anthony Bathurst. As Major Whittaker isn't here to introduce us, I'll introduce myself. I'm Colonel Nicholas Fane. This is my wife and this is my niece, Miss Pennington. Mr. Anthony Bathurst—*the* Mr. Bathurst." He effected the introduction with an air.

Anthony shook hands with him and bowed to the two ladies. Mrs. Fane was a blonde, a fair-skinned, fluffy-haired little woman, somewhere in the early forties. She had an odd trick of fluttering her eyelids quickly and nervously whenever she spoke. Anthony formed the opinion that as a girl she must have been rather winsomely pretty.

"I am delighted to meet Mr. Bathurst. I really had no idea that you were a friend of Major Whittaker's, Mr. Bathurst. I can never remember hearing him discuss you in any way. Can you, Nick?" She turned impulsively to her big husband.

"No, my dear, I can't say that I ever did—until last night, that is. Dear old Guy told me about him last night. They have a mutual acquaintance, Edith, that's where the connection comes in. You've met Dick Arkwright, haven't you? Married Sir Charles Considine's elder daughter, Helen. Well, Dick Arkwright was at Sandhurst with Whittaker and me. He was in the eleven. Rattlin' good wicket-keeper he was, too, Dick Arkwright I'm talkin' about. And he knows Mr. Bathurst. That's how Guy comes into it." He dropped his eyelid momentarily at Anthony as he embarked upon the explanation.

"So that's that, Mrs. Fane," laughed Anthony. "I hope I'm explained satisfactorily. I was knocking round in the district and I thought I'd give Major Whittaker a look-up. He's often asked me to."

"I believe you're going to be a God-send, Mr. Bathurst," said the girl, coming forward. "What's your handicap?"

Anthony laughed again.

"I'm a perfectly rotten golfer, Miss Pennington, so don't thank Heaven for me yet. The proof of the pudding lies in the eating. You may yet rue the day that I blew into Swallowcliffe Hall. My driving's not too bad, but my short game makes Cherubim and Seraphim very, very lachrymose, I assure you."

Enid Pennington laughed and Anthony was struck by the rich beauty of her contralto. Seemingly carelessly, he took a good look at her. She was a tall, dark girl, slim and of very graceful carriage. Her dark eyes were proud and a whit disdainful. But if the observer missed the disdain in Enid Pennington's dark eyes, he would be remiss indeed to miss it on her mouth. The curve of the lips was alluring and semi-provocative, but the disdain was there, plainly to be seen. At the same time it was attractive. But as she laughed at Anthony, it was instantaneously lost and Mr. Bathurst realised that here was, without any doubt whatever, an attractive and beautiful girl.

Colonel Fane laughed with her.

"Modesty, Enid, sheer, unadulterated modesty! I'll lay a wager Mr. Bathurst's a dark horse, if you only knew. Probably give us all two strokes a hole. We've met 'em before, haven't we, Edith?"

Before Mrs. Fane could reply, Major Whittaker and Mrs. Whittaker entered the breakfast-room.

"'Morning, everybody! Surely you've started? Goodness gracious, there was no need for any of you to wait. What's come over you, Nick? Please help yourselves from the sideboard."

The Major seemed outwardly in the best of spirits, but a look in his eyes betrayed him. Anthony walked over to him quietly and unobtrusively. The Major listened with great attention to whatever it was Mr. Bathurst told him.

"All the time I'm here, mind you! When I leave, I hope the danger will have been averted." Anthony's voice was so low that only the Major could possibly have heard him. That was Mr. Bathurst's intention at least.

"What are you doing this morning, Nick?" Mrs. Fane asked the question of her husband.

"Stopping in, my dear. I've got something to talk over with Guy. I suggest you and Enid breeze up to the links and have a round. Perhaps, after a spot of lunch, we might have a four-ball in the afternoon."

"How far away are your links here, Major?"

"A couple of miles—about—Bathurst, and quite decent, too. Do you play?"

"I've already described my golf form to Miss Pennington," laughed Anthony. "But I'm glad it didn't put her off her breakfast."

The lady in question smiled back a reply.

"As a matter of fact, Mr. Bathurst, I'm very partial to my 'brekker'. It's evidence of a well-spent youth and a frantically fervent desire to retain my schoolgirl complexion. How do you think I'm succeeding?"

"The two terms are surely somewhat contradictory, Miss Pennington. Still, I'll accept your word for it. Your success is amazing!"

"What about you, Con?" asked Major Whittaker. "Are you staying in?"

"I think so, yes. Mrs. Fane and Enid will be all right without me."

Mrs. Whittaker appeared to make up her mind very quickly and as the men passed into the library, her eyes gave Anthony a look of eloquent appeal which it was impossible to miss. Inside the room, Anthony immediately took charge of the situation.

"How long have you been staying here, Colonel Fane?"

"Came up at the end of June, Mr. Bathurst. We were up here last summer and the Major was keen on us repeating the visit this year. We're very old cronies, he and I."

"I see. Major Whittaker tells me you are aware of the present position."

"I am, sir. I was here of course when the Major got the first of those damned messages."

"You are also aware, then, that, according to the text of the messages, the peril is imminent? The time limit, if I may describe it as such, expired, we think, at midnight last night."

"I suppose that's what it really amounts to, Mr. Bathurst. Major Whittaker and I came to that conclusion before you arrived."

Whittaker laughed grimly.

"Well, I'm prepared for them." He tapped his pocket. "I've got my service revolver here—and fully loaded. They won't be the first dirty Russians I've—executed. When they come, they won't find it a tea-party. Fane's ready too, aren't you, Nick?"

Fane nodded in confirmation.

"Rely on me, my boy. I'll see you through."

"Good!" put in Anthony. "And I'm also in like condition." Mr. Bathurst, in turn, touched his pocket significantly. "There is just this, however," he added. "If they attack in that way, it probably won't be in broad daylight. The attack, when it does materialise, may be much more insidious. That's what tends to disturb me. We must be prepared to cope with almost any emergency. We must also be ready to recognise the attack directly it is launched against us. Do you follow what I mean, Major?"

"Yes, I see your point, Bathurst. I did when you spoke to me at breakfast this morning. But I think that, provided we take reasonable care—"

Colonel Fane cut in impatiently.

"I propose, Bathurst, that the Major doesn't leave the Hall at all. That seems to me to be by far the best plan to adopt. Then after a time, if these murdering devils really do mean business—"

Mr. Bathurst was as unceremonious as the Colonel himself had been just previously.

"I'm very much afraid that they do mean business, Colonel Fane. We can put any other possibility out of our consideration. I watched from my bedroom last night—or this morning would be more exact. They were on the *qui vive*—take it from me." He walked to the French doors that commanded the lawn and beyond that the tennis-court. "Come here, gentlemen, will you?" Anthony pointed out to the courts.

"There was a man out there, plainly visible from my bedroom window."

It seemed to Anthony that Colonel Fane regarded him with some degree of curiosity.

"What sort of man, Bathurst? Could you describe him? Could you see enough of him to form any opinion?"

Anthony shook his head gravely.

"Unfortunately I couldn't. First I saw his shadow and then just the outline of his form. Still, he wasn't there for very long. As I watched him, he cleared away out of sight. But I have no doubt that he was there to see if the demands of the Silver Troika had been complied with. I wouldn't say that he seemed very pleased about it either."

Major Whittaker shook his head with some show of foreboding.

"In my opinion, then, they may be on us at any time."

"You must take no risks certainly." Mr. Bathurst thought hard for a moment. Then he asked a question. "Are *all* the windows of the Hall shuttered and barred?"

"Every one, Bathurst. I told you that I have never felt quite safe since I left Russia. I knew I should have to take precautions. I had it done directly I came to live here."

Anthony looked at the French doors of the library. "These are the only ones then that are not protected? For we can almost class them as windows, can't we?"

Whittaker acquiesced.

"That is so. But we couldn't—or we shouldn't—be taken by surprise here. There's the wall at the end of the garden and grounds. They'd have to show to get over that. To get in here this way, they'd have to come out in the open."

"Where are Neville and Richardson?"

"Looking after the front of the house, and armed as we are."

"Inside the gates, I presume?"

"Yes, inside the gates. They'll have something to do to get inside—Verensky and Co., I mean. It won't be as easy as walking the plank."

"That's what I'm thinking, Guy," put in Fane. "It seems to me that this side is our vulnerable point. That's what Bathurst here means, I take it?"

"Exactly," said Mr. Bathurst. "I am entirely in agreement with you, Colonel. This is the point we must watch, and I think it ought to be moderately easy to do so efficiently. But bring Richardson, the chauffeur, round to the back here. Let Neville see to the front by himself. When the light begins to fail to-night, we can review the situation again. All the same, I'd give a lot to know what's become of Daventry."

"Let's hope he'll turn up before to-night, Bathurst," declared Major Whittaker. "It looks to me very much as though every one on our side is going to count."

"Against this choice little outfit—every time. We can do with all the help we can get," contributed Fane.

He paced the room rapidly and the asperity in his nature seemed to manifest itself more and more. The situation was undoubtedly playing havoc with his nerves. Anthony watched him for a moment or two and then turned to Major Whittaker.

"The man that met your car last night, Major—the carrier that drove us over Ugford Moor to Little Knype Wood—was that Coppinger himself? I saw the name on the side of the cart—that's how I happen to know it."

"It was, Bathurst. Mrs. Whittaker arranged for his help through Richardson, my chauffeur, and Neville. Neville speaks highly of him. He's a thoroughly reliable man in every way. Why do you ask?"

"Just to satisfy myself that it was Coppinger himself, that was all. I like to know exactly where I am." Anthony pulled at his upper lip. "Upon mature consideration, Colonel Fane, I agree with you on your suggestion that the Major stays inside Swallowcliffe Hall—for a time that is, at least. They must show their hands sooner or later. When they do, it will help me to form an opinion as to our future policy. Perhaps, Colonel, you would be good enough to send for Neville."

The Colonel bustled out. The moment he had gone, Anthony spoke to Whittaker.

"I have one more suggestion to make, Major. Be guided by me. Put another letter on the tennis-court tonight. Repeat emphatically what you said before—that all the required papers have been destroyed. Be as earnest and explicit as you can. Let there be no possibility of any misunderstanding whatever. It may have a salutary effect. On the other hand, it may not. But at any rate, whatever happens after you have done it, I think it should prove of distinct assistance to me."

The Major looked very doubtful and translated his doubt into words.

"You're more optimistic than I am, Bathurst. You don't know these scum like I do. They'll never fall for that—true though it is. I've got as much chance of being believed as a celluloid cat has of getting out of a petrol-flooded Hades. It's the Koh-i-noor to a caraway seed against it."

Anthony gripped his arm.

"Nevertheless, do as I say, Major Whittaker. Believe me, I have an excellent reason for asking you."

"All right, Bathurst. Have it your way." Whittaker, realising the strength of the speaker's personality, gave a pessimistic assent to the proposal. "Very well, I'll do it—no doubt you know what you're—"

Neville entered, piloted by Colonel Fane. Despite his artificial leg, Mr. Bathurst could see that Major Whittaker's personal servant was still a fine, robust, soldierly man.

"Everything quiet, Neville?" asked the Major.

"Yes, sir. Nothing to worry about at all so far, sir." He coughed. "But I'm thinking it's to-night that we'll be meeting trouble, sir. Just a song at twilight, so to speak, when the lights are low. That's when we shall have to keep our eyes skinned, sir."

"Send Richardson round to the back here, Neville, will you? We think he will be more use round here. That's all. Then you get back to your post, Neville. We'll see you again before this evening. I may want you to do something special for me."

Neville saluted and made his way from the room. Anthony turned again to his two companions.

"I think I'll have a look round generally, Major, if you don't mind. There are still one or two points with regard to the house itself that I haven't yet mastered. If you go anywhere—to other rooms, I mean—take Colonel Fane with you. Go nowhere absolutely alone. I shan't be away very long."

In the hall he looked at his wrist-watch. Half-past eleven—and still no sign of Daventry! The situation to Mr. Bathurst, whichever way he looked at it, didn't seem to be improving. But what could he do, save wait and see what time brought forth? His present intention was to take a careful look round the servants' quarters.

Swallowcliffe Hall was an old, rambling building something after the shape of a squat T inverted. Towards the foot of the letter were the kitchens. As he arrived, he could see two figures standing talking by a door that appeared to open on to what was evidently the kitchen garden. Mr. Bathurst could see a row of cucumber frames close to the line of hot-houses. As the first sounds of the voices reached him, something prompted him to stop. He could see that if he went any closer, he would be seen, and that was what he did not want to happen. The voices he could hear were those of a man and a woman. Beyond that he could say nothing, for the woman had her back to him and the man was now hidden by the angle of the door. But all the same, from the glimpse he had caught of her costume, Anthony was inclined to think that she was one of the maids. Surely nobody else would be likely to stand talking in this part of the house! Suddenly he stiffened into magnetized attention. The woman, whose back he could see, was speaking.

"Yes, I do mean it. You'll get no mercy from him," she said in a low, tense voice. "When I say murder, I mean murder. If *he* gets you—and he will get you if you try this game on any more, take it from me—he'll crush you like that."

Anthony saw her raise her clenched hand with dramatic intensity.

"Like an egg-shell—so."

She suited the action to the words, snapping her thumb and second finger. But it appeared to have no effect upon her companion. The man's low tones came in reply. Anthony was unable to hear what he said, for the woman's words came again.

Her voice was now aggressively scornful, almost contemptuous, in fact.

"Do you think I'd take the trouble to tell you this if I didn't? What sort of precious fool do you take me for? Have some sense, man! I tell you, he'd stick at nothing. God knows I wish it was all over, but go!"

She turned impetuously away. As she did so, Anthony retreated quickly and noiselessly. But he could bear steps up the path that led away from the door down to the kitchen-garden, and then a clanging sort of noise, peculiar to his ear situated as he was, albeit familiar.

He strode quickly back to the other part of the Hall, thinking deeply. Which of the maids was it—Fothergill, the girl whom he had seen before, or the other one the Major had mentioned, Appleton? Or was it by any chance Mrs. Chamberlain, the cook? There had been three of them mentioned. Mrs. Chamberlain was the widow of a man who had seen service with Major Whittaker! Altogether an engrossing little problem!

CHAPTER IX
ENTER MR. GARLAND-ISHERWOOD

AS HE PASSED along towards the library, Mr. Bathurst could see the figure of a girl in front of him. She moved ahead of him lightly and gracefully. It was not Miss Pennington—he was certain of that. It was not tall enough. It was somebody, he thought, whom he had not encountered before. He decided it must be the Miss Whittingham whom the Major had mentioned upon the previous night, the lady secretary whom Whittaker employed for his political work. Mr. Bathurst thought, from what he could see of her in the distance, that she was wearing a plain white blouse over a neat navy blue skirt. She was about the same height as the girl whose figure he had just seen at the door, but Anthony did not think that it was she, although it might have been possible for her in some way to have slipped ahead of him. Her clothes in general colouring were not unlike the clothes of the other girl. He determined therefore not to dismiss altogether this possibility. Suddenly she opened the door of a room on the opposite side to the library and entered. It was the secretary, no doubt! Perhaps the person who had the greatest liberty of access to the Major's correspondence! On that account Mr. Bathurst found her interesting. Still, he would retain an open mind on that score. Deliberately he paused with his hand on the handle of the library door. As he stood there, he heard a shout. Then he heard an exclamation from Colonel Fane, followed by another shout. He identified this last as being in the voice of Major Whittaker.

"What is it?" he heard him cry. "What is it, Richardson? Keep him covered, man, for the love of Heaven!"

Anthony pushed open the door and entered. A strange sight met his eyes. Colonel Fane and the Major stood in the centre of the room. At the French doors stood Richardson, the chauffeur. The revolver in his right hand covered a man who was apparently on the point of entry. This man presented an extraordinary appearance. He was of middle height, with long, straight, lank hair that fell in black strands untidily over his forehead. His eyes shone brightly behind a pair of horn-rimmed glasses of very large pattern. In his left hand he carried an antiquated specimen of a straw hat, "boater" shape. In his right he waved a huge and business-like-looking butterfly net. His elfin face was creased and puckered into a kind of peering, wistful expression. His clothes gave the impression of having been purchased somewhere out of England.

As Anthony entered, the stranger made a sweeping bow with his straw hat to the occupants of the room and embarked upon what was evidently an explanation.

"You will pardon me, gentlemen—of that I am sure! For I am in the wrong, I know! I abase myself! At the same time, my reception somewhat surprises me, for although I intrude upon your privacy and break your great national tradition that an Englishman's house is his castle, hear my excuses before you condemn me to the lowest dungeon beneath the castle moat. And I think you will hear them better if this gentleman stops poking his six-shooter into my ribs. I find it a distinct drawback to the quality of my elocution."

At a nod from the Major, Richardson lowered his revolver. But as he did so, Mr. Bathurst, intending to take no chances, stepped a little closer to the central group. A semi-humorous expression flitted momentarily across the intruder's mischievous features.

"Thank you, gentlemen. That certainly makes the atmosphere a little less strained, shall we say, and me a trifle more comfortable. But I forget. I digress! I owe you an explanation. May I sit down?"

Colonel Fane looked askance at Mr. Bathurst. Anthony nodded agreement, but ranged himself at the intruder's side, as that person took a chair that Fane indicated. There was something about this diversion that he was unable at the moment to understand. Also it was not Mr. Bathurst's habit to run unnecessary risks. The man next to him placed the butterfly-net on the floor at his feet. Anthony watched him carefully as he laid it on the carpet.

"My name, gentlemen, is Horace Garland-Isherwood. I am an American, a citizen of the land of the free! My home is in Philadelphia. I have plenty of money, an aversion to all women, and one other hobby. This!"

He pointed to his collecting net. "I am an ardent entomologist."

As he spoke, Anthony was irresistibly reminded of the fairy stories of Knatchbull-Hugessen.

"I am staying in England with a friend near your Buttercross. Ugford Moor and the woods round Knype offer me a very happy hunting ground for the prosecution of my—er—other hobby and the collection of my specimens. Yesterday, I may tell you, I nearly captured the very finest Machaon it has ever been my lot to see. If you are unversed in butterfly lore, gentlemen, let me inform you that the Machaon, or swallow-tailed butterfly, is of the Lepidoptera order of Insecta Haustellata. Its wings are black and variegated most beautifully with gorgeous yellow markings. Near the extremity of each hinder wing is a circular red spot surmounted by a crescent of blue and the whole surrounded by a fine black ring. But although not what I should call uncommon, gentlemen, they are somewhat difficult to capture, because they fly with exceeding rapidity and in a nearly straight line, which is somewhat unusual. Unlike the Sambucaria of the Ourapteryx family or even the smaller Acberontia—"

"And what was it you nearly captured to-day, Mr. Garland-Isherwood?"

Anthony's questioning interruption appeared to occasion the entomologist a measure of surprise.

"Really, sir, your sagacity is amazing! However did you know that I was chasing a most gorgeous Red Admiral, the very first I have seen this summer? But I am no sap. That was why I climbed your wall. A most inhospitable wall too, gentlemen. If I had not had an intensive course of athletics at Harvard, I think it would have handed me the frozen mitten. But however did you know, sir? You were not in the immediate vicinity—at least, if you were, I failed to observe you." He peered inquisitively at Mr. Bathurst.

Anthony smiled.

"I did not know. All I knew was that that would be your explanation of having climbed the wall of Swallowcliffe Hall. I was right. What other explanation could you have?"

The grey eyes of Mr. Bathurst regarded the American steadily. Mr. Garland-Isherwood seemed a trifle disconcerted at the directness of Mr. Bathurst's reply, but after a brief interval he affected to rid himself of the discomfiture. His own rejoinder was accompanied by another of his elfin smiles. He nodded his head up and down two or three times.

"Really, sir, really! Permit me to offer you my congratulations on your perspicacity. I address no doubt a disciple of your immortal Sherlock Holmes? Yes?" He bowed and smiled.

Colonel Fane took a hand.

"When I tell you that this—"

His words were abruptly cut short by a resounding crash. A big brass Benares bottle that usually stood on the mantelpiece had fallen heavily into the fireplace. Mr. Bathurst was the unhappy culprit. Usually alert and adroit in all his movements, he had on this occasion been responsible for the occurrence through an awkward motion of his elbow. Embarrassed, he apologised profusely.

"Your pardon, Major Whittaker. And yours, gentlemen, too. It was extremely careless of me. I hope the damage is infinitesimal."

Mr. Bathurst stooped to pick the bottle up. As he did so, the Major caught the intention that his eyes reflected. Major Whittaker walked across to the intruder.

"Your explanation is accepted, Mr.—Isherwood. But there have been two or three very strange burglaries in this neighbourhood fairly recently and my chauffeur has been instructed to deal unceremoniously with any suspicious-looking characters that he finds knocking about. You will pardon me if I seem to include you in that category. But that was the reason why you were received in such cavalier fashion. I do not think we need detain you any longer, sir."

The entomologist seemed about to say something but stopped suddenly. He pulled himself up with a certain amount of dignity.

"Thank you, Major Whittaker. You have accepted my explanation. I, in return, will accept yours. It would be exceedingly ungracious of me to do otherwise. The worst enemies of Horace Garland-Isherwood shall never call him a curmudgeon, even though an ancestor of his sailed with the Pilgrim Fathers." He made a sweeping gesture with his straw hat, similar to that with which he had first greeted them.

"See this gentleman off the premises, will you, Richardson?" The Major, with peremptory abruptness, gave the affair its closure.

The entomologist turned and followed the chauffeur. Colonel Fane, Major Whittaker and Mr. Bathurst watched them.

"Now I wonder what exactly his game is?" declared the Colonel.

"Yes, and where he's off to now?" said Major Whittaker.

Mr. Bathurst smiled at the similarity of the two questions.

"Come to that," he answered, "I think that I can tell you better where he's *not* off to." He paused, awaiting the inevitable and wondering from whom it would first come.

"Where's that, Bathurst?" demanded the Colonel.

"Philadelphia in the morning," replied Mr. Bathurst.

CHAPTER X
MAJOR WHITTAKER ANSWERS THE CALL

LUNCH, tea and dinner passed uneventfully.

There was nothing to indicate that anything out of the ordinary was even in the nature of a possibility at Swallowcliffe Hall. Also there was still no sign of Peter Daventry. Anthony's eyes were ever on the alert and the best of his mental processes always in active employment.

After dinner, he tactfully suggested that the ladies withdrew, Mrs. Whittaker receiving from him special and confidential instructions. He, Major Whittaker, Colonel Fane, Neville and Richardson, the chauffeur, repaired to the library.

"Now, gentlemen," said Anthony, "Colonel Fane's plan shall be adopted. Major Whittaker is not moving from here until to-morrow morning. I do not think that there is any particular danger to be feared before darkness sets in—actually in my opinion before midnight. But we are going to remain in this room with the Major all the time. I am of the opinion that you, Neville, and you, Richardson, will be of greater service to us in here, in this room, than outside. If it gets very dark, your chances out there of stopping them will be considerably lessened. Here you can help to form a bodyguard round your master. Colonel Fane and I will be with you. What do you think of the idea yourself, Major Whittaker?"

"I don't think you can better it, Bathurst. I have implicit faith in whatever you decide. What do you say, Colonel?" He turned in the direction of his friend.

Colonel Fane nodded an affirmative.

"Yes, you know I agree with the idea. I don't think we can beat it."

"Right then." Anthony looked at his wrist-watch. "You and I, Richardson, will take up our positions by these French doors. You, Neville, will guard the door on to the corridor by which we have just entered. Colonel Fane will remain here and his actions will be guided by us. If anything untoward happens, he will know all about it at once. He will be in a position to act instantaneously. You are all armed, gentlemen, I take it?"

The men addressed nodded and the vigil against the Silver Troika began. Whittaker seemed now to have fully recovered his nerve. The intimate presence of Bathurst and of his own friends had without doubt considerably heartened him.

"I am in your hands, gentlemen," he said simply.

Fane took a book from the bookcase and seated himself at the table in the middle of the room. Whittaker sat at his desk, writing. The others took up their positions as Anthony had arranged. For a considerable time, there was silence, save for the scratching noise of the Major's pen upon the writing-paper. It was nearly dark now and Anthony motioned to Richardson to keep continually upon the *qui vive*. Whittaker, after a time, finished his correspondence and went and sat opposite to Fane.

"I have a torch," said Anthony, "that will give us immediate illumination of the room should we want it, without, of course, any one of us moving. Put the light off now, Neville, will you?"

Neville extended his hand and touched the switch.

"Thank you, Neville. Silence, everybody, now, please."

"Before we settle down, Bathurst"—it was the Colonel who spoke—"can't we have a little more air? There's no reason why we shouldn't, is there? It's insufferably hot in here. How about the small window there—over the French doors?"

Anthony looked up, considered the request, and then assented.

"All right, Colonel. It certainly is very hot in here. Open it, will you, Richardson?"

The chauffeur reached up and obeyed immediately.

As Mr. Bathurst had seated himself, not only could he watch the garden, but he was also able to see the position of everybody within the room. Neville was at the corridor door, the Colonel one side of the centre table and the Major on the other, facing the Colonel. Whittaker seemed tired and worn out with the suspense and anxiety, but he accepted the cigarette that Colonel Fane offered to him across the table. Richardson, the chauffeur, after opening the window as he had been ordered, resumed his seat opposite to Anthony and on the other side of the French doors.

For a quarter of an hour or so, there was complete silence. Then Anthony thought of something and resolved to alter the seating arrangements.

"Major Whittaker!" he exclaimed. "Change your position, will you? Come and sit behind me—against the wall here. I think you will be safer away from the middle of the room. There is just the chance of a shot finding you as you are sitting now."

Whittaker rose and crossed to where Anthony had indicated, turning to glance at the clock on the mantelpiece as he did so.

"I feel done to the world, Bathurst. The worry of it all has worn me to a shred. My fingers seem numb. I'm all of a tingle and my head's all of a buzz. Seems as big as a football. But I'll sit where you say. I think it will be a better idea myself." That the affair was mastering his nerves was evident. He seemed to be repeatedly swallowing.

Five minutes or so passed, the only noise in the room being a cough from Neville from his position by the door. Then suddenly there came a sharp exclamation from Richardson, the chauffeur.

"What's that, sir?" he cried. "What's that noise? There's something in the room, sir. It's been in the room too for some little time."

Anthony listened intently. There was a strange beating, whirring, flapping, fluttering sort of sound. It seemed above them, high up in the air somewhere.

Quick as lightning, Anthony whipped out his torch and flashed it towards the ceiling. Everybody's eyes anxiously followed the white circle of light. Then a hoarse, constricted sort of cry came from Whittaker.

"Curse it. Something's touching me! What is it?"

Quick as thought, Mr. Bathurst swept the torch on to the Major. Then he laughed, and the laugh held a note of relief.

"Nothing to be alarmed at, Major, although I've no doubt that it would please our visitor of this morning more than it has pleased you. It's what they call a specimen of the Nocturnal Lepidoptera. It's just a common Death's-Head Moth, that's all. Its proper name, I believe, is Atropos. Notice the singular marking on the thorax? Almost exactly a representation of the skull and cross-bones."

"It's a beastly thing, Bathurst. I knocked it off directly I felt it touch me. It fairly startled me. Its two eyes were shining like stars as it flew towards me."

"I can quite understand that, Major, especially in these present circumstances. Anyhow, it's gone now." Anthony's eyes followed it as it fluttered away again through the open space at the top of the French doors.

Colonel Fane laughed hoarsely.

"It seems a funny thing for a soldier to say, but the infernal thing gave me a shock, Bathurst, for the moment. Of course I know we're all keyed up to concert pitch and all that, but there seemed something unclean and loathsome about it—to say nothing of its beastly name. It sent me all of a shiver."

Anthony made no reply. He was carefully watching the windows. He could hear the occasional movement of Neville's feet whenever he slightly shifted his position at the door. He could also hear the deep breathing of the Colonel and the quicker, shorter exhalations of his own *vis-à-vis*, Richardson. Whittaker had put his head in his hands. Thus they sat, the minutes winging by with their inevitable relentlessness.

Suddenly Mr. Bathurst raised his hand with a gesture enjoining silence. He was certain that he could hear footsteps.

"Revolvers ready, gentlemen, please."

His voice was quite steady, but every one of his nerves was tingling with suppressed excitement. No sooner had he spoken than there was a strange sighing sound from immediately behind him and the body of the man who had sought his help slid almost noiselessly from the chair on to the floor. Major Whittaker had answered the call!

CHAPTER XI
THE EMISSARIES OF THE SILVER TROIKA

SIMULTANEOUSLY with the fall of the Major's body, Richardson's revolver cracked viciously, shivering the glass of the French doors into countless fragments. To Anthony's ears, Neville and the Colonel seemed to cry out in unison. As they did so, there flooded through Mr. Bathurst's mind a sickening and humiliating sense of failure. An emotion that, translated correctly, meant that somebody had appealed to him for help, had trusted him implicitly, had put faith in his plans, only for him to fail ignominiously and let the appellant come to his death just as simply as though he himself had not raised a finger in defence. To a death, moreover that had come to him in Anthony's own immediate presence, for he knew, without being told, that Major Whittaker was dead. Never before had he felt so hopelessly humiliated, and his humiliation was not yet complete.

Torn between two emotions—to turn to the body of the Major on the one hand and to join Richardson in the defence on the other—he followed the former inclination, although not altogether instantaneously. Before he could get to the body of Whittaker, several revolvers seemed to crack simultaneously in the garden and only just outside the doors. He heard Fane utter a curse of execration as the Colonel's revolver dropped to the floor. The Colonel clapped his left hand to his wrist and Anthony could see the blood welling from the wound. Just as co-incidentally—or so it seemed to him—for each incident crowded so quickly upon the one that preceded it that there seemed no period of intervening time—he saw a stabbing circle of light flood the room and Richardson borne back from the French doors by sheer weight of numbers. The doors themselves had given way for the same reason. The messengers of the Silver Troika had kept their tryst! A woman's scream came from the house—it was from Mrs. Whittaker. He heard her voice outside the door leading on to the hall corridor.

"Guy! Guy! What is it? Whatever's happening? Where are you?"

Fane replied to her.

"For God's sake keep out of it, Constance. This is no place for you. And be quiet—be quiet! Leave it to us."

The moment—or fraction of a moment—that Mr. Bathurst had spent in turning towards the body of the Major had effectively turned the scale against the defence. Because of it, the emissaries of the Silver Troika, seizing the psychological moment, were enabled to assume the whip-hand. As they burst through the defences so unceremoniously, the man with the brown beard covered Richardson, the gentleman with the withered arm did likewise to Neville, whilst the sleek slug-man favoured Colonel Fane with a similar courtesy.

"Red Lids" performed the dutiful operation upon Mr. Bathurst himself. The man that wielded the electric torch stepped into the middle of the room.

"So!" he said, and then turned to the "Slug", speaking rapidly and almost breathlessly in a foreign tongue. It was Russian, Anthony decided, after hearing the first half-a-dozen words. Immediately following, the man broke out in English. "Keep your hands up, every cursed one of you, if you want to see the sun rise to-morrow. I will relieve you of your revolvers, all of you. Keep them covered, *mes enfants*, and give me the rope. I shall feel safer if they are bound. See to it, Schmidt."

Schmidt chuckled oleaginously and Anthony was reminded once again of a fat slug just regaled with a banquet of lettuce-leaves.

The leader walked to the square light-switch in the wall and pressed it, at the same time pocketing his electric torch. He threw the revolvers he had taken on to the table.

"Hold your hands out," he cried to Fane, "behind you!"

The Colonel submitted, helped towards the submission by Schmidt's revolver. Neville and Richardson, in similar plight, were served alike. As he walked towards Anthony, Mr. Bathurst could see him well. He had no difficulty in identifying him as the "President" whom the Major had described to him the night before. He passed the length of cord round Anthony's wrists and knotted it tight. Whittaker had been right. He was by no stretch of imagination an oil-painting. Part of each of his lips had been cut away, just as the Major had said, leaving two rows of evil, yellow-looking fangs protruding from scarlet gums. But the condition had been his so long that he had evidently mastered the difficulties of labial-less speech. He looked round the circle with a leer.

"So!" he said again, and his voice was silky with malevolence. "Where is our kind host? Is this English hospitality? Why is he not here to greet us—some of his old friends of Red Russia? Have we not come many miles to see him?" Then, just as suddenly, his voice changed again, and this time it bore a viciously relentless note of crackling menace. "Where is he, I say, you English swine? Where is he? If you play tricks with me, I'll serve you as the Tartar served me." He motioned towards his mouth. "I'll hack you into a thousand slices, you hairless dogs. Where is he, I say, where is he?" His eyes glared, the epitome of rampant wickedness.

Mr. Bathurst's grey eyes met his unflinchingly.

"If you want an answer to your question, I shall be pleased to answer you."

The "President" swung round on to him instantaneously and vindictively.

"If I want an answer—what in hell do you mean? Do you think I'm playing? Out with what you know—and quick at that."

Anthony nodded to the floor behind him.

"Very well then. If by the term 'our host' you allude to Major Whittaker of Swallowcliffe Hall, you will find him here. I am afraid that he has fulfilled his last duty of hospitality and I offer you apologies upon his behalf. But if you will accept me as his deputy, I am sure you will permit me to express my regret at the coldness of your welcome. Believe me, I would have wished it to have been very much warmer."

Neville grinned at the irony in Mr. Bathurst's voice. The "President" glared at Anthony with a mixture of malevolence and doubt. Then he walked across to Whittaker's body.

"Get up, you scum!" he growled, saluting the prostrate form with a vindictive kick. "You Judas," he continued, "get up and show your white-livered face!"

An oath burst from Colonel Fane's lips, but Schmidt poked his revolver at him ominously and he became silent again.

"You will pardon me," put in Mr. Bathurst, "—I assure you that I hate disturbing you—but you still fail to appreciate the true position. I thought I informed you that Major Whittaker had discharged his last duty as a host. Even the most savage tribes have learned to respect the dead."

As he spoke, the "President" dropped on his knees beside the body and put his ear to the heart.

"Dead?" he cried. "Dead? And not by my hand, by God! Then he died too easily, by the Holy Ikon!" He sprang to his feet and faced them all again. "Which of you killed him? Which of you took the prey from my jaws? Come, speak, you nest of traitors! I'll promise an easy and comfortable passing to the man that killed him. No torture—no pain. Just a friendly bullet." He pulled a revolver from his pocket and tapped the barrel lovingly. The thick utterance of his speech, with the tongue doing most of the work of the missing lips, put an additional horror into his words.

Here the huge man with the brown beard interposed. He spoke in a torrent of Russian. He appeared to be arguing with the lipless horror in the middle of the room. The "President" listened for a time and then answered in English, somewhat grudgingly, Anthony thought.

"All right, Verensky! I grant you there's sound sense in what you say. But if he'd had a hundred lives for me to take, I'd have plucked them delicately from him one by one—and slowly! With no hurry in my hands! As plucking the feathers from the fatted goose! I'd have—" He broke off and thought for a moment before proceeding. "Still, perhaps you're right, Verensky. What do you say, Schmidt? It is strange hearing no opinion yet from you. Is it possible that you are not yourself? You heard what the chicken-hearted Verensky said. Do you agree?"

The brown-bearded giant growled at the unflattering reference, but Schmidt ignored the taunt thrust at him and bridged the situation.

"Yes," he hissed, "I think Verensky is right. If the arch-traitor and despoiler is dead, and you should know death when you look upon it too well to be deceived, why then he is dead and already burning in the special hell that the good God has prepared for him. For my part, I say let him burn there. He has kept his appointment early, that is all. And let us get on with the more important part of our business. Ask Krakar and Loronoff. See what they say, and then, my blood-brother, I will tell you something, something that you do not know, something that I, Otto Schmidt, have already seen in this chamber of death."

The "President" frowned at this last piece of egotism. Anthony listened intently, determined not to allow a single word of the conversation to escape him. He was beginning to form theories about the case that he had been unable to consider before. He found himself wondering if Mrs. Whittaker were still in the hall and if so, how much of the affair had reached her ears. But as far as he himself and the others with him were concerned, he was unable at the moment to see from where their own succour was likely to come.

Krakar, his red-eyed companion of the public walks and pleasure grounds of the City of Liverpool, answered the "President's" query with a spate of Russian. Loronoff, the man with the withered arm, was less voluble, but from the expression on the face of each of them and from the look that flitted across the countenance of the "president" as he listened to them, Anthony felt certain that they agreed with the gospels according to Saint Otto and Saint Verensky.

"All right, then," muttered the "President". "The majority shall have it. I will fall in with what you say. So that you can tell us at once, Schmidt, what has been discovered by your wonderful intelligence, by your altogether marvellous sagacity! Behold, I listen! We all listen! Now, friend Otto!"

"If you then listen," hissed Otto Schmidt, "then surely you shall hear and afterwards see. Look, my comrades, look! Look at that man by the door there."

All eyes, including those of Anthony, looked in the direction that he indicated.

"Loronoff," cried the "President", "march your man over here quickly! I can see him better over here and there will be less risk." He laughed mirthlessly and mercilessly. "I have not come these thousands of miles to run unnecessary risks. It is my enemies who will run the risks."

The man with the withered arm obeyed the "President's" order. He pushed his revolver into the small of Neville's back and Neville limped stiffly into the middle.

"Now, President," exclaimed Schmidt, "look at him! Look at his face. Don't you recognise him?"

Anthony craned forward to see exactly what was going on, but his eagerness was not to the liking of Krakar. With an oath and a threatening gesture, he brandished his revolver in Mr. Bathurst's face and forced him back to his original position.

The "President" swore softly under his breath.

"Otto Schmidt," he said quietly, "I make you an apology. As President of the Silver Troika to a faithful member, I make it to you. I do know this man. You are right. It is the cursed Neville. He is Whittaker's servant, as he was Whittaker's servant in the glorious days of 1918, when our mighty country freed its limbs from the shackles. He may know the truth. If he does, he shall tell us. Oh yes, his lips shall speak." He walked up to the late Major's batman and thrust his evil face into the face of Neville. "My friend," he said very softly, "where are they—what we have come for? Tell me or I'll pull your tongue out by its roots, and that will be a joy to what will come afterwards." He laughed, but the laugh was soft with a sense of horror. "Tell me, I say! Where are they?"

Neville, the imperturbable, shook his head stolidly.

"I don't know what you are talking about," he answered.

"So," said the "President", "is that really so? Shall I then have to find you something to assist your knowledge and loosen your tongue? Are you forgetful? Tell me, you dog, *where are they*, or at least what is left of them? We know that very few have gone."

He hurled the last words at the man whom he menaced and as he did so became more than ever the incarnation of active and belligerent evil. But Neville refused to be shaken by the force of mere words.

"I told you before, I don't know what you mean, or even what you're referring to. If I don't know what 'they' are, I can't very well tell you where 'they' are, can I? I should think even you have got common-sense enough to see that." He tossed his head contemptuously at his questioner as he spoke.

The "President" looked straight at him, his eyes glittering with cold cruelty and malevolent desire.

"You liar!" he said slowly and deliberately. "I'll burn the truth out of you, if that's your game! I'll make you wish you'd told the truth at first. I'll bring you to your knees screaming for mercy. Krakar!"

He turned quickly and hurled another mouthful of Russian at the red-eyed gentleman. The latter grinned unpleasantly and nodded quickly two or three times in succession at what his chief said. Mr. Bathurst, however, was not done with yet. He had caught the word *"nachaiok"*—one of the few words of Russian that he knew.

"Why do you still harp on this?" he asked almost persuasively. "You have already been informed by Major Whittaker as to what actually has happened with regard to the things you want. Why pursue a subject that is already closed and which it is absolutely impossible for any one of us here to re-open? Major Whittaker wrote to you on the sixth of August telling you that the things you so urgently desire had been destroyed by him some considerable time ago. There is no doubt that that message was received by you or at least by someone acting upon your behalf."

He paused to see the effect of his words upon the other's face. The "President's" face twisted into a repulsive and contemptuous leer.

"Lies! Destroyed! Tell that story to a babe at the breast. I should be imbecile to believe that, as you yourself must be, Mr. Cunning Postman." He flicked his fingers under Anthony's nose with vehemence. "But I cannot think that you do believe it. I stand in a house of lies and the father of them is dead. May he rot in his grave, the despoiler!"

Suddenly he seemed to think of something. Dropping down again by the side of Whittaker's body, he felt carefully in all the pockets of his clothes. But the disappointment was plainly to be read upon his features when he sprang to his feet again. He fixed his eyes upon the man whom Schmidt had recognised.

"Neville," he cried, "you know where they are! I know that you know, you lying dog. And do you know *how* I know? Eh? I'll tell you." He sidled towards the old soldier with wicked craftiness, looking like an evil bird about to swoop down upon its prey. "If he makes the slightest movement, Loronoff, put a bullet through his arm. Do you hear me? I don't want to kill him—yet."

He crept close to the helpless Neville and then, with savage suddenness, gave him a merciless buffet on the mouth. Neville fell back, bleeding freely from the blow.

"You cowardly swine!" cried the Colonel. "If only my hands were free—"

But the "President" heeded him not.

"I'll tell you *how* I know, my dear friend Neville. I caught the look of triumph on your face when I found nothing in that dead dog's pockets. You weren't cunning enough to hide it. And as you know, you shall tell me! Krakar, give me the 'Persuader'."

The gentleman addressed produced something from his coat pocket and handed it almost lovingly to the "President". The latter walked to the rear of Neville and seized his right hand. Anthony watched him and his movements curiously and then felt a wave of horror sweep over him. The lipless man caught hold of Neville's thumb and did something with the "Persuader" that Anthony was unable to see. Neville shrieked and Anthony heard a cry of horror break from the lips of Richardson, the chauffeur, who was in the best position to see what was actually happening. The operation seemed to be repeated and this time all the colour was drained from Neville's face and he gave a low moan. Anthony jerked at the bonds which bound him in a fierce, unreasoning sort of passion, so much so that Krakar, who had returned to his place, growled menacingly and pointed his revolver straight at Mr. Bathurst's heart. Anthony could hear the voice of the "President", silky and then stiff again with the savage lust of cruelty.

"Well, my friend, are you going to speak? I'm listening if you are. Where are they? Where are they, you—"

Neville screamed again, wildly and uncontrollably, and as he did so, the electric light bulb in the centre of the room flew into a thousand pieces. The crack of the revolver shot outside and the bursting of the bulb seemed to happen together—instantaneously! As he had prophesied the evening before, Mr. Daventry was certainly 'bang' on the premises!

CHAPTER XII
PETER DAVENTRY JUSTIFIES HIS SELECTION

A SHOUT of exultation from outside and a wild roar of triumph, another shout, and then there came two more quick revolver shots, seemingly very close at hand. Simultaneously with the latter of these, Mr. Bathurst's foot flew up and caught the red-lidded Krakar beautifully upon the point of the elbow. Timed to a nicety and directed towards the arm that held the revolver, the effort was completely effective. Mr. Bathurst had the supreme satisfaction of seeing the threatening instrument fly high into the air and its owner draw back with a howl of pain. At the instant, bound though his hands were, he flung himself upon his opponent. His physique was such that the Russian went down under his weight like a house of cards. Anthony wound his legs round the legs of his antagonist and pushed his head with all the strength and force at his command against the point of Krakar's chin.

From the other parts of the room came strange sounds, for the tables had at least been partly turned. With a muttered curse, the "President" turned from his attentions to Neville and flooded the room with the light from his electric torch. As he did so, he uttered a yell of pain and execration, for another bullet from the unerring hand of Mr. Daventry, still unseen, plugged him neatly through the wrist, so that the torch fell to the floor. The "President" cried an order in Russian and rushed through the French doors into the darkness, followed, so Anthony presumed by the noise that succeeded his exit, by Loronoff, Schmidt and Verensky. With an adroit movement of the knee, Krakar squirmed from under Anthony's heavier body and rolled away from its weight. Then he picked himself up from the floor, looked wildly round, and dashed out in the wake of the others.

For a moment—a brief, palpitating moment—all was silence. Nobody in the room seemed to have breath left to speak. A silence that Mr. Daventry broke as he stepped jauntily through the doors into the room.

"Bathurst," he cried, "are you here?"

"I am, Daventry," replied Anthony. "I'm on the floor, and there's a torch in my pocket—right-hand side. I can't get to it because my hands are tied. And besides being on the floor, my dear Daventry, I am extremely pleased to see you. Let me hasten to assure you that you are far from being *de trop*."

Peter bent down and possessed himself of Mr. Bathurst's torch. "Great snakes!" he exclaimed. "You're all trussed up. I seem to have made my entrance in the nick of time."

"You have at that!" cried the Colonel. "You've taken the very words from my mouth. I'm in a similar predicament to Bathurst, as well as two others of us. Be as quick as you can, sir, with your knife, if you please. There's a man fainted here and over there is a man who has fought his last fight. Hurry, man, those swine may be back at any moment."

From the light of the torch, Peter slashed at the cords of the four men.

"Richardson," said Anthony, as soon as the chauffeur was freed, "get half-a-dozen candles—the damage to the light may be extensive. We must look to Neville and to your master."

The chauffeur hastened to obey the order, returning quickly with six big candles, which the Colonel lit at once. Anthony gave the two prostrate men a quick but comprehensive glance.

"Daventry," he said, "you and the Colonel carry Neville into the other room—the dining-room. Richardson and I will bring the body of the Major."

"But suppose they come back?" remonstrated Fane.

"We must chance that," responded Mr. Bathurst. "But I don't think they will—to-night. Lock the door, Colonel," he said, when the two burdens had been safely brought in, "in case any of the ladies should venture down. I don't think it's likely. They must be frightened out of their lives if Mrs. Whittaker has told them. Anyhow we won't risk it. We shall be far better alone." He looked at the body of the Major, as it lay on the floor where Richardson and he had placed it, and covered the face reverently.

An exclamation from Peter Daventry arrested his attention.

"Bathurst," he cried, "look at this poor devil's thumb! It's in a ghastly mess."

As he spoke, Colonel Fane forced some brandy between Neville's clenched teeth and down his throat. The colour came slowly back into his features and he opened his eyes. His own glance, like that of all the others, went down to his right thumb. The top joint was not a joint any longer. It was a piece of red, raw pulp. The "President" had wielded the "Persuader" most skilfully. No doubt experience had taught him the trick of the trade. Peter Daventry failed to repress a shudder, but Neville apparently was game to the last.

"Never mind me, gentlemen," he said, and his voice was fairly strong, considering the ordeal through which he had so recently been. "Look to the Major. He wants help more than I do."

The Colonel joined Anthony and Peter.

"Bathurst," he said with suppressed emotion, "you were there—nearest to him. What in the name of Heaven killed him? Or was it just a natural death?"

Mr. Bathurst hesitated for a moment before he answered:

"We shall not know what killed Major Whittaker until a doctor has seen him. When that has happened—if it is then necessary—we can turn our attention to how he was killed. Certainly no one was near him when he died. He maybe had an ordinary seizure. There may have been heart weakness—brain trouble possibly. He has recently gone through an unnerving experience, remember, and it may have told on him." He shrugged his shoulders. "To assert or to consider anything at the present time must of necessity be merely conjecture, which never makes any appeal to me at all. If when the doctor sees him he tells us that Major Whittaker died a natural death, my own heart will be very much lighter, because he called to me for help, and I am not sure that I haven't failed him. Who was the Major's medical man, Colonel Fane? Do you happen to know?"

"Dr. Searle, of Buttercross. Not that he ever worried him much. The Major wasn't a man who liked doctors messing round him."

"Make arrangements then, Colonel, please, for Dr. Searle to come over here as quickly as possible, and please tell Mrs. Whittaker as much as you deem politic."

The Colonel looked at him doubtfully.

"Do you think we'd better wait till the doctor actually comes, or shall I tell her at once?"

Anthony thought for a moment.

"Tell Mrs. Fane. She will break it to Mrs. Whittaker better than you will be able to. Tell Daventry here where the 'phone is. He can telephone to Dr. Searle for us. I'll stay here with Neville while you go."

Fane paused on the threshold, irresolute.

"There's another point," he said. "What are we going to tell Searle when he comes?"

"I have thought of that," replied Mr. Bathurst. "I am going to take a risk. I am going to say nothing about our visitors. Major Whittaker was found dead on the library floor by me—that's all I'm going to let out for the present. What may happen after that depends to some extent upon what Searle tells us. Until I know that, I'm holding my hand. Get along, Daventry, will you, and 'phone him."

Neville's voice broke in upon them.

"The doctor's telephone number is Holmedale 2244, sir, if you don't know it."

"Thank you, Neville. It will probably save time to know it. Now, Colonel, see Mrs. Fane while Daventry speaks to the doctor."

Left with Neville, Richardson and their dead master, Anthony bent over the body again and looked carefully at the dead man's face. He pulled down the lower lids of the eyes and looked at the two pupils. Then he sniffed at the lips and mouth. A whitish mark on the left wrist next attracted his attention.

"H'm!" he muttered. "If so, where is the—"

Before he could follow up his train of thought, the door opened to admit Mr. Daventry.

"No communication possible *via* telephone, Bathurst. I've tried several times, but there's nothing doing at all. I should say the wires have been cut."

"They were pretty thorough then, the scoundrels. Meant business, didn't they, and doing the job properly? And haven't finished yet by a long chalk, I'll wager." He thought for a minute. "Get the car ready, Richardson, and get off to Dr. Searle's surgery hell for leather. If he asks why we didn't 'phone to him, tell him we're under repair or something and the 'phone's gone wrong. He may not think to ask you, though, when he hears your news. He may be too startled. You heard what I said to Colonel Fane just now? Tell the doctor the Major's dead—died very suddenly—and no more."

"Right, sir. How about if those murderin' devils try to stop me? If they're still on the watch, you know, sir—"

"Take your revolver, Richardson, and Mr. Daventry here will accompany you with his. He's ridden in your car before, you know. As a matter of fact, I don't anticipate that you'll have any more trouble to-night. Get to the doctor's at all costs."

Peter and the chauffeur made their exit immediately, the former glad to have the opportunity of action. Anthony turned to Neville as the door closed.

"Had the Major any heart weakness of which you knew, Neville?"

"No, sir. I never knew the Major to be ill, sir—leastways, not for years, sir."

"Never heard him complain, eh?"

"Never, sir. If that's what you're thinking, sir, perhaps you wouldn't think it disrespectful if I gave you my opinion. My master was murdered, sir, in a way that we couldn't see! Murdered by those perishers just as surely as though they'd cut his bloody throat, begging your pardon for the use of the adjective, sir."

"You think so, Neville, do you?" Anthony looked him over carefully.

"I do more than think it, sir. I'm positive, although of course I've got no proof. But I'd like to be as sure of a thousand quid." His voice sank to a whisper. "You remember that 'orrible moth, sir, that was flutterin' round the room, not long either before the Major toppled over? Well, just as—"

The door was pushed open again. Colonel Fane entered the room, his face showing signs of extreme agitation.

"Thank God I've got the worst over. My wife had heard nothing of the affair until the shots right at the end of it. It's a big house, you see, and the bedrooms are a good distance away. It was very sporting of Connie Whittaker to have kept what she knew to herself for so long. Lots of women would have found the temptation to talk irresistible. But she had obeyed me implicitly. Mrs. Fane tells me that she took the worst news splendidly, considering everything. They're together now and Enid, my niece, is with them. The two of them will help her to bear up."

"Did she ask to see her husband, do you know?"

"She seemed inclined to want to at first, so my wife says, but eventually was persuaded not to. Why do you ask?"

"I wondered, that was all. How far away is this doctor's place, Neville?"

"A matter of about four miles, sir, not much more. Half-an-hour should see them back, sir, providing, of course, that the journey's all plain sailing."

Anthony paced the room for a moment or two. Eventually he paused and, turning to the others, said—it must be confessed somewhat to their surprise:—

"I'm going back into the library for a moment or two. After all, it's where the poor chap died, and if there's any evidence at all—" He left them without waiting to complete his sentence.

Inside the library he could see nothing of any great significance. The candles were burning very low, so he took his torch from his pocket and let it play round the room. The revolvers were on the table where the "President" had thrown them and there were the lengths of cord lying on the floor as Daventry had slashed them from the wrists of the four of them. Otherwise the room seemed quite ordinary. The wind through the broken glass of the French doors caused the last dying flames of the candles to gutter fitfully and cast strange, eerie and at times monstrous shadows in and across the apartment. The setting seemed eminently suitable to what had gone before. The three letters that the Major had written prior to his death lay on the desk at which he had sat to write them. Mr. Bathurst picked them up, gave them a hasty glance, and put them into his pocket. He would hand them to Mrs. Whittaker in the morning. In the act of pocketing them, his ear caught the sound of the wheels of a car.

As he left the library and walked back to the dining-room, he met Peter Daventry with the man whom he presumed to be Dr. Searle. The doctor was a little, red-faced, 'jumpy' sort of man, his 'jumpiness' being noticeable in his speech as well as in his manner, for his voice was high and squeaky.

"Ah, Colonel Fane, I believe! We met once before if you remember. This is bad news I hear. I am indeed sorry to think that we should meet again under such dreadful circumstances. Where is the—"

The Colonel pointed to the heap on the floor.

"Who found him?"

Mr. Bathurst replied at once.

"I found him on the library floor. My name is Bathurst— Anthony Bathurst. He had apparently gone in there to write some letters and had fallen from his chair to the ground. We carried him in here."

Dr. Searle made his examination. After putting the stethoscope to the heart, he felt the wrists and looked at the dead man's eyes.

"H'm!" he said. "Quite dead—no doubt about that. Stone cold." He undid the Major's clothing, loosened the collar and exposed the neck, throat and chest. "H'm!" he muttered again. "Slight excess of thyroid perhaps—hardly enough, though, I should have thought, to—" He rose and faced his audience.

"An ordinary case of cardiac failure, I should say, gentlemen, to all appearances. Very likely the Major stooped down suddenly or made an impulsive movement of some kind and—" Dr. Searle shrugged his fat little shoulders. "We shall never know exactly what it was, gentlemen. We seldom do in cases of this kind. There is a slight thickening of the mitral valve of the heart and just the slightest condition of stenosis. There was nobody with him or near him, you say, when he died? Ah well, it's a shock for those left behind, but for himself—well, there might have been many worse passings. Entirely painless! I'll come over again in the morning and see Mrs. Whittaker. In the circumstances, I shall, of course, be quite prepared, as the Major's medical adviser, to issue a certificate. Gentlemen, I am sorry. It is most sad, but I can do nothing. It's very late. I will wish you goodnight. Perhaps your chauffeur would run me back? Thanks! Good-night, Colonel! Goodnight, Mr. Bathurst! Good-night to you, sir!" He bowed to the three of them.

"I will find Richardson for you," volunteered Mr. Daventry.

"Well, Bathurst," said the Colonel, "the doctor's opinion must have removed a load from your mind."

Anthony shook his head doubtfully.

"Good-night, Colonel Fane!" was all he permitted himself to say, as he walked from the room.

As he went, Colonel Fane stared at him curiously!

Chapter XIII
MR. DAVENTRY'S NARRATIVE

AT THE DOOR he ran into Peter Daventry on his way back from the chauffeur.

"Has he gone?" inquired Anthony.

"The doctor? Yes. What's your programme now?"

"Bed, laddie, or rather bedroom, and you're coming with me. I imagine that you have quite a lot to tell me. Also there are several things I want to talk over with you. I'll explain your presence here to Mrs. Whittaker in the morning. I had anticipated it to her."

"How is she? Heard any more?"

Anthony shook his head. "No, nothing. This way—and then straight on. First door on the left. Tread softly. There's been quite enough excitement tonight without attracting any more."

Once in the bedroom, Anthony closed the door.

"You have much to tell me, and I have much to tell you. It is imperative too that we should each know what the other knows. Also it is not certain what is going to happen next. But there is one fact that emerges from the mist that I cannot ignore. I have failed in my mission. The man who sought my help is dead. I shall never forgive myself that." There was an unmistakable bitterness in his voice.

Peter Daventry's sympathy went out to him immediately.

"For the love of Mike don't take the blame for that! You heard what Dr. Searle said. An ordinary case of heart. Might have happened at any time. Nobody could justly accuse—"

Anthony stopped him.

"I heard what Dr. Searle said. Yet I am not satisfied. I'm afraid that I was not convinced. I say to myself the man was murdered. All the intelligence I have drums it into my ears. My instinct tells me the same story—the man was murdered. Here he is threatened with death at a certain specified time. The death occurs. The organisation that has threatened him appears on the scene coincidentally. It seems obvious that there must be a connection. The inference is far too plain for any other possibility to be even considered. And yet—" He paused, evidently weighing the whole affair in his mind.

"And yet what?" intervened Peter with eagerness. He had seen Bathurst in this mood before—it usually presaged something important.

It was some time before the reply came and when it did come, Mr. Bathurst spoke very slowly.

"And yet, Daventry, I'll swear that Whittaker's death was a surprise to the amiable villain who criticised the conditions of his hospitality. When he realised that the Major was dead, there was an unmistakable look of thwarted spite on his face. I'm certain of it. The man's rage touched bestiality. I'd swear it was the real thing in disappointment. Now what went wrong with their precious plans, if anything? Tell me that. That's my problem, Daventry!" He sat on the ottoman at the foot of the bed and then continued: "That's the point that is beating me in this case, Daventry! One half of my senses tells me I'm investigating a most cunning murder. The other half tells me that the murderers were cheated and baulked of their victim. So where am I in the end?" Rising from the box, he paced the bedroom a time or two, then took out his cigarette-case and handed Peter a cigarette. "Let's smoke on it," he said, "and you listen carefully to me while I tell you exactly what's happened since we parted company in Little Knype."

Daventry listened attentively. He attempted to treat the narrative in the same way as he had known Bathurst himself treat similar narratives upon various occasions in the past. At one or two of the more important incidents he whistled incredulously. When Anthony had finished—and he finished on a note of sincere congratulation concerning the most timely arrival of Mr. Daventry upon the scene—Peter himself took up the thread of his own story.

"Well, I'm afraid, Bathurst, that I started by making a rather priceless bloomer. I'm afraid I ran well up to form there. When you left me—you buzzed off rather quicker than I had been anticipating for the moment—I temporarily lost my nerve. Not much—just a little. But sufficient to rattle me and to get the old brain-box a bit woolly in the clear. I knew there was only one precious thing would put me right—you know the idea, balm in Gilead and so on and so forth. I lit a cigarette."

Anthony failed to repress an exclamation of wonderment. But Daventry went on imperturbably.

"Oh, yes, I agree it was a pricelessly fat-headed thing to do, especially situated as I was, but there you are. Even Homer waggled the old bonce sometimes, you know. As the bloke said the other day in the play, 'It's no use crying over spilt milk—there's enough water in it already.' I lit a jolly old 'gasper'. Well, of course, I don't know exactly what happened, but I suppose the fat little feller with his mammy's eyes and the other gentleman with the dirty face-fungus were nearer to me than I had anticipated. I've certainly very good reasons for thinking so. You remember they had given us a bye and had strolled on—er—treading the primrose path of the gladsome old dalliance, don't you? Anyhow, it's even money that the dear old lads spotted me light up and it's a caravan of camels to a cock-eyed caterpillar that they started sleuthing me. The bright idea may even have occurred to them that I was A. L. Bathurst, Esquire, although I admit you don't possess my singularly graceful figure. Well, I was trundling along, all merry and bright and gaily practising saying 'Diana' as charmingly as I knew how, when I heard a low whistle from somewhere in the undergrowth quite close at hand. 'Pon my soul, Bathurst, when I heard it my jolly old blood wouldn't have disgraced a Polar bear. You could have poured it into a sieve. It reminded me of the old whistle that called back the winsome cobra-chap in 'The Speckled Band'. You remember that, don't you? I remember as a nipper I used to wake in the middle of the night and imagine that I'd just heard it! I stopped, changed my legs or something, like dear old 'Tishy', and it was a bit of luck for me that I did, I can tell you! For as I did so, a couple of bullets whistled past my ears like two little bits of real, genuine Larwood. Without stopping to think what my best course was, I bolted into the undergrowth like a shot bunny. Talk about dust!" He stopped and looked quizzically at Anthony.

"Go on," said the latter. "I don't blame you in the least, if that's what you're thinking. I should probably have done exactly the same."

Peter grinned appreciatively.

"Stout fellow! You've taken a weight off my mind by those truly noble words. I ran, Bathurst, quicker than I've ever hopped it in my life. No stout old lady or cripple could have lived with me. My action was simply superb. But a peculiar noise behind me caused me to turn round as I ran. If my blood had been cold before, Bathurst, it was all jolly old stalactites this time. Talk about Club Row! There was a screamin'ly friendly-looking bow-wow after me about the size of a saloon 'bus. I can tell you he was a proper twenty-eight seater and no error. But he failed to digest one of Daventry's Little Lead Pills. Made quite a fuss about it too before he took his single ticket to the jolly old huntin'-grounds."

Anthony nodded.

"I heard him—twice! Talk about *your* blood running cold! Mine did when I heard his dying yelp!"

Peter nodded in return.

"It was a joyful note, wasn't it? Well, anyhow, I dropped Mr. Bloodhound, Morris Minor or whoever he was, in his tracks. Then I decided to put as much daylight (or nightlight, if you like it better) between myself and his carcass as was humanly possible. I was doing even time comfortably like a young Applegarth when something caught me a most juicy and appetising biff on the back part of the old thinking-apparatus and life interested me no more." He rubbed the back of his head ruefully. "It's still sore too, my little greeting from the Silver Troika, as you call them. When I came to, feeling like the morning after the night before—you know, dark brown taste in my mouth and all that—there were four men standing over me—King Beaver, the fat swine who talks like the last thing in snake-charmers, the fruity fellow whose lips have fared badly on their amorous journey through life, and your pal with the pink peepers. They gabbled something at me in Russian, I think. I wasn't having any, of course. I played Simple Simon to that. Then the 'President', as you call him, asked me who I was and what I wanted in Little Knype Wood at that time of night? What was my place of call? Would I kindly pass on the news? Then I had a brain-wave. Perhaps it will be a permanent one—you never can tell with yours truly. I told 'em I was Anthony Bathurst. Struck me all of a sudden that if they really thought that, it would help you in your endeavour to cross the jolly old line. Why had I shot their Pekingese was the next question on the examination paper. Pretty cool that, wasn't it? Piece of darned H.P., I call it. I replied asking why had they had a pop at me? This caused them to gabble again amongst themselves like a bazaar committee. I fancy I was the bone of contention. The point was, what should be done with me? Judging from the sincere and impassioned earnestness of the leader, he was all for my walking the plank or something on the jolly old spot. Seemed to be an authority on boiling oil and things. But dear old 'Slug-face' didn't see eye to eye with him and he chin-wagged a bit about it. 'Whiskers' seemed to me to be at one with 'Slug-face', but the other two appeared to be on the side of the 'President.' Eventually, however, 'Slug-face' said something to the 'President' that made an impression, because it made that priceless old Anglo-Catholic very taciturn for a few minutes. Properly down in the mouth he was over it, I can tell you. As a result, 'Whiskers' and 'Starry Eyes' tied my hands behind my back and I was quick-marched for about a mile and a half, I should think, till we came to a sort of disused gardener's hut—or tool-shed—on the edge of Little Knype, as I found out afterwards. I was flung in and the door fastened. There I stayed the night through, cursing my confounded luck, you bet. Some time in the morning, 'Whiskers' arrived with half a loaf. There was a kind of rough bench inside the hut, so the old Beaver did the Old Mother Hubbard act, broke the old Bermaline up in dinky little pieces, put them on the top, and I had to eat it after the manner of an unassuming quadruped."

Anthony grinned as he tried to realise the position.

"'Pon my soul, Bathurst, when I'd finished I nearly let out a melodious whinny. I got no lunch, but at tea-time—or at what I imagine was round about the time for the refreshing old Orange

Pekoe—Beaver boy blew in again with more of the dainty Hovis and a few pieces of Gorgonzola cheese. Same performance! Same performance by P. Daventry in his world-famous animal imitation act! Two performances daily! Well, time flew by, I don't think, and gradually it began to get dusk—but very gradually, believe me! I couldn't tell how the old *tempus* was 'fugiting'. My watch had stopped—I discovered that afterwards—and, of course, with my hands as they were, I couldn't wind it, even if I had known. But all of a sudden I had another of my superfine brain-waves. Standing up against the wall on one side of the hut was a spade—you know, one of the kind that dear old Adam delved with when Eve span—and the sight of the side of it caused the jolly old grey matter to revolve most healthily. The revolutions sent me almost dizzy. I sat on the floor—back towards it—and wriggled and wriggled like a Trade Union lizard till I got the rope that bound my wrists up against the edge. Then, as the dear old Bard of Stratford said during the intervals when Anne hadn't a way, 'there was the rub!' It was a ticklish job, Bathurst, take it from me, but little Peter's long suit was always perseverance. I gritted my teeth and filled my soul with pensive thoughts of the gallant though disconsolate old Bruce and the indefatigable old web-spinner. But, joyful to relate, I got through the knots one by one and at last stood up—a free man."

"Well done, Daventry!" put in Anthony. "Go on! What did you do next?"

"Felt in my pocket for my revolver. I was a cheery optimist."

"It had gone, of course."

"It had," returned Peter, "but even there my luck held. I looked round for a weapon of sorts. Spades and brooms seemed to be the only things the hut held. Made me think of Jack Cade's army. And although brooms may be bright little fellers for the jolly old Admirals, they made but slight appeal to little Peter. I was just giving the idea up as a bad job when I spotted my revolver! It had been chucked into a corner when I had undergone my induction. The rest was supremely easy. I biffed the door one of my best and juiciest with the old spade and was soon hieing me away. I guessed I was still in Little Knype, but I found a path that led me eventually to a widish bit of road. I kept my eyes skinned, I can tell you, for any of my old playmates, but happily (for me, that is) they seem to have been engaged elsewhere. My most pressing little problem now was—which way? As I was commencing the old council of war with Peter Daventry Esquire not only in the chair but also forming the snappy old quorum, an angel blew along. His face was red, his nose snub and more red and his breath singularly redolent of 'Spearmint.' I fell on his neck like unto the old prodigal and in response he directed me to Swallowcliffe Hall."

"How far were you actually from it when you asked him?" Anthony cut in.

"Less than half-an-hour's walk, I should say. I had to come straight down the road, as easy as falling off the Christmas tree. Anyhow, just as I made my objective, the old shooting-gallery started. So I skirted round to the back as hard as I could pelt. On the wall was the cunningest little thing in rope-ladders on which you ever clapped eyes. Ten times out of nine, rope-ladders are like the friendly old undertaker—they let you down in the end. But this one was a winner all over. I executed a graceful ascent, negotiated the spiked gallery, and made my way like a master of wood-craft towards the theatre of operations. Like the cheery old executioner, it didn't take me long to get the hang of things. When I saw what was happening, I didn't know quite what to do, though. The 'President' chap was just getting to work on your man, Neville. I was afraid to fire in case I hit you or one of your people. The 'President' and one or two of his precious gang were dodging about so. But when they got well on the job with that torturing business, the old brain-box revived again and I conceived the really snappy notion of having a shot at the electric light. Little Peter's hand never wavered. He was himself again. Taking his revolver from his pocket—ahem!—with the utmost *sang froid*, realising that the lives of his trusty comrades depended upon his skill, our young hero, in the straight line of descent from William Tell—"

Anthony smiled and, leaning forward, patted him on the back.

"You did well, Daventry, and it was a damned good shot on your part. You hit the bulb, as far as I could see, plumb in the centre. But we still have at least two problems to solve and undoubtedly one awkward situation to face. Now tell me, did you get any inkling from these beauties as to what they're after? Do you remember any chance remark, any phrase or allusion, either while they were round you or when you were in the hut, that would help me?"

Peter Daventry shook his head with some despondency.

"I don't, Bathurst. Most of their talk—if not all of it—when they were discussing the brightness of my future, was in Russian. It was, if I may be allowed to suggest, caviare to the—er—corporal."

Mr. Bathurst smiled again at the sally.

"Very well, then, we'll sleep on it for to-night. Don't forget it's to-morrow already. We shall have another visit from the Silver Troika—I haven't the shred of a doubt about it—but it won't be for a few hours yet. I'm certain of that. Also, I have to face Mrs. Whittaker in the morning, a job to which I'm by no means looking forward. So for the moment, I'm for bed. I'm not anticipating the morning at all pleasurably, Daventry! I feel that I have betrayed my trust—miserably too!"

"Don't see what else you could have done beyond what you—"

But Anthony was impervious to Daventry's well-intended sympathy.

"I underrated the strength of my opponents—also their intelligence, which is always a fatal mistake. That's where I blame myself. I, of all people, should have known better."

"I see your point," returned Peter, as he got between the sheets. "Still, all the same, I—" He broke off suddenly and fired a question at his companion. "What puzzles you most about the whole affair? The death of Major Whittaker or the—"

Mr. Bathurst interrupted him to reply to the first question.

"What puzzles me most, Daventry," he said, "is the part played in the affair by a certain Mr. Garland-Isherwood, the gentleman from America that chases butterflies. For the moment I can't place him at all."

Chapter XIV
THE WRIST-WATCH AND THE LETTER

On the following morning, Mr. Bathurst was the unwilling recipient of yet another shock. He had risen early, dressed quickly and come downstairs to breakfast with Mr. Daventry. None of the ladies had put in an appearance when he and Peter arrived in the breakfast room, and Colonel Nicholas Fane seemed but a shadow of his former rather aggressive self. When he had finished a somewhat meagre meal (for him), Anthony claimed his attention.

"Mrs. Whittaker? How is she this morning, Colonel? Have either you or Mrs. Fane seen her yet?"

"I have not, Bathurst. To tell the truth, I don't want to—in fact, I have shirked the encounter. What can I say to her? What can one ever say in affairs like this? But I believe my wife is with her now. I left her under the impression that she was going to Mrs. Whittaker." He shrugged his shoulders in a kind of helpless resignation. "Why do you ask? Had you any special reason?"

"Yes, Colonel Fane. I fear that it is necessary for me to see her as soon as possible. Perhaps you would be kind enough to ask her for the interview? Yes?"

The Colonel nodded acquiescently.

"All right, I will. Can I help you at all, my boy? If so, by all means command me. I've had poor old Whittaker moved into one of the bedrooms."

Anthony rose and thrust his hands deep into his trousers pockets.

"Thank you, Colonel. It seems to me there is one thing certain. The ladies must be got away from here some time to-day. There is no doubt in my mind that those devils whom we entertained last night like us so much that they are bound to call again. It will be no place for women when they do. Make arrangements with Mrs. Fane, will you, Colonel? I'll leave that to you and her."

"What about the women on the Major's staff?"

"Whom do you mean—the people in the kitchen?"

"Partly, and I was partly thinking of Miss Whittingham, poor old Whittaker's secretary. What about her?"

"I haven't had the pleasure of meeting her yet," returned Anthony. "Perhaps you would remedy the omission some time this morning? But in reply to the query you raise concerning her, I certainly think she had better get out of it for the next couple of nights, say, at least. I think the kitchen staff—the maids and so on—can remain here with us. I can't see that any peril overhangs them." He pursed his lips as he came to the decision. "Tell Mrs. Whittaker I'd like to see her as soon as convenient, will you, Colonel?"

Colonel Fane nodded and promptly withdrew.

"Seems properly down in the mouth over the job, doesn't he, Bathurst?" It was Peter Daventry's first contribution since he commenced breakfast. "Were he and the Major very close, do you know?"

"According to the dead man, they were at Sandhurst together. Fane looks a good deal the senior of the two—or rather did—but I understand that actually there was very little in it. So perhaps it's not so surprising that he's so upset. Major Whittaker seemed to hold a high opinion of him."

As he spoke, there came a tap at the door. Before Anthony could extend the usual invitation, the door opened and a girl entered. She was wearing a white blouse over a navy blue skirt and Mr. Bathurst was able to recognise her without difficulty as the girl who had preceded him in the corridor on the previous day. Colonel Fane had evidently lost no time in acceding to Anthony's suggestion. She was of distinctly striking appearance. Of medium height, her black hair was parted in the middle and brushed down flat on either side of her head. Her eyes were a rather unusual dark blue, which only served to intensify the pallor of her complexion. Her whole aspect was so serious and in her eyes there reigned such a sadness that to Anthony she suggested the tragedienne.

"Mr. Bathurst?" she said very quietly in a tone of inquiry supported by her look. Then she caught the unspoken answer from Anthony's eyes. She went on without waiting for him to speak. "Colonel Fane told me to come along here. He said that you wanted to speak to me. What is it you wish to—" She paused and again there came the query in her dark blue eyes.

"I presume that I am addressing Miss Whittingham?" Mr. Bathurst was all courtesy.

"Yes, I am Pamela Whittingham, secretary to the late Major Whittaker." Her voice was low but the words came very clearly and distinctly from her lips. Seeing Mr. Bathurst's expression as she spoke, she hastened to explain. "I am indebted to Colonel Fane for the knowledge that Major Whittaker is dead. He has just told me."

"I see. It was a shock to you, no doubt?" Anthony watched her carefully as he asked the question and he did not take his eyes from her as she answered it.

"A shock in one way, perhaps, and yet not in another. To a certain extent I was in Major Whittaker's confidence, more so perhaps during these last few days. I knew something of the danger that menaced him. I think it relieved him somewhat to talk about it sometimes, and I was there, close to him. But of course I hoped, as no doubt we all hoped, that it would be averted."

"When you say you knew something of the danger that threatened the Major, are you speaking particularly or in general terms?"

"Quite generally. I knew—I have known for some time— that he had made enemies during his life and I also knew that he feared that they would revenge themselves upon him. In fact, he told me as much. But he told me nothing more." Miss Whittingham made her statements one by one with the utmost composure and complacency.

"Did the Major tell you that the danger which he feared had become imminent?"

She nodded her head gravely.

"He hinted at it about a week or perhaps ten days ago.

Anthony announced his interest.

"Tell me exactly what he said, Miss Whittingham, if you can. Try to remember the actual words that Major Whittaker used. Facts are so much more useful than conjectures."

Miss Whittingham considered this question for a moment or two before she ventured her reply. When this came, she spoke very slowly indeed.

"I think—mind you, I could not swear to it or anything like that—I only think that he said: 'Well, Miss Whittingham, it's come at last. The beggars are hot upon my trail.' If they were not the actual words he used, they are near enough to give you the information that you are seeking, Mr. Bathurst."

"H'm! What was your reply when the Major said that to you?"

Miss Whittingham looked very surprised at the question. She contented herself at first with an almost imperceptible movement of the shoulders.

"I think I just expressed my regret, that was all. After all, it was hardly my place to comment on it, was it?"

"I see. You had no idea, I suppose, as to why these enemies of the Major wished to be revenged on him? What was the nature of the trouble between them and him?"

Here Miss Whittingham became very emphatic.

"No, Mr. Bathurst. I have no idea whatever. I thought I had made that clear. The Major never confided in me to that extent."

"Thank you then, Miss Whittingham. That is all that I have to ask you. If you think of anything else, if anything comes to you suddenly from the repository of your memory, as it were, that you consider it would help me to know, please come to me and tell me. Sometimes these things are almost unconsciously stored, you know. Thank you again."

The secretary slipped out of the room almost silently.

"Not much information there, Daventry, say what you like about it. I get nothing particular from anybody. It's all so vague—'enemies', 'papers'. What papers can be so valuable that men are prepared to murder for them? Tell me that, if you can."

"Strikin'-lookin' girl that, don't you think, Bathurst?"

Anthony waved the opinion away unsympathetically.

"That wasn't the question I was asking, Daventry. I scarcely looked at her face. I was more interested in her hands—particularly her finger-tips. My question was what could the papers have been for men to murder—"

Peter cut in with some contrition in his tone.

"I'm sorry, Bathurst, but her expression reminded me very much of Pauline Frederick. I couldn't help thinking so all the time you were talking to her. I nearly always found myself feeling sorry for her—sympathetic, you know. As to the question of the papers—well, there you are! That's the old conundrum! How about a marvellous invention that Whittaker may have scrounged from these honest workers, these hardy peasants who wrest a frugal living from the bare—"

Colonel Fane's voice outside the room and Anthony's admonitory finger brought his suggestion to an abrupt but well-merited conclusion. They could hear what the Colonel was saying.

"I'll come in with you, Constance. I don't suppose he'll want you for very long."

As the door opened, the Colonel ushered in Mrs. Whittaker. Mr. Bathurst rose to greet her.

"This is my friend, Peter Daventry, Mrs. Whittaker, of whom I spoke to you the night before last. You will remember?"

The lady inclined her head and bowed in Mr. Daventry's direction. Peter returned the bow. Mr. Bathurst proceeded. He seemed to speak very gently.

"I should like to express my most sincere sympathy with you in your trouble, Mrs. Whittaker. I feel that I owe you a tremendous debt, the whole of which it is impossible for me ever to repay to you. But believe me, I shall endeavour to repay as much as I can." There was a ring in his words that betrayed a wealth of infinite purpose.

Mrs. Whittaker held out her hand to him.

"Thank you, Mr. Bathurst," she said very simply. "I know that."

"Sit down then, Mrs. Whittaker. I have just one or two things to ask you before you go and perhaps one or two things to tell you. We will deal with the former first. The servants, Mrs. Whittaker, excluding Neville and, of course, Miss Whittingham, your late husband's secretary—tell me about them. How long you have had them and so on. Major Whittaker did give me some details the night I arrived. I should like you to add to them."

"Besides Neville and Richardson, we have three servants, Mr. Bathurst. They are Mrs. Chamberlain the cook, and Fothergill and Appleton, the two maids. Mrs. Chamberlain is the widow of a man in my husband's old regiment. She has been with us ever since we came to live up here. Appleton and Fothergill have been with us four months and seven months respectively. I am quite satisfied with all three of them, Mr. Bathurst. Mrs. Chamberlain is a treasure and the other two seem good, reliable girls. Fothergill at times may be a trifle sulky, but—"

Here Mr. Bathurst intervened.

"What references did they have? You had some, of course, from them?"

Mrs. Whittaker nodded.

"Oh, yes, I would never think of engaging a servant without. Appleton was recommended to me by a friend of Mrs. Fane's, a Mrs. Rigby-Clissold of Clymping, Sussex. Appleton had been with her eighteen months before she came to me. Fothergill came with a local reference—I forget from whom, but I know it was quite satisfactory."

"How about Richardson, the chauffeur? What about him?"

"Well, as a matter of fact, Major Whittaker got him through Miss Whittingham, his secretary. We had a previous chauffeur who left rather hurriedly, obtained employment in Venice—he was very clever at stained-glass window work—and the Major fixed up with Richardson through Miss Whittingham, who knew that our other man had gone. But he's entirely reliable and trustworthy, Mr. Bathurst. We have never had a single complaint against him—in any shape or form."

"I see, Mrs. Whittaker. There seems no trouble then in that direction. Now another question! Was Major Whittaker in the habit of wearing a wrist-watch?"

"Yes, Mr. Bathurst, on the left wrist—always! Why do you ask?"

"There is a whitish mark on the left wrist that suggests unmistakably the habitual presence of a wrist-watch. That fact was what prompted my question. But, strange to say, the watch itself is not there. Neither is it in any of the Major's pockets.

That fact is what really prompted my question. Of course, it may be nothing—there may be nothing at all in it and the explanation may be very simple—but it struck me as being unusual. There is a difference between the unusual, for instance, and the extraordinary. You see what I mean, don't you?"

Mrs. Whittaker's face puckered into a mixture of surprise and reflection.

"I can't account for the watch's absence, Mr. Bathurst. Have you looked for it anywhere?"

"No, Mrs. Whittaker, not yet. But there is a clock on the mantelpiece of the room in which the Major died. That touches the matter just a little, I think, don't you, Colonel?"

Fane glared.

"Hanged if I see your drift, Bathurst. There certainly was a clock there. I saw Whittaker look at it more than once."

"Exactly! So did I. That *is* my drift, Colonel. Still, as I said to Mrs. Whittaker just now, there may be nothing at all in the incident to cause us any worry." He put his right hand into the breast pocket of his coat and again addressed Mrs. Whittaker. "Major Whittaker wrote three letters last night, Mrs. Whittaker, in the room where he died during our period of waiting there. I found them on his desk and kept them to give to you this morning. The question of whether you forward them to their respective addresses, in the light of what has happened, or prefer to retain them yourself is one for you to settle. Read them and decide for yourself. That will probably help you to come to a decision. They may be important—they may not."

As he spoke, Peter Daventry noticed a curious expression of something like surprised annoyance come over his face. Mr. Bathurst drew the letters of which he had spoken from his pocket. There were but two. The third was not there. He handed the two to the widow.

"I am exceedingly sorry, Mrs. Whittaker," he said, "but I am very much afraid that the third letter that I mentioned has been stolen from my pocket during the night. I have no doubt, therefore, that these two are relatively unimportant. Once again, please accept my apologies."

Peter Daventry could see that once again Mr. Bathurst felt a sense of failure.

CHAPTER XV
THE NAME ON THE ENVELOPE

MRS. WHITTAKER took the two letters somewhat curiously and opened them. She read them rapidly and then handed them back to Anthony.

"There is nothing important here that I can see, Mr. Bathurst," she said. "Look for yourself."

Anthony did as he was bid. The first was a short note to a Colonel Hilton Keatley of Ormskirk Grange, Lancashire, accepting an invitation to a dinner of the Lancashire Unionist Association on the 2nd of September, while the second was addressed to a Leslie Chadwick Esq. of 17, Crossland Mansions, Aintree. It contained but a few lines to the effect that Major Whittaker was unable to do anything in the matter that excited their joint interest for some weeks at least. Mr. Chadwick was to wait until he heard from the Major again. The Major also hoped that Mr. Chadwick's health continued satisfactory.

"Thank you, Mrs. Whittaker," said Mr. Bathurst, after a few minutes' scrutiny of the two sheets of paper. "Certainly neither of these appears to help us very much or throw any light on our darkness. But tell me, was it the Major's habit to attend to certain correspondence himself? For instance, consider Miss Whittingham, his secretary—why was it, do you think, that she didn't deal with the letters that occasioned these replies? Or might it be that she would hand certain correspondence over to the Major to answer? Have you any idea what the Major's system was?"

Mrs. Whittaker paused to consider the question before giving Anthony his answer.

"I don't know that I can answer that in the way that you want me to, Mr. Bathurst," she returned at length. "I shouldn't say that my husband had any definite system, as you called it, to which he would invariably adhere. What I should say usually happened is this. What you would describe as personal letters he would answer himself, leaving Miss Whittingham to type the political and ordinary routine correspondence. Still, if you asked her the question herself, no doubt she could give you much more detailed information than I can." She looked at Anthony with a kind of appeal in her eyes.

"Perhaps I can help you a bit there, Bathurst." The interruption came from Colonel Fane.

"Yes, Colonel?" Mr. Bathurst gave him the invitation.

"Well, with regard to what Mrs. Whittaker just said about personal letters, I can speak from experience. Take my own case, for example. Guy Whittaker always wrote to me in his own hand—has done so for years. If I wrote to him, he always replied himself—in writing."

"I can understand that, Colonel. I think it's what I should have expected to happen. Was this Colonel Hilton Keatley a close friend of Major Whittaker's?" Mr. Bathurst turned again to the lady as he put the question.

"Yes," she said, "I think I could say that. Guy and he used to meet each other quite a lot over matters of politics."

"I see. And this Mr. Chadwick to whom your husband wrote—Mr. Leslie Chadwick—what about him?"

The lady shook her head.

"I have never heard of him," she said most emphatically. "If he were a friend of my husband's, it was entirely without my knowledge. I have never heard him mention the name."

Mr. Bathurst looked inquiringly at the Colonel. The latter sensed the precise nature of the inquiry at once.

"No, I've never heard Whittaker mention the name either. My sentiments in that direction are exactly the same as Mrs. Whittaker's."

Mr. Bathurst seemed unperturbed.

"We shall find an explanation, no doubt. Send for Miss Whittingham again, Colonel, will you, please?" Before the Colonel could stir, Anthony went on: "Don't you trouble, sir. Daventry will go. Do you mind, Daventry? Find Miss Whittingham and bring her along here as quickly as possible."

Peter slipped out with alacrity. He had had many worse errands than that. A matter of a few moments saw him back with the desired lady. Anthony lost no time in opening.

"I'm sorry to trouble you again, Miss Whittingham, but a little matter has arisen that very probably you can settle for us better than anybody else. Did Major Whittaker make a point of dealing with certain of his correspondence himself or were you instructed, shall we say, to refer certain matters to him?"

The blue eyes opened wide.

"Do you mean with regard to letters and things that came in?"

"Yes. What was your ordinary procedure over letters?"

"The Major always went through the post himself—*first*. I don't mean that he opened all the letters when I say that, because he wouldn't. I think he looked at the envelopes—at the handwriting perhaps. By far the greater number of them he would hand to me unopened for answering. Others he would open and hand to me for the same purpose. Some, no doubt, he would open, retain and reply to himself—I might not see them at all."

"I follow you, Miss Whittingham. I anticipated your reply would be on those lines. There is one other question that I wish to ask you while you are here. Have you ever come across the name of Leslie Chadwick in the Major's correspondence?"

She half-frowned for just the fraction of a moment before replying. Then she shook her head.

"No. I can't remember the name. I have a fairly good memory for names too."

"You can't remember ever typing a letter to a man of that name?"

"No, never."

"Or ever seeing a letter from him?"

"No, not even that. Where does he live—do you know?"

"In Liverpool, Miss Whittingham. In Aintree, to be exact."

She shook her head more vigorously.

"That makes me certain of what I have told you. I have never met the name Leslie Chadwick in any way in the Major's correspondence."

"Thank you, Miss Whittingham. That is all that I want to ask you."

She turned to go.

"Colonel Fane will be giving you instructions within a very short time from now."

"Thank you, Mr. Bathurst."

Miss Whittingham withdrew and closed the door behind her. As she did so, Mrs. Whittaker came forward impulsively across the room and touched Anthony on the arm.

"Mr. Bathurst, I am very worried. What did you mean just now when you said a third letter had been stolen from you? You can't mean a letter of my husband's? How is such a thing possible? I don't—"

"Last night, Mrs. Whittaker, your husband wrote three letters, which I found on his desk, as I have already told you. I placed the three of them in my pocket in order to be able to hand them to you. But one has gone. I have no doubt that it has been stolen—stolen for its importance."

"Might you not have dropped it? Or perhaps mislaid—"

"No, Mrs. Whittaker, I have done neither. The letter has been stolen."

"But why? Why should anybody steal it, Mr. Bathurst? What value could it possibly have to anybody else?"

Anthony shrugged his shoulders.

"That is what I hope to discover, Mrs. Whittaker, that is the problem. If I knew, I should have much less—"

She interrupted him.

"Besides—here's a point, a most important point too, it seems to me—how could anybody have known that you had the letter in your possession? It is impossible that anybody *could* have known. You can't steal a thing from anybody unless you know—"

"I admit the force and truth of all that, Mrs. Whittaker. I have considered that aspect of the matter myself. That is another problem which I have to consider." He glanced at his wrist-watch. "Has Colonel Fane told you what I suggest is the best and safest plan for you to adopt? I hope that you are in agreement?"

The lady nodded, with a look of infinite sadness.

"I am leaving as early as possible this morning—before lunch at any rate. Mrs. Fane and Enid are taking me to stay in Liverpool with some friends. We shall remain there until the funeral."

"That's an excellent idea. I can't think of anything better. Before you go, Mrs. Whittaker, I have one more question to ask you. Doubtless you remember my first interview with your husband on the evening that I arrived, and what he told me concerning the Government and the Police. Is it your wish that I should still respect his desires in those directions?"

As he put the question to her, she shot him a half-scared glance, her hands working in obvious agitation.

"My husband is dead, Mr. Bathurst. Nothing else matters very much to me when I think of and remember that. But if you can, without imperilling any other lives, for instance, or jeopardising any other interests, I would prefer you to do as Guy asked you. I like to think that he knew best."

"Even though by so doing, I may minimise the chance of avenging his death?" Mr. Bathurst's voice was incisive.

"You use the word 'avenge,' Mr. Bathurst. No doubt you use it from deliberate choice. You think my husband was murdered then? I thought Colonel Fane seemed—"

"Even if his death were natural, Mrs. Whittaker, it would be fair to say that his enemies encompassed it. Nevertheless you are right. I used the word 'avenge' quite deliberately."

The lady's reply came low and tense.

"I would like his death to be avenged, but I feel that I must obey his wishes. Keep the Police out of the case if you possibly can. It is sufficient for me to realise that that is what he wanted."

Anthony bowed.

"I will remember what you say, Mrs. Whittaker. By the time I next see you, I hope I shall have cleared up some at least of the mystery." He held out his hand to her.

When the door closed upon Colonel Fane and Mrs. Whittaker, Anthony turned quickly to Peter Daventry.

"There are two things I must do at once, Daventry, although I very much fear I'm too late. How could I tell—how could I guess? The whole affair is—"

He paced the room under the influence of some excitement. "Go into the library, Peter, and hunt all round the desk where the Major wrote the letters last evening. If there's a waste-paper basket underneath or near, look in it—search all round for any scraps of paper there that may be lying about. I don't suppose for a minute that you'll find anything. Still, there's just a chance."

Peter started upon his errand. But the question in his brain went irresistibly to his lips.

"Why don't—"

"Why don't I go, were you about to say? Because, my dear Daventry, I'm going somewhere else. Once again we'll divide our forces."

Anthony followed Peter out and made his way quickly upstairs. He had no difficulty in finding the bedroom where the body of the dead man had been laid. Major Whittaker was dressed exactly as he had been when death had come so quickly to him. Nothing appeared to have been touched. Anthony bent down quickly and felt inside the pocket of the dress jacket. It was empty—there were no letters or papers of any kind. He shook his head with some impatience.

Leaving the bedroom as noiselessly as he had entered, he stood on the heavily-carpeted landing for a moment, lost in thought. Neville, a few yards away, watched him curiously and wondered what Mr. Bathurst was doing. Anthony placed his left hand over his closed eyes and stood there motionless.

"I picked up three letters last night," he said to himself. "Two I have handled this morning—the third has gone. What was it that was different about the third from the other two? For I am emphatically certain that there *was* something."

Memory, which is the power to revive at will ideas that have been impressed upon the mind, depends very much upon the vividness of the initial impression, which in its turn comes from a process of concentration. But Anthony, when he had picked up the letters, had done so with his mind full of other things—things which he had considered at the time as of greater importance. He was forced now, therefore, to rely upon the power of visualisation. There is a great difference between visualisation—that is to say, visual remembrance—and mental vision. By the latter a person may visualise ideas through the medium of words, but by the process of visualisation the actual words originally seen may be remembered. It is a question of the operation of the law of optics. At the back of the lens of the eye is a nerve screen—the retina—upon which the objects before the eye may be said to be photographed. The objects themselves are not seen, but the images or pictures of them. Mr. Bathurst applied this principle to the pictures of the three letters he had picked up from the desk on the previous evening. How had the third letter differed from the two he had handed to Mrs. Whittaker? That was the precise point which it was necessary for him to visualise.

Suddenly, with a quick stab of remembrance, it came to him. The address on the envelope had been typed!

The other two were in the Major's handwriting, or at least in the handwriting which he presumed was Whittaker's. He could now see, by this process of revival, the actual words that had comprised the name and address. The ink had been of a faintly palish shade and the words on the envelope had been "Messrs. Thornton and Jackson, Dale Street, Liverpool."

As he took his hands away from his eyes, he saw Neville still standing and watching him from the end of the landing. He beckoned to him with rapid decision.

"Neville," said Mr. Bathurst, as the servant approached with his usual stiff gait, "tell me something if you can. Do you happen to know of a firm in Dale Street, Liverpool, of the name of Thornton and Jackson?" He watched Neville's face closely before the man answered.

"No, sir," was the reply. "I can't say that I have ever heard the name, sir. Why did you want to know, sir, if I may ask? Because no doubt—"

"I just thought that you might be able to help me, that was all. As you can't, never mind."

He descended the stairs quickly and found Peter still on the hunt in the library.

"Well, any luck, Daventry?"

"None at all. There's not a sign of anything having been left behind here."

"Where's the waste-paper basket?"

"Not here. Been removed, I expect."

"Whom by, I wonder?"

Peter shrugged his shoulders doubtfully.

"Can't say. How about trying to find out?"

Without waiting to respond verbally, Anthony walked over to the side of the room and pressed the bell. Neville was quick to answer the summons.

"Neville," said Mr. Bathurst, "perhaps on this occasion you will be able to help me. Is there a waste-paper basket usually kept in this room?"

"Yes, sir. There should be one here, sir."

"Well, there isn't one at the moment."

"Been removed then in all probability, Mr. Bathurst, by one of the maids. I will inquire for you, sir, if you will wait for just a moment."

"Thank you, Neville. If you would, I should be obliged. Be as quick as you can, won't you?"

Anthony's eyes met Peter Daventry's as Neville closed the door.

"What," said Peter, "What are you thinking?"

"That I'm too late again. I'm making a habit of it this journey. But how was I to know—how could I possibly foresee? A man must work on the things that lie in front of him. If I lie in bed at night and hear fog-signals, I may surely be forgiven if I deduce the presence of fog. I cannot be reasonably expected to deduce that the atmosphere is perfectly clear and that the noises I hear are from a new kind of fog-signal that the railway authorities are testing on certain lines, can I? But . . . thank God things are beginning to straighten out at last." Peter looked mystified. He felt that he would very much like to know where the straightening was to be observed. Everything looked precious crooked to him.

A tap on the library door stopped the remark that he had been on the point of making. Neville entered again at Anthony's invitation. He carried the waste-paper basket in his hand.

"Here is the basket for which you inquired, Mr. Bathurst. It was removed by one of the maids this morning in the ordinary way when she tidied the room. All the contents, I understand, have been destroyed."

"I see. Just as I expected. Who removed it, Neville? Did you discover which maid?"

"The basket was taken out by Fothergill, Mr. Bathurst. I interrogated her on the matter myself."

"Is Fothergill the maid who habitually sees to this room?"

"Yes, sir." He winced as though in pain and looked down at his bandaged thumb.

"She takes the basket every morning and destroys the contents?"

"That is so, Mr. Bathurst." Neville answered the question so emphatically that Anthony could entertain no doubt upon the point that he had raised.

"Thank you, Neville. If Miss Whittingham is still in the house, tell her I should like to have another word or two with her."

Neville bowed and withdrew. When he returned within a matter of a few moments, it was to tell Mr. Bathurst that the late Major Whittaker's secretary, acting upon the instructions of Colonel Fane in the capacity of Mrs. Whittaker's representative, had left Swallowcliffe Hall about twenty-five minutes previously. Mr. Bathurst accepted the situation philosophically.

CHAPTER XVI
MR. BATHURST AND THE SILVER TROIKA

"I HAVE something else to say," said Neville, "something Mrs Whittaker has asked me to tell you. She was anxious that I should not forget. She has found Major Whittaker's wrist-watch. I gathered from what she said, Mr. Bathurst, that you had been making inquiries with regard to it. As a result, she had a good look round to see if she could find it. She was successful. She found it in the Major's bedroom, sir. He had evidently left it in there."

"Purposely, do you mean—or carelessly?"

"Mrs. Whittaker didn't say, sir. But I have it here, Mr. Bathurst. Mrs. Whittaker thought that you might care to examine it."

He thrust two fingers into the pocket of his waistcoat and handed over the wrist-watch to Mr. Bathurst. In shape, size and appearance it was ordinary. It was attached to its strap just as it had been taken from the wrist. Anthony looked at it curiously. It had stopped at nine minutes to seven. He tested the winding apparatus in order to see if the watch required winding. It was almost fully wound. The watch was out of order. He handed it back to Neville.

"Thank you, Neville. That's all right. How's the thumb this morning—very painful, I suppose?"

The man nodded.

"I know I've got it, Mr. Bathurst, if that's what you mean— but it might have been worse. That's how I look at it. The devils might have had a go at the other one as well. There's no knowing the tortures their minds can invent."

"I suppose not. You were of course in Russia with your late master?"

"Yes, Mr. Bathurst. That's how that swine of a Schmidt recognised me last night. Many's the time I've thought me and the Major wouldn't have left Russia alive."

"Had some ticklish times, eh?"

Neville nodded again.

"Which I shan't see any more, now the master's gone. I can't tell you all that his death will mean to me, sir. I stood by him the whole of the time he was up against them Silver Troika merchants. I only wish I could stand by him now. But it's too late."

"When did you first know that the Silver Troika was on his track?"

"As soon as the Major got the first of the messages, sir. I was probably the first person he confided in. He sent for me and told me."

"Did he tell you also of the message he sent them in return—that the documents and papers that they so badly wanted had been destroyed, and that he couldn't possibly fall in with their demands?"

Neville nodded an affirmative.

"You agreed with his policy?"

The servant moved his shoulders expressively.

"What else could he do, Mr. Bathurst? You can't give people what you haven't got, however much you'd like to, can you? That stands to reason, don't it?"

Anthony didn't answer. He walked across to the desk where the Major had sat writing the night before and took a piece of notepaper from one of the pigeon-holes therein. Taking his fountain-pen from his pocket, he scribbled a sentence or two upon it. He then read carefully what he had written. Folding the paper in half, he gave it to Peter Daventry.

"Find the nearest telegraph office, Daventry, and get that off at once. Prepay the reply. Ask Richardson to direct you. Time is valuable."

Peter slipped out and Anthony turned to Neville again.

"I intend to deal with these Silver Troika gentlemen in my own way, Neville. What I intend to do I'll inform you of later. But I am going to accept their challenge, as it were. In the meantime, help me over this. Who arranged the terms of my visit?"

"The terms, Mr. Bathurst? I don't quite—"

"The actual arrangements and their details, Neville—who made them? The meetings with Richardson and Coppinger, the sentences by which our respective identities could be proved, the various steps which were taken to frustrate the 'President' and his little gang—who was responsible for them?"

"I see what you mean now, Mr. Bathurst. For the moment I didn't get you. Mrs. Whittaker was the real originator of the plan—and I helped her."

"Richardson, of course, was an obvious choice of auxiliary. Who suggested employing Coppinger? Mrs. Whittaker herself or you?"

A slight flush surged over Neville's face.

"I was responsible for him, Mr. Bathurst. We wanted somebody besides our own chauffeur and I knew Coppinger to be a reliable man. I suggested his name to Mrs. Whittaker."

"How long have you known him?"

"Coppinger? Long enough to trust him, Mr. Bathurst. He's done several little jobs for me in the past. I know that he can be absolutely relied on. I've proved his worth in several ways, come to that."

"I don't doubt that for a moment, Neville, but you haven't exactly answered my question, have you? I asked you how long you had known him."

"Getting on for a year, Mr. Bathurst. But don't worry—he's as straight as a gun-barrel."

Anthony smiled at Neville's enthusiasm.

"All right, Neville, that's all I want to know. How long will Mr. Daventry be, would you say? He's gone to send a telegram for me. Where's the nearest telegraph office?" Neville looked a trifle anxious.

"Over at Holmedale, sir—a matter of about three miles from here. But if he asked Richardson, as I think I heard you tell him to, sir, the chauffeur would probably take him along in the car. He should be back therefore any minute now."

"Good!" Mr. Bathurst paced the room several times. Turning to Neville, he said at length: "Bring me the attaché case that your master used when he delivered his messages to the members of the Silver Troika. The Major told me that at midnight on the 6th of this month he put a letter inside an attaché case and placed the case on the tennis-courts. He informed me also, at the same time, that you kept watch that night and saw two of the Silver Troika fraternity, who were evidently deputed for the job, remove the letter and leave the case behind. I understand that you recognised them as the 'President' and the gentleman who calls himself Verensky, the brown-bearded specimen. You knew them, of course, from your operations with the Major in Russia?"

Neville hesitated for the fraction of a second before he answered.

"Yes, Mr. Bathurst, that is so. I saw Verensky and the 'President'—there's no mistaking them. I had run up against them when in Russia with Major Whittaker."

"Naturally. I think I begin to understand matters a little more clearly. You'll bring me the case, won't you?" Neville bowed his assent. Shortly after he had made his exit, Anthony heard Peter's voice in the doorway.

"All right?" queried the former, as Mr. Daventry entered.

"Everything O.K., Bathurst. Should be there before midday. So says the bright young damsel with the post-office manner. Will that suit you?"

"Very well, Daventry, very well indeed. As long as he's here by to-morrow, I shall be quite satisfied."

"Whom will the Commissioner send? Any idea?"

"Sir Roderick Hope, I expect. He usually does in cases of this kind. Sir Roderick is the Commissioner's pet pathologist at the moment."

"You have your doubts then, I presume, after all?"

"S'sh!" said Anthony, as the door opened again.

It was Neville, carrying the attaché case that Mr. Bathurst had requisitioned.

"Here is the case, sir, that you desired. It was in the Major's bedroom. I have also taken the liberty, after consultation with Colonel Fane, to communicate with the telephone authorities with regard to them making the necessary repairs. I presume that I am in order, Mr. Bathurst? There is no objection?"

"Certainly not, Neville. Quite the reverse, in fact. Put the case on here, will you?"

The man obeyed.

"This time, Neville, I am going to send a message to the Silver Troika. The case bearing it will be placed on the tennis-courts for them to find at midnight tonight. No doubt they will see it there, for I think that they are bound to be on the watch.

This is the message that I purpose sending to them." He took a sheet of notepaper from his pocket. On it he had written the following message:

"To the Servants of the Silver Troika.

"Major Whittaker, as you know, is dead. You have looked upon his dead body. It is obvious, therefore, that he is beyond the reach of what you have called your 'justice.' But it is believed by those that still represent him and safeguard his interests that you are determined to have 'what you came for.' It is proposed that you confer with the Major's representatives upon this matter at some time during the evening of to-morrow— shall we say at midnight? A guarantee is given that the conference will be entirely friendly and conducted upon reasonable and equitable lines, and it is sincerely hoped by all concerned that the entire matter will be brought to a satisfactory conclusion. If you agree to this suggestion place your decision in the attaché case.

Friends of the Dead Man."

He handed it to Peter Daventry, who read it silently and then handed it back without comment. He then passed it on to Neville. The man, so Mr. Bathurst thought, appeared to be a little perturbed at the tenor and direction of the message.

"Well, Neville," inquired Anthony, "what's your opinion? Tell me, I should value it."

Neville seemed irresolute—undecided. Eventually he committed himself.

"It goes against the grain with me to parley with murdering devils of their kind, Mr. Bathurst, especially as we can't give 'em what they want. That's my opinion, since you asked me for it. I've only one way for dealing with that outfit. I'd like to put a bullet through every man-jack of 'em. Not that that treatment wouldn't be a jolly sight too good for 'em. What's the idea, though, Mr. Bathurst, behind it?"

Anthony smiled.

"To find out a bit more than I know at present. When I've found out—well—" He shrugged his shoulders expressively.

"Well, what?" chorused Neville and Peter Daventry.

"Well, what? That is difficult to answer. But after that, it's quite on the cards that I might be disposed to go in for a little course of Neville's suggested treatment." Mr. Bathurst placed the message carefully inside the attaché case. "I confess that I find the prospect distinctly pleasing," he added.

CHAPTER XVII
MRS. CHAMBERLAIN'S NARRATIVE

As NEVILLE went from the room, Anthony heard another voice addressing the servant in the corridor. It was a voice that was unfamiliar to him—the voice of a woman—and he was positive that he had never heard it before.

"Who's that?" queried Peter.

Anthony shook his head and held his finger up for Peter to keep silent. Mr. Bathurst was listening to what the woman was saying. He heard Neville answer, the words he used being:

"I've no doubt the gentleman will see you if it's as important as you say it is. He's in here now. At any rate I'll ask him if he'll see you."

A tap came on the door and Anthony walked over to admit the visitor. Neville stood there and behind him a woman. She was a middle-aged woman with a pale face and dark red hair, a trifle over average height. The expression she wore on her face was tired and worn. From her white overall and white cap, Mr. Bathurst formed the opinion that this must be Mrs. Chamberlain, the cook of Swallowcliffe Hall. Neville acted as spokesman for her.

"I beg your pardon, Mr. Bathurst," he said, "for troubling you, but this is Mrs. Chamberlain, the cook here. She tells me that she feels she would like to tell you something about the master. Will you see her, sir? Shall she come in or are you too busy to see her now?"

"Let her come in by all means, Neville. What is it she has to tell us?" His eyes met the woman's with some encouragement. "Come in, Mrs. Chamberlain. You want to speak to me, I understand."

Neville ushered the woman into the room and then followed her. Anthony motioned her to a chair that stood close handy. She took it, looking anxiously at each of the three men in turn.

"Well, Mrs. Chamberlain, what have you come to tell me that Neville says you regard as so important? Take your own time over it and tell me the story in your own way."

The woman nodded.

"Yes, sir. I will, sir. I feel that that is what I should like to do. My trouble is that I don't quite know how to start. But I've heard from the mistress this morning, sir, that the Major's been taken and I know how upset she is over it, poor lamb, as is quite natural, of course. I remember how I was myself when my man went west." She sniffed at the reminiscence. "Well, since she left me this morning, I've been doing things."

"Doing things?" queried Mr. Bathurst.

"Yes, sir. By 'doing things', I mean thinking things over. Well, it's like this. I've thought things over and I've decided to come and tell you something, something that somebody ought to know. What with what I know and them shots that was fired somewhere round here last night, I think it's about time somebody took a bit of notice. Do you see my meaning, sir?"

Anthony had encountered this type of person before and his experience had taught him that people of this particular kind told their stories better when interruptions were few and far between. He therefore determined to allow Mrs. Chamberlain a loose rein and give her her head. His reply therefore was:

"Of course. Please go on."

"Well, sir, I said to myself, when the mistress told me the sad news this morning, 'Now that's very peculiar, a thing like that coming on top of the other.' I thought it over and thought it over and then the idea entered my head to tell one of the gentlemen. So I came up and asked Neville all about it—where I could find you, sir, to tell you what I know. Begging your pardon if I've taken a liberty."

Anthony put her at her ease and expressed his understanding of the position.

"That's all right," he murmured encouragingly.

Mrs. Chamberlain was now beginning to feel her feet better.

"What I'm going to tell you, sir, happened a month ago—or thereabouts. It happened on the ninth of July. I can remember the date, sir, because of the terrible thunderstorm we had that night in these parts. My memory's like that, sir. I can remember last March the twelfth, to give you an instance, because I burnt my elbow on the edge of the frying-pan. See what I mean, sir?"

Anthony smiled.

"Not at all a bad method, Mrs. Chamberlain. Go on."

"Well, sir, on the ninth of July, we had this terrible thunderstorm that I spoke of. The thunder was horrible and the lightning worse. Fair shook me to pieces, it did, sir. It lasted from about half-past six in the evening till past ten o'clock. We all of us thought it was never going to stop. You remember the night I'm talkin' of, don't you, Mr. Neville? It 'ud take a bit of forgettin' by anybody what was up here at the time." She paused for Neville to corroborate her description of the storm.

"I remember the thunder and lightning, if that's what you mean," he said curtly.

"Of course you do. I can tell you, you'd have fair surprised me if you hadn't. I never remember a storm like it. Well, me and the other two maids, Liz Appleton and Fothergill, was proper terrified. I thought the last day had come. I'd been reading a lot about that sort of thing in the papers and I suppose it had got into my head a bit—all about the Pyramid and such-like. Anyhow I came along from the kitchen and crouched against the wall of this very room where I'm sitting at the present moment. It seemed to be lighter here than anywhere and I couldn't see the lightning so vivid. I stopped where I was for a long time—until the storm was over, to tell the honest truth about it. Just as I was thinking it was all pretty clear and of getting back to the kitchen, congratulatin' myself on having been spared, I heard a cry from this room."

Mrs. Chamberlain looked intently at Anthony, as though to give point to her last words. But if she expected him to question her immediately concerning the origin of the cry, she was at least temporarily disappointed. Mr. Bathurst made no sign. He waited for the narrative to be continued. Peter Daventry watched him and then surveyed the woman again. He was beginning to feel extremely interested in the dark problem into which he had been so suddenly drawn, the more so because he was unable to estimate accurately the relative importance of the various evidences he had been called upon to consider. Realising that she was expected to proceed with her narrative, Mrs. Chamberlain proceeded.

"It was a strange sort of cry, sir, a hoarse, strangled sort of cry. Then directly after I heard a voice calling out and I recognised it at once. It was the voice of the master, Major Whittaker. I heard him say, 'What are you doing there, Forrester? Get away from me! My God, someone take it away from me! Get back to your grave, Forrester.' They were the exact words, as I remember them, sir."

She paused and looked up once again at the face of the man to whom she spoke. On this occasion she was rewarded in the shape of a question, a question that ultimately became a series of questions and eventually caused the look of triumph to pass from her face.

"In your opinion, Mrs. Chamberlain—and please think very carefully before you answer—was the cry that you first heard in the voice of Major Whittaker?"

Mrs. Chamberlain pushed her hair up from her forehead with the back of her hand before she answered.

"I couldn't be sure, sir. A cry's a funny sort of noise to recognise—one cry's very much like another—but I *think* it was."

"Two of the words you mention that you say the Major used were the word 'grave' and the name 'Forrester.' Would you swear that they were the actual words spoken? Think carefully, especially with regard to the name. I can't over-estimate the importance of your answer."

Mrs. Chamberlain moved her head vigorously. Nobody could have been more emphatic.

"Yes, sir, I'm certain he said 'grave' and I'm quite sure he said 'Forrester.' And I'll tell you how I know. The word was by way of being familiar to me. I sort of recognised it. My old father was a Forester, one of the Ancient Order. And right proper he looked in his regalia, I can tell you. Just as though he'd come off the Christmas tree. There was a time when he thought of becoming a Druid, but the Foresters had it. I remember a Sunday in one November. Mother had put a bit of pudding under the meat—"

"Thank you, Mrs. Chamberlain. What happened after you heard what the Major said?"

"There was a dead silence for a minute or two and then I thought I heard a low, jeering sort of laugh. Then, sir, after that, I took a bit of a liberty, but I couldn't 'ave stopped myself if you'd offered me all the treasures you could think of. I opened the door of the library to see who was in there. I felt as though I simply couldn't resist it."

"Well, and who was in there? Did you discover?"

"Major Whittaker, sir, and no one else. There wasn't a soul in the room besides the master. He was crouching all of a heap up against the wall, just as though something had scared him very badly. I think he must have got out of his chair."

Anthony pondered over what the woman had said. Then he asked her another question.

"Which way was he looking? Can you remember that?"

"Yes, sir, I can. The Major was looking over in the direction of the French doors leading into the garden, starin' out, you might say. I can see him now, sir, looking that way with a most strange look in his eyes." Neville's impatience, against which he had been struggling for some time now, mastered him. He came forward impetuously.

"Look here, Mr. Bathurst, this woman—"

Anthony held up a hand to check him.

"Let Mrs. Chamberlain finish," he said quietly. "What happened when you entered the library? Did the Major say anything to you? Was he annoyed with you, for example, for coming in?"

Mrs. Chamberlain shook her head in strong denial of the suggestion.

"He was too frightened to be annoyed with anybody, sir. Seemed more like glad to see me. I asked him what was the matter—if I could help him at all."

"What did he say to that?"

"Asked me if the man was still there, and he pointed out towards the garden as he said it."

"Could you see anybody?"

"Not a soul, sir. Take it from me, sir, there wasn't nobody there at all. The Major was imagining things. P'raps he'd been dozing off like and had waked suddenly, thinking he was seeing things—back in the Army, like as not."

Anthony regarded her curiously, a gleam in his grey eyes.

"Did you tell your master you could see nobody?"

"Why, of course I did, sir. I turned round to him at once and said that there was nobody there. Neither there was. I told him he must have seen a ghost."

"What did he say to that, Mrs. Chamberlain?"

"Well, sir, if you'll believe me, it seemed to make him worse than ever. His face went the colour of a bit of dough under the rolling-pin and it was as though he was trying to speak to me and couldn't. His mouth opened, but no words came."

"He didn't appear relieved in any way at your suggestion then?"

Mrs. Chamberlain shook her head rather lugubriously. "No, sir, far from it, in fact."

Anthony turned to Neville.

"I take it from your attitude, Neville, during the time that Mrs. Chamberlain has been telling us this story that it is news to you. You are incredulous with regard to it. That is so, is it not?"

"I should think it was, Mr. Bathurst," replied Neville impatiently and almost contemptuously. "I never heard the like of it."

"The Major obviously never motioned anything of the kind to you?"

"Of course not, Mr. Bathurst."

Mrs. Chamberlain bridled at the old soldier's incredulous tone.

"One would imagine, sir, from the way that Mr. Neville has received my account of the incident that I'd been givin' way to a little romancing. I should like to say that I'm almost a total abstainer. This is the last time that I ever—"

Anthony cut into her protest.

"That you ever what, Mrs. Chamberlain?" He looked at her very seriously.

"That I ever come forward with what I always understood was evidence. It seems to me that Mr. Neville here might just as well call me a liar straight away and have done with it. The idea!" She clasped her elbows in a state of turbulent indignation.

Neville smiled at her with satirical commiseration, but said nothing in reply. He evidently considered that the accusation of Mrs. Chamberlain concerning himself was too much in the nature of an absurdity to need refutation.

Anthony determined to attempt to pour the necessary oil upon the troubled waters.

"There, there, Mrs. Chamberlain! You misjudge Neville, no doubt. Your story has surprised him, I expect. After all, it isn't a story that one hears every day."

"That's not to say it isn't true, is it?" she rejoined with more than a soupçon of sulkiness.

"Certainly not, Mrs. Chamberlain. By the way, Neville, it's only fair to Mrs. Chamberlain for me to ask you this question. You will admit that readily yourself, I've no doubt whatever. Is this surname Forrester that she has mentioned familiar to you at all?"

Neville jerked his head up quickly as he answered the question.

"No, sir. I'm pretty familiar with all the people round here and there's nobody of that name round this quarter, I'm positive."

"Go back a bit, Neville. Leave the present circumstances. Never mind about immediate surroundings and who lives round here. Is this name Forrester familiar to you from any other part of Major Whittaker's life or career, say years ago? Think carefully, because it may be extremely important."

At first the man addressed seemed just as emphatic in his denials he had appeared to be previously.

"I can't say that I've ever heard of the name, sir, in connection with the Major, certainly not in what you might call recent years. I've cast my mind back over the time we spent in Russia together and even beyond that. Of course when we were over the other side in France—"

Suddenly his face changed and an expression of doubt came into it. Mr. Bathurst was quick to see the working of his mind and seized the opportunity.

"Well, Neville," he questioned, "have you thought of anything interesting?"

"Well, sir," returned Neville, "that's funny and no mistake. It's strange how one thing brings up another. Me mentioning the word 'France' did the trick. I've called to mind a Forrester that was in our mob—the Northshires." Neville grinned at the reminiscence. "We used to call him 'Mud-guts'—he always seemed to be in the thick of the mud and slush wherever we happened to go. Nice young feller, though, for all that."

"What happened to him?"

"He stopped one," replied the old soldier tersely.

"Killed?" The question came from Anthony very quickly.

The old "sweat" nodded.

"Too true. I didn't see it. I wasn't there. We was counter-attacking at the time. But I know Forrester got put out of mess. We lost a rare lot of men that day. Fair slaughter it was."

Mr. Bathurst pondered for a moment.

"What connection did this man have with your master? Any?"

Neville shrugged his shoulders.

"Don't suppose the Major even knew his name, sir. Just a full-blown private, he was, that and nothing more. Major Whittaker may have known him by sight, but there was no more in it than that—at the most."

"Think carefully again, Neville! Did you ever hear the Major mention the name of Forrester at any time, either recently or during those years ago? At any time—anywhere?"

But in replying to this question, Neville seemed more certain of his ground.

"Never, Mr. Bathurst, never once all the time that I've been with him. If I had have done, sir, I should have remembered the name long before I actually did, sir."

"Yes, I follow you there. That seems sound," agreed Anthony.

"Of course it is, sir. I can't see any connection of the Forrester I spoke about with Major Whittaker at all."

"Still, there was a man in his regiment that name—you admit it yourself," broke in Mrs. Chamberlain semi-triumphantly. "Looks to me as though there's something in it. Perhaps my story ain't such moonshine, after all." Her last remark was tinged with scorn. She continued at once, anxious to strengthen her position and drive her point home. "The man you speak of quite likely knew the Major unbeknown to you. I don't suppose you know everything by a long chalk."

Mrs. Chamberlain tossed her head with exultant indignation. The situation between the two of them looked to be developing awkwardly. Mr. Bathurst made haste to alleviate it by intervention.

"Whatever may come of it, Mrs. Chamberlain, there is no gainsaying the fact that your information is most important and at the same time most valuable. We are indebted to you for it. But I want to ask you one more question before you go. I can't altogether account for what seems, on the face of it at least, to be in the nature of a contradiction in your story. When you first described what happened on the night of the thunderstorm, you mentioned that you heard a low, jeering sort of laugh. To the best of my remembrance, that was the actual phrase that you used."

He was interrupted by Mrs. Chamberlain, who, nodding her head repeatedly, at last broke in.

"Quite true, sir! Quite true! I've no wish to withdraw one word of what I said. I said 'a low, jeering sort of laugh' and I meant 'a low, jeering sort of laugh.' For I'm pretty certain that was what I heard. The kind of laugh I should think might have come from Mr. Neville here, judging by his hattitude to-day." The superfluous aspirate on this occasion completely mastered her.

The man to whom she referred let go an impatient exclamation of denial.

"What the—"

Anthony extended a protesting hand.

"Quiet, Neville, please! Let me finish what I want to say to Mrs. Chamberlain." He turned again to that lady. "Yet, Mrs. Chamberlain, although you claim to have heard this laugh, you say afterwards that you told the Major he 'must have seen a ghost.' By that I presume you to mean that there was nobody there, either in the room or outside, and that Major Whittaker was suffering from an hallucination. If so, who was it whom you heard laugh? I confess that part of your story puzzles me."

The cook inclined her head with an almost bovine approval.

"I quite agree, sir. I know it sounds a bit contradictory. I've asked myself the same question more than once and I don't know that I've ever been able to answer it satisfactorily. But the conclusion I've come to is this. I think that the low laugh I heard came from the Major himself. That's the only way I can explain things."

She rose to go and Anthony opened the door for her.

"I suppose we must consider it a possibility," he conceded, "although I don't know that as a solution it altogether—"

Mrs. Chamberlain departed without waiting for him to finish, inwardly gratified at Mr. Bathurst's courteous attention.

Peter Daventry grinned at him as he came back into the room from the door.

"You have your uses, Bathurst," he said. "I've noticed it more than once."

But Mr. Bathurst received the pleasantry somewhat gravely.

"Don't forget my instructions about to-night, Neville," he said.

Neville bowed and, making no other reply, walked stiffly from the room.

Chapter XVIII
PETER DAVENTRY REMEMBERS
HIS HOOD

DINNER that evening was a very different meal from that of the previous evening. Every lady was, of course, absent. Consequent upon Mr. Bathurst's plan as outlined to Colonel Fane, Mrs. Whittaker, Mrs. Fane and Miss Pennington had gone into Liverpool to stay at the house of a friend of the lady first named. Miss Whittingham had been told to report again at Swallowcliffe Hall when summoned. The kitchen staff had remained on duty, to Peter Daventry's extreme satisfaction. As he said to himself, 'Man must live,' and two meals in one week of dry bread and stale gorgonzola cheese were quite enough (of their kind) for him. Mrs. Chamberlain had not allowed her annoyance with Neville's reception of her story of the 'phantom intruder' (as Peter Daventry put it) to interfere with the quality of her cuisine. She had had her instructions from Mrs. Whittaker before that lady left and had done her level best to obey them implicitly. In the circumstances and taking into consideration the difficulties under which the meal had been prepared, the menu was nothing short of excellent. To have found fault with any one of the courses would have been hypercritical. Even Colonel Fane, who justly prided himself upon the discrimination of his epicurism in this particular direction, expressed himself as being more than satisfied.

"Mrs. Chamberlain has surpassed herself," he declared, "considering everything." He drank his wine and repeated his assertion. "Don't you agree, Bathurst?"

"Yes, Colonel, I do. I only wish the atmosphere of the house was more conducive to enjoyment. By the way, I haven't seen a lot of you since this morning. Did you see Mrs. Whittaker and the other ladies off?"

"I did, Bathurst. Everything went off as you suggested—and pretty well too. As well as could be expected, anyway."

"Good! Now I have one or two things to discuss with you."
Colonel Fane looked at him somewhat apprehensively. "I shall
be ready. Consider me at your service. But before you do that,
there's something that I should have told you. Dr. Searle has
been over to see me this evening." The Colonel paused—he
seemed a trifle uncomfortable—and Peter Daventry formed
the opinion that the pause was to give him time to see how Mr.
Bathurst received this last piece of information. But Anthony
controlled his feelings perfectly and Peter could see that the
Colonel learnt nothing.

"Really, Colonel? Why didn't you tell me?"

"Well, I didn't quite know where you were at the time and as
the doctor was in a tremendous hurry, I let it go. I'm upset. I've
lost an old and dear friend. I can't quite realise it. I hope that I
have done nothing particularly blameworthy?"

Anthony returned question for question.

"What did the doctor say?"

Colonel Fane twirled his moustache with an air.

"Come to that, no more than he told us last night after his
first examination. There will be nothing in the way of his issuing
a certificate."

Mr. Bathurst took a creased telegram from his pocket. "In
the light of that then, Colonel, you may find this interesting."

The Colonel frowned as though unable to understand either
the remark or the position. Mr. Bathurst handed him the
message. The Colonel took it with a puzzled look and read it.

"Hope?" he said questioningly. "Who's Hope? And how does
this affect Dr. Searle? I'm afraid I don't—"

Anthony extended his hand for the telegram to be returned
to him.

"Hope," he announced gravely, "is Sir Roderick Hope, the
eminent pathologist who has appeared so many times for the
Crown during recent years. Perhaps you recall his masterly
evidence in the case where the laundress was found dead in the
swimming-pool at Lewisham? I sent for him this morning. I
imagine that it is quite on the cards he may be able to help me."

"You sent for him?" inquired the Colonel. "Is it possible for you to control a—"

"Perhaps I put it rather carelessly. I enjoy the confidence of Sir Austin Kemble, the Commissioner of Police at New Scotland Yard, and I have been able to arrange with him for Sir Roderick Hope to come up here. I expect him in the morning, as you saw from the telegram I showed you."

This time Colonel Fane's frown was unmistakable and the tone of his voice indubitably frigid.

"You are not satisfied, I suppose then, with Dr. Searle's—er—diagnosis?"

"I mean having another opinion, Colonel, and an expert one. Let us leave it at that." He sipped his liqueur brandy. "So it doesn't matter much after all my not having seen Dr. Searle again."

The Colonel grunted unintelligibly.

"What were the things you wished to discuss with me, Bathurst? I should like to hear them."

"I was just coming to that myself, Colonel. In the first place, have you ever heard Major Whittaker mention the name of Forrester?"

"Forrester? Never! That's soon answered. He knew nobody of that name to my knowledge, Bathurst. At least, he's never spoken to me about it."

"Thank you. That's point number one. The second point concerns our friends of the Silver Troika. You agree with me, I know, that we have not yet seen the last of them. But I think that what I purpose doing will have the effect of delaying their action for, say, a matter of about twenty-four hours. To that end I have prepared this."

A copy of the letter that Anthony had drafted earlier found its way into Colonel Fane's hands. He read it with a similar air to that which he had worn when reading the telegram from Sir Austin Kemble. Then he placed it by the side of his dessert plate.

"I don't get you, Bathurst," he declared. "How the blazes can we 'confer', as you call it, over the question of what these poisonous blighters have come for when we know that poor old Guy destroyed every single paper he'd got? Seems to me we're asking for more trouble, and screaming for it pretty loudly at that. How can you conduct the conference, for instance, when you're crass ignorant of the whole bally caboodle? Whittaker's told 'em once what happened. They didn't fall for it. You're not going to shove into me that there's the slightest chance of them falling for it this time."

"I grant you all that, Colonel. But I don't know that I want them to. That isn't my main idea. You speak of me quite justly, perhaps, as being ignorant of many things. I will not attempt to contest that statement. My handling of the case so far has been far from brilliant, but unhappily there have been very palpable reasons for that. Reasons, mind you, not excuses. But I don't think that I shall be quite so ignorant if my conference with the Silver Troika materialises, because out of it I look forward to learning something." He rose from the table. "I'm going to have a word with Neville and Richardson. Stay here till I come back, will you, Daventry?"

"Seems pretty sure of himself, doesn't he?" remarked Colonel Fane, as Mr. Bathurst made his exit.

Peter nodded sagaciously.

"You can bet your bottom dollar he means real business this time, Colonel," he contributed. "The death of Major Whittaker last night in old Bathurst's presence has touched him on the raw. He'll see the affair through now to the bitter end for a 'stone ginger.'" He settled himself in his chair, the picture of serene confidence.

"You seem very sure of your friend's ability." For his part, Colonel Fane appeared to look unimpressed. Peter, regardless of the fact, burbled on merrily.

"Take it from me, at the sleuth game he's 'it.' The absolute ultimate syllable! Look at the cases he's handled successfully when Scotland Yard's been whacked to a frazzle. Five times in succession, mind you! There was the case of the Oxford cricket blue found dead on the billiard table at Sir Charles Considine's place in Sussex, there was the affair that I dragged him into down in Berkshire with its strange secret of the screens, the famous dentist's chair murder at Seabourne, the red bon-bon tragedy at Mapleton during a Christmas dinner, and the extraordinary murder of Julius Maitland, the well-known South African millionaire, just before the Derby in the disused cowshed in Wiltshire. All of 'em triumphs for A. L. B. Triumphs, Colonel, that's the only word!"

"I remember one or two of them," conceded the Colonel rather grudgingly, "but they were all what I should term 'ordinary' cases of apprehending a criminal and essentially different from this affair up here. There's no mystery here, as far as I can see, that Bathurst is called upon to solve. Personally, I am quite satisfied with Dr. Searle's opinion of the Major's death—in fact, I should have been inclined to regard any other opinion as fantastic. Moreover, the case is different in other ways."

"How do you mean?" inquired Peter. "I don't quite—"

"Well, what I mean is this. Look at it for yourself. It's a plain and straightforward issue. There are these devils of the Silver Troika to be dealt with. What is it they want? What are these papers and documents exactly that they desire so much? How can Bathurst do anything with them? He's got nothing to give them, even if he wanted to."

Here Mr. Daventry looked profoundly wise, but he contented himself with the shelter of a platitude.

"Those that live longest will see the most, Colonel Besides, don't forget we've still got to hear what Sir Roderick Hope has to say about the Major. Take it from me, Bathurst has got a pretty shrewd idea in his head concerning that. I won't pretend to know what it is, because quite frankly I don't! But if Major Whittaker did get 'bumped off' by somebody—mind you I only say 'if'—take it from me that A. L. B. will swing the jolly old Eugene Aram stunt on to him before he's very much older. I'd like to be as sure of a sackful of Jimmy o' Goblins."

Colonel Fane looked puzzled.

"The old Eugene Aram stunt? I'm afraid I don't altogether—"

Peter grinned at his companion.

"Gyves upon his wrists, Colonel. Don't you remember the old lad, how he walked between?"

Before the Colonel could form an adequate reply, the door opened and Anthony entered.

"I don't think we shall have any trouble to-night, Colonel. I think my plan of campaign will avert it," he said, "but it's always as well to take precautions. Carry your revolver with you wherever you go. I should advise you to do the same, Daventry. I'm going to myself." He patted his pocket significantly.

The Colonel rose and stretched his arms.

"I'm for early bed to-night, Bathurst. Last night's operations took it out of me. Half-an-hour with a book and then I'm toddling up. If the Silver Troika want to interview me to-night, I'll oblige them in my pyjamas. I can shoot just as straight in silk as in serge. If you want me before I go up, I shall be in the library."

"I shan't interfere with the gallant Colonel's arrangements," said Anthony a moment later, as the door closed upon him. "I expect he's pretty well through by now. I've seen Neville and I've also seen Richardson. My letter to the Silver Troika will be placed on the tennis-court a few minutes before midnight. What happens after that is on the knees of the gods. But I'm certain we shall gain twenty-four hours. If I'm wrong—" Mr. Bathurst shrugged his shoulders.

Peter Daventry looked at him eagerly. There seemed to him just a possibility that he might be in at the death, so to speak, after all.

"Will they come?" he whispered.

"I think so," returned Anthony. "At any rate, we shall know if they don't."

"How?" questioned Peter.

"Because we shall be very close to the spot, watching—you and I, Daventry, and three others."

Chapter XIX
MIDNIGHT OF AUGUST THE FIFTEENTH

"Three others?"

"Yes, three—Neville, Richardson and Coppinger, our old friend of the carrier's cart. I've collared him to equalise matters a trifle. The other party may number five—it may be reasonably expected to. I'm quite prepared to find it mustering six even. There are the 'President,' Loronoff, Schmidt, Krakar and Verensky, and possibly one other. So Neville prevailed on me to rope in Coppinger. Neville suggested that he'd be useful in a crisis, and I agreed it would even things up considerably."

"Good!" said Peter. "Here's to a nice, cosy little scrap."

Anthony shook his head.

"I've no wish to damp your enthusiasm, Daventry, but I'm afraid you'll be disappointed. To-night we hold what may be well termed a watching-brief. We shall be armed, I agree, but I don't think we shall be called upon to demonstrate the fact. At the moment, I'm all on the side of peace with the Silver Troika."

Peter waggled his head judicially.

"What hast thou to do with peace?" he quoted with a pretence at censure. "Turn thee behind me."

Anthony smiled in acknowledgment of the aptness of the remark.

"I suppose Coppinger will come," went on Peter. "He won't let us down?"

"Neville's gone over to him in the car. He feels confident that he can persuade him."

"Where do we take up our position?"

"We shall be in the tennis pavilion, very close to the actual courts. That will be our place of concealment. It is there, I understand, that Neville hid himself some few days ago when the first reply was sent to our continental friends. So there's no doubt it will be quite suitable for the task we have in hand to-night. We'll get down there, I propose, about half-past eleven."

Neville's mission to Holmedale for the services of the carrier did not prove fruitless, and at half-past eleven the five men, headed by Anthony, made their way from the library down to the tennis pavilion. Coppinger, although by no means a conversationalist, as Anthony and Peter had discovered before, tapped a healthy-looking truncheon in his pocket and expressed his willingness to serve.

"As a Britisher," he said, when Neville had escorted him from his shop at Holmedale, "count on me against any foreign muck. There's too many of 'em allowed to run amok in this country by far—taking the bread from the mouths of Englishmen too. It was bad enough years ago—it's a sight worse now. One of 'em had the audacity to say to me a week or two ago, 'You can say what you like, Mr. Coppinger, it's your damn king, but it's our damn country.'" He took his pipe from his mouth and put it in his pocket.

Peter Daventry admired the sturdy independence of the man and Anthony could see that the Silver Troika would receive short shrift from the Holmedale carrier, should Fate ever throw him into contact with them.

Mr. Bathurst placed the attaché case in the middle of the court. He had determined, after a great deal of consideration, to fulfil that duty himself. Returning to the pavilion, he and the other four took up their stand. The pavilion lay to the left of the tennis courts and from the window everything that happened could be plainly seen.

The minutes passed. Everything remained almost uncannily silent. The moon was now well up and flinging its white brilliance across the patch of grass. Anthony was unable to refrain from thinking that the scene, as he was looking at it, was almost exactly the same—for conditions—as when he had watched from the window of his bedroom on the first night that he had spent under the roof of Swallowcliffe Hall. He looked up at the bedroom window, which he could just discern in the distance, almost idly, and at the same time endeavoured to calculate the distance.

In the midst of this occupation, he felt somebody gripping his arm tightly above the elbow. It was Neville.

"Somebody has climbed the wall at the end of the garden, sir," whispered the old soldier. "One person I fancy. I saw the shadow moving along the front of the wall as he got over."

"Quiet then, everybody," returned Anthony in a similar whisper. "Range yourselves in a line along by the windows of the pavilion and have your revolvers ready in case they should be wanted. But no man is to fire or take any action unless I give the word."

The men expressed their understanding silently. The five of them watched the figure of a man creep stealthily down from the shadow of the wall and pick his way lightly—almost mincingly—towards the tennis courts. To Peter Daventry his figure was entirely unfamiliar. But as he crept nearer and nearer and at last emerged, as it were, out of the haze of the distance into the circle of moonlight that bathed the dark stretch of grass where the case lay, Mr. Bathurst was able to recognise him at once. The man who had climbed the wall had done so at least once before. It was Mr. Garland-Isherwood!

"See what he does," whispered Anthony. "This is getting interesting."

Neville's eyes were almost starting from his head with curiosity and excitement, but Richardson and Coppinger, standing side by side as they were, appeared to be comparatively unmoved. Silver Troika or eccentric entomologist—it was all in the day's work for them and to be confronted with the same imperturbability.

"Who is it?" asked Peter in the lightest of whispers.

"The butterfly expert," replied Mr. Bathurst just as quietly. "But s-sh, watch him—we may learn something!"

Mr. Daventry did as he was directed—indeed, he needed no instructions or incentive to do so—and he saw the gentleman from Philadelphia bend over the case and pick it up from the ground. To open it was the work of a moment and the watchers in the pavilion saw him take out the paper and read it. Anthony held out his arm and looked at his wrist-watch. It still wanted four minutes to midnight. Mr. Garland-Isherwood appeared to read through the message at least twice. Then he pushed his long, quivering fingers through his streaky hair impulsively and, in Peter Daventry's opinion, somewhat impatiently. Standing there on the grass under the moonlight, he gave the more observant watchers the impression that he was unable to make up his mind thoroughly as to what should be his next step. He seemed to be undecided about something. He held the case in his left hand and tapped it nervously and irresolutely with the fingers of his right, as though seeking inspiration from unknown sources. Then they saw him replace the case on the grass and take a step or two in the direction of the house. Mr. Bathurst's fingers were just closing round the butt of his revolver when the man whom he and the others were watching suddenly stopped. A change had come over his mind. They saw him turn in his tracks impetuously and listen. What he had heard it was impossible for them to say, for at that precise moment Richardson sneezed—Peter Daventry described the effort afterwards as eminently full-blooded. The entomologist ran like a startled hare towards the direction from which he had come and in a few seconds was lost to sight.

"Try to control yourself, Richardson," said Anthony. "That gentleman's movements interested me considerably. Now I'm afraid we've lost him for some time."

"Sorry, sir," returned the chauffeur, "but my nose started to tickle all of a sudden and I couldn't stop myself. Take my word, sir—"

"Hist!" said Anthony. "Look! What's that?"

"More of 'em! More visitors," growled Neville.

"Two more men have climbed the wall at the end," said Coppinger very quietly. "They're coming down in very much the same manner as the previous chap did. Had they been a bit earlier, they would have met him."

"Watch!" commanded Anthony curtly. "The 'President' and Schmidt," he whispered to Peter. "Recognise them?"

"Too true," replied Daventry. "I've been to one of their 'At Homes.' Had time to study their personal beauty."

The 'President' walked swiftly towards the case and jerked it up impetuously from the grass. As he did so, his face was under the full light of the moon and Anthony saw a look of malevolent disappointment take temporary possession of his features. He snapped an exclamation of some kind at his fat companion, for they saw the latter swing round abruptly and shake his head vigorously in evident reply. The 'President' opened the case with an almost vindictive abandon, took out Mr. Bathurst's message and flung the case with a contemptuous movement back on to the grass. Then he beckoned the 'Slug' to his side. The latter bent over and read the letter with his companion. Then two facts showed plainly to the company of watchers. The two fell to argument, pointed by gesture and expostulation. Eventually, however, the 'President' took something from his pocket, picked up the case from where it lay on the ground, and was seen to write with the case as a foundation. As he did so, he appeared to address a number of questions to Otto Schmidt, judging by the motions of the latter's head and hands. Suddenly the case was opened again and replaced and the two emissaries of the Silver Troika turned on their heels and walked rapidly away.

"Now for their reply," said Peter, when an appreciable interval had elapsed. "What about me for retriever?"

Anthony caught him by the arm.

"Not yet, Daventry. I want to wait a little to see if anything else happens."

"What? What do you expect may happen? Will they come back?"

"I don't think so, but I want to see if Mr. Garland-Isherwood does, because I think that he may do. Just for the moment, that assumes to me the greater importance." Mr. Bathurst smiled as he made the statement.

"Who is he? One of the Silver Troika or—"

Anthony shrugged his shoulders at Peter's question. "I'd give a lot to know. We'll wait a quarter of an hour. If he doesn't show by then, I am going to conclude that he isn't coming again."

Fifteen minutes later, Anthony issued the evening's final instruction.

"Neville," he ordered, "you and Coppinger bring me the case, will you? I have reasons for not showing myself at the present moment."

The old soldier walked stiffly across the grass, accompanied by the dour and sturdy carrier of Holmedale. Mr. Bathurst opened the case that his two assistants brought back. In it lay his own letter—nothing more. But across his letter was scrawled in an ugly, sprawling and ill-formed handwriting the reply that he wanted.

"Accepted on behalf of the Silver Troika. Midnight to-morrow.—'The President.'"

Anthony turned to the men round him.

"We shall be there, gentlemen!" he exclaimed. "The Silver Troika shall not find us inhospitable."

CHAPTER XX
THREE HOURS LATER

AT TWENTY-NINE minutes past three that morning, Mr. Bathurst suddenly sat up in bed and listened intently. Somebody was outside his bedroom door! He hadn't the slightest doubt about it. As has been stated before, he possessed the happy knack of getting to sleep almost instantaneously and also the complementary faculty of awakening at the lightest and slightest of sounds. He looked towards the door and, to his amazement, saw it open gradually.

Sliding noiselessly from the bed, he snatched his revolver from the pocket of his coat and flattened himself against that particular portion of the wall that was behind the door as it opened. But his anxiety and precaution were short-lived. For here was no marauder, no silent strangler of unsuspecting sleepers, but Colonel Nicholas Fane.

"Bathurst!" he called in a low, tense voice. "Bathurst! Are you asleep, man?"

Anthony emerged from his place behind the door, the incarnation of apology.

"My dear Colonel, please forgive me for receiving you so unceremoniously and with such an absence of the ritual of hospitality, but to tell the truth, the fault is at least partly your own. You will admit that you didn't inform me that you were coming."

But Fane was in no mood to bandy words.

"I'm sorry if I startled you, but I'm uneasy over something. There's been a strange noise under my bedroom window for some time now. In fact, I'm certain it woke me up. I should think I've listened to it for over an hour—it seems more like a day— but I believe now that I know what it is. I've puzzled and puzzled over it. First of all I thought it was a dog, then I fancied it must be the wind, then suddenly it came to me like a revelation."

He stopped and, from the working of his features, Anthony could see that the Colonel was speaking with sincerity and with no small amount of agitation. But before Mr. Bathurst could reply to him or ask a question even, Fane proceeded.

"In my opinion, Bathurst, there's a man in the grounds under my bedroom window, either ill or very badly hurt. The noise that I've been hearing is the man groaning."

Anthony's reply this time was quick and to the point. He walked rapidly towards his clothes.

"Knock on Daventry's door, will you, Colonel? I'll slip on a dressing-gown and a pair of shoes and be with you in a brace of shakes."

"Which way—left?"

"No, to the right. Rout him out. Tell him what you think's doing, and I'll join you in his bedroom. Give me two minutes."

Five minutes later, the three of them were descending the stairs, Anthony with his electric torch in one pocket of his dressing-gown and his revolver in the other. The house was as silent as the dead man lay in one of the bedrooms.

"Is Neville about, Colonel?" he asked.

"Haven't seen him," rejoined Fane who led the way. "I came in to you first. Why? Do you think it's Neville we shall find outside? Do you think the Silver Troika have nobbled him?"

Anthony shook his head by way of reply.

"Can't say. It may even be a member of that distinguished circle. The position may have been reversed—Neville may have 'nobbled' him. Or there is yet another possibility. When thieves fall out, you know—this way, Daventry."

"Come out through the kitchen-garden," supplemented the Colonel, "and then work round to the left. I think I can walk straight to where I heard the groaning coming from. Follow me, will you?"

The Colonel walked ahead in silence, Anthony and Peter but a few paces behind. The former found that he did not need his torch, for already it was beginning to get light. They skirted round the side of the house in accordance with Fane's directions and suddenly Mr. Bathurst stooped to pick up something from the gravel. It was a glove—very small and obviously a woman's. As he did so, he heard a low groan that came from only a short distance ahead. Colonel Fane turned to them.

"I was right, you see, Bathurst. There's a man here right enough. He's lying in the shadow of the wall there unless I'm a Dutchman."

They made their way to where the Colonel had pointed and soon saw that the Colonel's statements were correct. A man lay on his side, his face covered with blood. There was a wound on his head that was still bleeding and every now and then he groaned heavily.

"Carry him indoors," said the Colonel. "We can attend to him better if we get him in there. We can get water for him and brandy too."

"Who is it?" inquired Peter. "Anybody you know?"

Anthony shook his head.

"He's a complete stranger to me, Daventry. I've never set eyes on him before, I'm certain. Don't know if the Colonel knows him."

Apparently Fane failed to hear, for he made no reply.

They carried him in and laid him on the settee in the dining-room. From his dress he seemed what may be described as an ordinary citizen. Anthony put him down as between twenty-five and thirty years of age. He wore a blue serge suit with a cheap soft collar and his socks, tie and boots were of but moderate quality. His hands were rough, suggesting that they were used to plenty of work. He seemed well-nourished and healthy and was of medium height, his skin being bronzed with the tint that tells of life in the open air. Colonel Fane obtained a bowl of water and wiped the blood from the man's face. He then started to bathe the wound, and as he touched it for the first time, the man groaned again and slightly shifted his position on the settee. The blow he had received was a severe one. From his place by the man's side, the Colonel looked up at Anthony. There was a puzzled look on his face.

"Do you know, Bathurst," he said, "I could swear I know this man. I'll take my oath I've seen him before somewhere."

"That's interesting, Colonel. Perhaps you'll be able to remember before long where it was. I'm curious to know. But how is he, do you think?"

"I think he'll be all right in a moment. He's coming round. He's had a bad bash from some heavy instrument, I should say, but I fancy it caught him a sort of glancing blow instead of connecting properly. It may have been from the butt end of a revolver."

Anthony nodded his acceptance of the suggestion.

"Very likely the attack came from behind him. He may have heard his assailant at the very last second of his approach and partly turned in an endeavour to escape what he saw coming to him. Perhaps he'll tell us when he recovers consciousness. The more important questions, Colonel, from our point of view as investigators are who is the man and what is he doing at this time of night in the grounds of Swallowcliffe Hall?" Anthony rubbed his hands.

As though in answer to Mr. Bathurst's two questions, the injured man opened his eyes and, following upon a first expression of dazed surprise, looked wonderingly round the room.

"Feeling better, my man?" demanded the Colonel.

The man addressed attempted to struggle into a sitting position, but failed. Putting his hand to his head, he sank back upon the settee.

"Where am I?" he muttered. "What's oop?"

"You are inside Swallowcliffe Hall," answered Colonel Fane, "the residence of Major Whittaker."

Anthony could have sworn that a look of fear—or, at the least, apprehension—crossed the face of the inquirer.

"Inside?" he demanded somewhat truculently. "Is that reet? Or is tha'—" He stopped, evidently conscious that all was not well with him, for he motioned again rather helplessly towards his head.

"You were found senseless inside the grounds," contributed Anthony. "Somebody had given you a crack on the head. What can you remember about that, eh? Anything?"

The injured man screwed up his face as though attempting to remember. Then he shook his head with a kind of hopeless resignation.

"Not much, Mestur, and that's a fact. I'd been for a country mooch and was makin' my way back to Buttercross—that's all I can recall. It was a champion night—I can well remember that. But dang it if I can remember how I came by this little lot."

"Where were you last? I mean at what place were you when your conscious reminiscence ends?" Anthony put the two questions promptly and decisively. The man rubbed his cheek with the back of his hand.

"Reckon I was somewhere near Little Knype. I can remember making t' main road from t' wood. But after that it's no use askin' me, Mestur, for my mind's a perfect blank. I must ha' got sandbagged or something. Good job t' skull's thick." He smiled ruefully.

"You weren't inside the grounds of Swallowcliffe Hall then by any chance?" inquired Anthony, giving the man a sharp look of inquiry.

"Si' thee now, what should I be doing there, Mestur?" returned the stranger with sturdy independence. "Didn't know I was on t' Major's visitin' list. But there, I'm always learnin' summat. When shall I be able to be gettin' along?"

"You lie there for a bit, my man," returned Colonel Fane. "You're not fit to move yet awhile. I'm going to fix this piece of lint on your wound, so keep steady. I don't think that there's a lot of damage done. But keep quiet and don't excite yourself."

Anthony fixed the injured man with a penetrating look.

"Your face seems familiar to me. Didn't I run across you over the other side in 1918 or thereabouts? What were you? Let me think for a minute and I shall have it." He stopped for a second, but then proceeded, his memory evidently coming to his immediate assistance. "I've got it! 'Emma Gees,' weren't you?" The man addressed gave an instant denial.

"No, Mestur, ye're wrong there. Reckon you're mistakin' me for somebody else. I was but fourteen when t' war broke out. I never got as far as France, so you're mistaken."

"I must be," returned Mr. Bathurst, "in those circumstances! But you are absurdly like the man of whom I was thinking. You and he are as like as the proverbial two peas. Wouldn't be your brother, I suppose?"

"Not unless mother kept it secret."

"You mean—"

"I'm t' eldest," came the terse reply. "Thank you, sir, that's a lot better. Reckon I'm fixed now, reet and proper. My head ain't half as buzzy as it was." This to Colonel Fane, who had made an exceedingly neat job of the bandaging.

As he spoke, the Colonel gave a start.

"Great Scott, man, I know now who you are!"

The man to whom he spoke grinned somewhat sheepishly. But before he could make any contribution concerning his identity, Colonel Fane had amplified his previous statement.

"You're the milkman that delivers milk to Swallowcliffe Hall. I've seen you knocking about here two or three times. I'm right, am I not?"

"Tha's reet," replied the man, relapsing more and more into his native speech. "There's no reason that I can see why I should be denyin' it. I've had Major and Mrs. Whittaker as customers ever since they've been this way."

"What's your game?" demanded Mr. Bathurst with a trace of sternness, but nevertheless with a note of enthusiasm. If the

Colonel's statement were true, it explained something that had been puzzling him.

"Satterthwaite," came the reply. "I'm Satterthwaite of Buttercross."

"You've no idea, I suppose, why you should have been attacked in this way?"

"Can't understand it, Mestur. Got no enemies that I know of."

"Seems so unreasonable, doesn't it? Don't you think so?"

The man got on his feet, still a little unsteady.

"T' blokes what did it may have meant robbery and made a mistake in the man. Maybe they thought I looked like Tommy Lipton or Rockyfeller." Satterthwaite attempted to grin at his touch of flippancy.

"And then took the trouble to carry you into the grounds of the late Major Whittaker's house? No, Satterthwaite, I'm afraid I can't quite—"

Mr. Bathurst plunged his hands into the pockets of his dressing-gown and stood thinking. Peter Daventry wondered what new train of thought had been started in his brain.

"Were you robbed at all?" The question was fired at the man very suddenly.

Satterthwaite shook his head.

"There was nothing on me worth the taking. I hadn't a lass with me. I don't take much brass out with me o' nights. I was taught better than that."

Mr. Bathurst looked at him doubtfully.

"The best thing we can do with you then, Satterthwaite, is to drive you back to your home. Buttercross way, isn't it? If you stay here with him for a few minutes, Colonel, Daventry and I will slip some more things on and run our unexpected guest over to Buttercross in the car. Fit to travel, Satterthwaite?"

The man shifted his feet uneasily.

"I think so, Mestur. I'm feelin' better certainly. But it's champion of you to take trouble—"

"That's all right," cut in Mr. Bathurst, "no trouble at all. But it's a good job for you that Colonel Fane here heard you groaning. You might have been there all night. Wait here for five minutes or so. Come on, Daventry."

Within a quarter of an hour, Satterthwaite, fortified for the journey with a draught of neat brandy, was seated next to Mr. Bathurst in the car. Mr. Daventry drove.

"Turn left and straight on," had been the milk-vendor's directions.

Arrived at their destination, Anthony and Peter Daventry assisted their protégé to alight. They found themselves before a small dairy.

"Thank you kindly, gentlemen," said Satterthwaite. "I can manage by myself now. It's been reet good of you to take t' trouble you have. But for you I might have been old Kelter by now. I'll give you good-night, gentlemen, or rather good-morning. But it's rememberin' your kindness I'll be."

"Well, Bathurst, what do you make of that?" demanded Peter on the journey back. "Struck me you didn't seem too satisfied with Satterthwaite's story. By Jove, I'd like to hear old Schmidt on that sentence. He'd have the old rattlesnake beaten to pulp that journey. But joking apart, were you?"

For a moment or two, Mr. Bathurst delayed his answer. When it came, it surprised Mr. Daventry, for it revealed Anthony in a mood of extreme gravity.

"Vice and virtue remain much the same in all places, Daventry. But decorum and propriety depend almost entirely upon the manners and observances exacted by the state of society. The bravest men have had their fears and the wisest have had their follies. One man to-night has made a grievous mistake. He told me something which has opened a door for me, a door too that looked to be impenetrable. The woman's mistake was of a different kind, but still distinctly illuminating." He extended his hand towards Peter. "Did you notice me pick this up?" he asked.

Peter looked and saw in his hand the lady's glove.

"I saw you stoop, but I wasn't sure what you were doing. So a coy damsel outed friend Satterthwaite, eh? Is that what you mean—a lady member of the Troika or the village milkmaid?"

Anthony shook his head.

"No, I don't mean either. But I am finding this a most remarkable case, Daventry. The light has been a long time drifting in, but I fancy there's a glimmer or so coming along at last. At any rate, certain things that puzzled me considerably have now cleared appreciably, as I hinted to you just now. But this, I fancy, is Swallowcliffe Hall. There is still much to do before we can say that our case is complete."

Chapter XXI
MR. BATHURST'S FEARS ARE WELL-FOUNDED

SIR RODERICK HOPE was not quite what Mr. Daventry had expected him to be. That is to say, in appearance. When he had been informed by Anthony Bathurst that the eminent pathologist from Scotland Yard was taking a hand in the investigation of the strange affair of Major Whittaker's death, Peter Daventry had formed certain clear-cut conclusions. Had he been interrogated, he could not have given any definite reason for forming such ideas. All that he knew was that he had formed them. It was, in fact, his invariable habit to do such things. He had imagined Sir Roderick Hope to be an elderly man, an obvious aristocrat of science. He had anticipated meeting a man who had given years and years to the exacting demands of his profession and who showed in his face and bearing the hostages he had made thereto, but instead of all that he found himself facing a man much more like an actor in appearance than a member of any other profession. Certainly—superficially—he would have made an admirable *jeune premier*. His manner was brisk yet charming and his features gave clear evidence that here was a man who could lead. He advanced towards Anthony Bathurst upon his entrance with outstretched hand and Peter Daventry felt that the murderer of Major Whittaker—if events proved that there was a murderer—would receive short shrift at this last combination of Bathurst and Sir Roderick Hope. In build and general appearance, the two men were not strikingly dissimilar. Each was tall and each possessed a clean-cut, clean-shaven face lighted by both determination and resolute strength. The chief point of difference lay in the eyes. Whereas Anthony Bathurst's were a steady grey, the famous pathologist's were light blue—steely blue. His greeting to the man who came forward to meet him was like every other quality that distinguished him—it was decisive and prompt.

"The Commissioner passed your telegram over to me, Bathurst. So here I am. What's your difficulty?"

He listened intently to Mr. Bathurst's opening words. Then he nodded an understanding of the position.

"You suspect foul play? That's the position, I take it?"

"Frankly, I do, Sir Roderick. That's why I telegraphed."

"Pardon me, gentlemen, but I feel that I should make one fact known." The interruption came from Colonel Fane and there was annoyance easily recognisable in his tone.

The suspicion of a frown passed over Anthony's face, but he allowed the Colonel to continue.

"I feel that I should inform you, Sir Roderick, before you intervene in this matter, that the Major was examined by Dr. Searle of Holmedale, his own—er—personal medical man, and Dr. Searle found absolutely nothing to excite his suspicions. He saw him, I may add, very shortly after his death. He is also quite prepared to issue the usual certificate. He will certify that the Major died of—er—ordinary heart failure."

"Many thanks, Colonel! As a matter of fact, I am quite aware of all those facts."

Sir Roderick's tone was courteous, but it definitely put the closure upon any supplementing of Colonel Fane's statement and it was very obvious to Peter, as he watched the Colonel's face, that that gentleman was quite aware of the fact. Sir Roderick Hope had the quality of suppressing people whom he considered unnecessary.

"Now, Bathurst," continued Sir Roderick, "tell me all that happened as you yourself saw it before Major Whittaker died."

Anthony obeyed the instructions implicitly. His recital of the facts of the affair immediately preceding the sudden collapse of the Major was a model of what such statements should be. The first interruption soon came. Sir Roderick Hope himself intervened crisply.

"When you requested the Major to move, Bathurst, to change positions in the room, I mean, repeat to me, if you can, his exact words." He looked sharply at Anthony. "You said that he mentioned something about his head buzzing, I believe."

Anthony considered the request.

"He said that he felt done to the world, worn to a shred was, I think, the actual expression that he used. I also fancy that he complained of feeling all of a tingle, that his head was as big as a football and his fingers numb. I can't remember anything else. Can you, Colonel?"

"I couldn't have remembered that," replied Colonel Fane. "I was far too anxious that night to notice the exact words people used when they spoke." He spoke somewhat sourly and with a distinct touch of impatience in his tone.

"Very good, Bathurst," cut in Sir Roderick. "Carry on, will you?"

Anthony described the coming of the Death's-Head moth and the effect that it had caused upon everybody in the room.

"It touched the Major, you say?" put in the pathologist.

Anthony nodded an affirmative.

"Undoubtedly."

"What happened after that?"

"The Major sat with his head in his hands for a while, gave an unusual sort of sigh as he collapsed, and slid to the floor from his chair—dead."

"I see. Now you've told me everything and I think I've got the facts in proper sequence. Let me see the body."

Directly they entered the bedroom where the body of Major Whittaker lay, Sir Roderick Hope got to work. He looked at the eyes, tongue and lips of the dead man.

"There was nothing, I suppose, in the nature of a violent convulsion preceding death?"

"None at all, Sir Roderick. The Major was quite quiet. Just a collapse, that was all."

"How long were you in the room before the Major died?"

Anthony looked at Colonel Fane for corroboration. "Two hours, Colonel?"

The Colonel thought it over before he answered.

"A trifle more, I should say, Bathurst."

"Take it at about two hours then, Sir Roderick."

"H'm! Thanks. Leave me for an hour or so, will you, please? I shall have to do a P.M. Fortunately I came down equipped, because you never know. Where's the bathroom?"

Anthony took Sir Roderick to the door of the bedroom and showed him.

"Straight along down, Sir Roderick."

"Right! I'll report to you again when I'm ready."

The time that followed seemed to Peter Daventry to be interminable, for it affected him in more than one way. He knew that Anthony Bathurst would make no further movement in the investigation until he had received the result of Sir Roderick Hope's post-mortem, and passivity annoyed Mr. Daventry as much as anything did. To him, all times were ripe for 'up and doing.' Delay discomfited him and caused him to chafe at the necessary restrictions that were imposed by such a condition. He lost count of the number of times he consulted his watch in his impatience. Anthony was reticent, the Colonel undoubtedly in a state of sulkiness. He was not used to taking a seat in the rear—the only times he had ever been behind in his life had been when his regiment had been in action. For a long period he sat in his chair, disinclined to speak to anybody, but at length his natural *penchant* for argument overcame his bad temper and he succumbed to the temptation.

"I'll lay a wager no Silver Troika touched Guy Whittaker. You can argue as much as you like, Bathurst. Not one of them was ever within a mile of him. The man died a natural death."

"Possibly, Colonel. Possibly not! Sir Roderick Hope will tell us who is right before very long, no doubt. Till then I suggest we possess our souls in patience."

Colonel Fane grunted evasively. Anthony in turn caught Peter's habit and looked at his wrist-watch.

"We may hear from Sir Roderick any minute now, I should say. Until then I am content to reserve my judgment, but all the same I claim the right to retain my opinion."

The words had scarcely left his lips when the door opened and Sir Roderick Hope came into the room. It would not be right to say that his face wore a look of anxiety, but there was an undoubted suggestion of trouble and apprehension there. He closed the door and came right up to the three men in the room before he spoke. When he at last did so, he spoke directly to Anthony Bathurst.

"Bathurst," he said, "I fear that your suspicions regarding the manner of Major Whittaker's death were only too well-founded. As far as I can judge from the P.M. that I have just done, the Major was poisoned."

"What?" cried Colonel Fane. "Poisoned? I can't believe it! How on earth could that have happened?"

Anthony received the information very quietly.

"I was afraid so, Sir Roderick. Your diagnosis is entirely as I expected. Poisoned by what?"

Sir Roderick Hope rubbed his cheek with his fingers.

"By Aconitum Napellus—tincture of aconite, to give it the name under which it is most usually used. In this instance, in my opinion, the alkaloid aconitine has been used. You will probably remember that it is one of the constituents of the famous African arrow poison. As little as four milligrammes of the alkaloid has been known to cause death. That would equal about one-sixteenth of a grain. I would describe aconitine as perhaps the most active of all known poisons."

Anthony was plainly agitated.

"What are the chief post-mortem appearances, Sir Roderick?"

"The mucous lining of the stomach and bowels is very congested and acutely inflamed. Those facts and the facts you gave me concerning Major Whittaker's symptoms before death confirm me strongly in my opinion. All the conditions of which he complained would be present in a case of aconitine poisoning. The question is, how was it administered?"

Anthony looked inquiringly at Sir Roderick.

"How would you suggest?" he asked.

Sir Roderick Hope shrugged his shoulders.

"Do you remember the notorious Dr. Lamson?" he countered. "Dr. Lamson, an unsuccessful medical practitioner, administered aconitine to his wife's brother. The youth—he was about eighteen—was exceedingly delicate, had been all his life, I believe, and paralysed in the lower extremities. Lamson gave the poison to him in the form of a capsule. Very possibly another brother-in-law of Lamson was disposed of in the same manner. There was a grave doubt about it. Scotland Yard thinks so, at any rate."

It was obvious now that Mr. Bathurst was thinking hard.

"Any other cases of it, Sir Roderick? Cases you can easily recall?"

Sir Roderick bit his lower lip in his attempt to remember.

"Yes, I can give you one other. There was a French doctor, but I can't recall his name at the moment, about a couple of years before the war, who attempted to poison a rival doctor. He sent him a liqueur in which aconitine had been dissolved. But I fancy the little plot failed. My memory on that's a bit hazy, though. Why?"

"What was the quantity—the least quantity—of aconitine that you said had been known to kill?" Anthony replied to Sir Roderick's question by asking another.

"Of the alkaloid?" said Sir Roderick.

"Yes."

"Four milligrammes, equalling about one-sixteenth of a grain."

Mr. Bathurst pondered over the answer before he swung round on to Colonel Fane.

"Well, Colonel, what have you to say now? Altered your opinion of the Silver Troika?"

The Colonel gave a movement of his shoulders simulating helplessness.

"I'm astounded at what Sir Roderick says. It would be presumption on my part to question his opinion, I know, but, to be truthful, I simply can't believe it."

Sir Roderick Hope did not allow the Colonel's remark to pass unchallenged.

"You are at perfect liberty to impeach my opinion, Colonel, should you so desire. But whether you do or you don't, it will make no difference to the facts. I will stake my professional reputation on the fact that Major Whittaker died of aconitine poisoning. Please inform the local doctor of what I say. It is right that he should know. I am sure that there is no need for me to say anything more." He turned to Anthony. "I will communicate to the Commissioner, Bathurst, the result of my examination. Doubtless he in turn will communicate with you. There is nothing more you want, is there?"

"No, thank Sir Roderick. I am greatly obliged for all that you have done—at such short notice too. Will you stay for lunch?"

"Thanks, no. I'll lunch in Liverpool. I intend staying there for a day or two. Will you arrange for the car for me in half-an-hour? I'll get you to run me over."

"Certainly. I'll see Richardson at once. He was the man who met you. Will you do me a favour?"

"Of course. What is it?"

"Let Sir Austin Kemble have a letter directly you get back. I'll put it into your hands before you go. I'll wire him in the meantime."

"That will be no trouble at all, Bathurst, because I'm due to see the Commissioner immediately upon my return." The eminent pathologist turned towards Peter Daventry and the Colonel. "Good-morning, gentlemen!"

They returned the greeting, the latter somewhat lugubriously.

"In half-an-hour then, Bathurst!"

When he had gone and the two of them were alone, Anthony drew Peter to one side.

"I've asked the Commissioner to arrange certain matters," he declared. "He is already in communication with the police up here, who will move when I give the word. If possible, I want to try to avoid an inquest. I think it will expedite matters a good deal for us. I also want you to do something for me, Daventry."

"You know I'm your man—always. What is it?"

"I am going into Liverpool this afternoon. If I am not back in time to assist in the interview with the Silver Troika that is expected to-night, carry on just as though nothing had happened. You won't be outnumbered. There will be the same number of you as last night, because I have asked Fane to turn up. Don't be alarmed at my absence, because it's quite on the cards that I may not be able to get back in time."

Peter screwed his face up a little doubtfully, for he didn't know that this new idea appealed to him very strongly. He certainly found no rapturous allurement about the prospect.

"Half a cock-linnet, old son! I'm guessing a bit in this gallery. I'm not worrying about being outnumbered. Didn't you promise those chaps a *reasonable* conference?"

"That's so, Daventry. Why do you ask?"

"Well, what was your game? You haven't told me up to the moment of going to press what your particular bright idea was going to be. I'm properly in the dark. The whole thing seems to me very much like shoving the old brain-box too darned close to dear old Leo's toosey-pegs."

Anthony grinned at him.

"I know what you mean, but don't worry. Have your revolver with you in case, but don't use it or show it unless things get very hot and it's a matter of sheer necessity. Got that?"

"I have, and I feel better. I'm feeling much more myself. What else do you want me to do?"

"Keep an eye on everybody here, particularly Neville."

Peter looked startled at the mention of the name.

"Neville? Is he a suspect then?"

"I'm not quite sure what Neville's actual game is, Daventry. But one or two points about him interest me considerably. That's why I want you to watch him for me."

"Right-o! I'll do my best, you know that. Where are you off to yourself, though? You ought to tell me, you know, in case of accidents."

"I intended to, Daventry. My task this afternoon is self-appointed. I am going to investigate a matter that I feel is overwhelmingly important. You remember the strange incident of the third letter, don't you?"

Peter nodded acquiescence.

"You mean the letter the Major wrote that you think was stolen from your pocket? Rather!"

Anthony corrected what he had said.

"The letter that I *know* was stolen from my pocket. I prefer you to put it that way if you don't mind, because there's no doubt about it. Well, I have been able, by a little process of mental photography, to remember the address that was on the envelope of that third letter. I'm very pleased to think I have."

Peter grew more interested.

"Oh, good man! That makes a difference. What was it?"

"The letter was addressed to a firm in Dale Street, Liverpool. The names on the envelope were Thornton and Jackson. The address had been typed and the typing-fluid that had been used was of a faint purple shade—a lightish purple would perhaps be a better description, something like a copying-ink pencil that has been wetted."

"You're going to Thornton and Jackson then, I take it?"

"Precisely my intention, Daventry, but as I said, I don't know when I shall be back. That will depend upon what I discover. But carry on for me with Verensky, Loronoff and Co. to the best of your initiative and resource."

Peter rubbed his chin.

"I wish I knew why you wanted me to trail old Neville. To tell you the truth, I'm a bit disappointed over that. Actually speaking, I'd taken a likin' to that trusty old retainer, especially after the thumbscrew episode! The old top I'd have liked to have sleuthed was old Gardener's-Underwear—Garland-Isherwood, or whatever his high-falutin' name is. I've got a shrewd idea that he annoys me considerably."

Anthony regarded him quizzically as he made the statement.

"Why?" he demanded pertinently. "Why particularly does he annoy you?"

Peter Daventry pushed his hand through his hair. How should he put it?

"Well, I've a notion that the dear old soul isn't all that he pretends to be. I don't think he spends all his time bug-hunting. Am I right?"

"As right as you always are," responded Mr. Bathurst.

CHAPTER XXII
THE NET TIGHTENS

AT ABOUT half past three that afternoon, while Peter Daventry, faithful to his trust, was keeping an observant eye upon ex-Sergeant Herbert Neville, Anthony Bathurst alighted from his car, dismissed Richardson at the corner by the Liver building and proceeded towards the establishment of Messrs. Thornton and Jackson. It did not take him long to reach his destination. He found that Messrs. Thornton and Jackson described themselves upon their shop-front as 'Gunsmiths and Rifle Specialists.'

Entering without hesitation, he asked to see the head of the firm, at the same time presenting his card endorsed by the Commissioner of Police, Sir Austin Kemble. The clerk that took him to the manager wasted no time in preliminaries. The manager followed his excellent example. As a result of this somewhat unusual procedure, within the space of about three minutes, Mr. Bathurst found himself in the presence of a gentleman who announced himself to be the head of the firm—George Thornton. He had Anthony's card on the table in front of him.

"Good-afternoon! I confess that your visit puzzles me, Mr.—er—Bathurst, especially when I realise the connection. In what respect do I interest Scotland Yard? Surely one of my guns hasn't killed anybody? Had it been Scotland Road now, I might—"

His keen, shrewd face lit up with an attractive smile which Anthony did his best to return.

"I can understand your wonderment, Mr. Thornton. I anticipated it. But I have not come to see you out of idle curiosity. I have come to ask you rather two or three important questions. I hope you will be able to answer them and by so doing materially assist me."

"If I can, Mr. Bathurst, I shall be most happy to do so. But what are they?"

Anthony looked at the chair by Thornton's table and the latter understood the meaning of the glance. He laughed.

"Your pardon! Please sit down—it was most forgetful of me."

"Thank you, Mr. Thornton." Mr. Bathurst speedily made himself as comfortable as possible. "In the first place," he inquired, "do you know a certain Major G. S. Whittaker of Swallowcliffe Hall, Buttercross?" Thornton shook his head slowly.

"No, I don't think so, although I must admit the name sounds familiar. Whittaker! Now, where have I heard that name?" He stopped to think. "I know!" he exclaimed suddenly. "Although I don't know the man, I know of him. I may even have met him. He's pretty prominent in political circles in this district—Unionist I feel certain."

"You don't do business with him then?"

Thornton looked blank.

"No, not to my knowledge, beyond, of course, a possible 'chance' purchase. That's always a possibility. Why?"

"He's certainly not a regular customer of yours then? You have no doubt on that point?"

Thornton shook his head emphatically.

"None whatever."

"Has he ever written to you?"

"Ever? Ever's a long time, Mr. Bathurst. To answer that question would—"

"I agree. Recently, then, shall we say?"

"No, I am absolutely certain of that. All the firm's correspondence ultimately reaches me, so I can make the statement with every confidence."

"My next question may surprise you, Mr. Thornton. Have you, on the other hand, recently written to him?" Thornton's denial of this question was in every way as forceful and emphatic as the others had been.

"Certainly not. I can vouch for that. Once again, why do you ask?"

"I'll tell you that in a few moments, Mr. Thornton, if you can bear with me till then. Your own trade envelopes, I believe—those you send out, for example, for reply already addressed to the firm—are typed in a lightish purple ink, are they not?"

The man that was being questioned smiled broadly and the smile held no small measure of amusement. It was accompanied by a shake of the head.

"On the contrary, Mr. Bathurst," he said, "our own envelopes are printed."

"Printed?"

"Printed. I'll show you one if you would care to have a look at it. Would you?"

"I should—very much, Mr. Thornton."

Thornton pressed the bell three times and a clerk quickly appeared in answer to the summons.

"Mr. Lacey is out, sir," he declared. "He's had to go over to Seacombe over that matter of Ware and Chandler."

"That's all right, Harvey. You will suit my purpose just as well. Bring me in one of the firm's printed envelopes—one addressed to ourselves, I mean."

"Yes, sir."

The youth disappeared with alacrity, to return again in a few minutes with the envelope in question.

"Thank you. That's all I want for the present, Harvey."

Thornton handed over the envelope to Anthony. Directly he looked at it, the latter could see that it in no way resembled the envelope that he had reproduced in his mind by his process of visualisation. He considered the change for a moment or two and the possibility that he might have made a mistake, but found himself unable to disturb the impression that he had at first formed. He was perfectly convinced in his own mind, despite the evidence of the envelope now in front of him, that the envelope that had been stolen from him after the death of Major Whittaker was exactly as he had since visualised it. He looked carefully at the envelope which Thornton had passed over to him. The paper was creamy-yellow in shade and the ink of the printer a bright black. The address shown was 'Messrs. Thornton and Jackson, 66, Dale St., Liverpool.' There were two discrepancies between the two envelopes as he saw them. There was a number shown on this envelope, whereas the other had mentioned none, and the word 'St.' here was printed with its ordinary and usual abbreviation. Mr. Bathurst was certain that in the other instance the word 'Street' had been typed in its full form. The ink of the full-stop after the word had been slightly smudged and he felt sure that the typed word before this slight smudging had been considerably longer than the two letters of 'St.'

"Satisfied?" he heard Thornton ask him.

"That's not too easy to answer. I am satisfied that this is nothing like the envelope that I had in my mind as being yours when I entered your office, Mr. Thornton. But as to being satisfied—"

Thornton broke in before he could finish his sentence.

"Pardon me if I ask you a question, because I must confess to a little bewilderment. But I suppose you are attempting to trace a certain letter. How is it that you are so certain that this envelope was what you describe as one of our firm's? What gives you that idea? I don't quite see how you could get it. I am at a loss—"

"I'll outline the position to you, Mr. Thornton. Major Whittaker of Swallowcliffe Hall, Buttercross, died the night before last. Before he died, he wrote three letters. I know that to be so without fear of contradiction, because I was in the room with him at the time and actually saw him write them. Two of the envelopes used for the letters were addressed by him in ordinary writing-ink—the third envelope was not. The address in this case was typed in the manner that I have described to you. Now, inasmuch as he must have had this envelope to hand when he had written the letter, ready for immediate use, so to speak, I formed the very natural conclusion that the envelope had been issued by the firm to whom it had been addressed and enclosed to him with another letter. Do you follow me, Mr. Thornton? Quite a logical inference, don't you think?"

The man addressed pursed his lips and nodded his agreement with Mr. Bathurst's explanation.

"Quite. I see your point perfectly. But now that you know that it was not so, there is another perfectly natural inference that you can draw, isn't there?"

Mr. Bathurst saw to where Thornton was heading. "Your meaning is that the envelope might have been typed for him in advance? By his secretary, for instance?"

Thornton smiled.

"Exactly, Mr. Bathurst. That seems to me to be a perfectly logical solution. Don't you think so yourself?"

Anthony rubbed his chin thoughtfully.

"It may be so certainly. But somehow, Mr. Thornton, in this instance I don't think that, though it may be logical, as you have pointed out, it will prove to be true."

Thornton seemed very interested at Anthony's remark. "Why not?" he asked.

Mr. Bathurst shrugged his shoulders.

"I can hardly tell you why. Call it instinct on my part if you like. 'Twill serve as well as anything else—or better!"

"You trust your instinct then implicitly, Mr. Bathurst?"

"Yes and no, Mr. Thornton. It is hard to answer absolutely accurately a question like that. It depends so much on the attendant circumstances. Would you do me a favour before I go?"

"If it is in my power, Mr. Bathurst, by all means."

"If it's no trouble, inquire of your staff if any envelope such as I have described to you has been delivered here during the last two days."

"I can do that easily. Harvey, the youngster you saw just now, will be the very man to tell you that. I'll send for him."

Thornton repeated the bell-ringing process and Harvey appeared again.

"Harvey," said his employer, "have you seen during the last two days an envelope addressed to us here typed in a faintish purple ink?"

"No, sir," came the prompt reply with a shake of the head. "I am quite sure that I haven't, sir. Our correspondence has been very light all the week, sir, ever since Bank Holiday. I've seen nowt of that kind, sir."

"Sure?"

"Yes, sir, quite sure."

Mr. Bathurst took a momentary hand.

"Does all the correspondence to the firm pass through your hands?"

"All t' incoming post, sir—yes, sir, every bit of it." Anthony turned to Thornton.

"These printed envelopes of yours—have they been in use for a considerable time? They're not an innovation of recent origin, for example?"

Thornton shook his head with direct emphasis.

"Used 'em for years, Mr. Bathurst. Ever since the war, to tell the truth. In the days before the war, we used to use a typed envelope, when our business wasn't as good or as big as it is now. We had one male typist then, now we've got four girls. That shows you the difference." Thornton smiled. "We've looked up a bit since then, Mr. Bathurst, I can tell you. Our typists' weekly wages bill runs round fourteen pounds at the present time. In the old days we used to pay a young fellow thirty-five shillings and that finished it." He smiled again at the savour of the remembrance. "And I'm not sure that young Forrester at thirty-five bob wasn't worth all the present lot put together, when you come to size things up properly."

Mr. Bathurst sat up and took immediate notice.

"Forrester, did you say?"

"Yes. Did you know him?"

"I knew a family of Forresters. I don't know whether—"

"This young fellow I speak of went across to France and never came back. Like thousands of others, of course—nothing unusual about that. So that he would hardly belong to the people that you know—you would remember it."

"What regiment was he? Any idea?"

"I can easily tell you. I used to correspond with all my employees that were overseas from time to time. I should have his address here somewhere." Thornton took his keys from his pocket and unlocked a drawer of his desk. From it he removed a file of old papers. "Should be here somewhere. I won't keep you a moment." He turned several over quickly but carefully, each one receiving a hurried but comprehensive glance. "Here you are, Mr. Bathurst!" he said at length. "Here it is. Forrester was in the Northshires. He was about twenty-two when he joined up."

"Thank you," said Anthony, "that settles it. He wouldn't be the man whom I knew then."

He rose from his seat. Thornton followed suit.

"Sorry I haven't been able to help you over the envelope, but at any rate I've told you what you wanted to know. I regret to hear of Major Whittaker's death—very sad indeed. We can ill afford to lose men of his stamp. The country needs 'em, Mr. Bathurst, needs 'em more to-day than at any time in its history."

"Thank you, Mr. Thornton. I can get a car to Aintree from here, can't I?"

Thornton grinned.

"That's right. But you're the wrong time of the year for the Grand National."

Mr. Bathurst smiled in return and shook him by the hand.

"I seem to be late all through this case," he said, "although I'm catching up now. That's a comforting thought, you know."

He closed the door behind him very thoughtfully.

CHAPTER XXIII
BOYS WILL BE—GIRLS

CROSSLAND MANSIONS were very close to the Aintree tram terminus and as he walked towards them, Mr. Bathurst thought of Thornton's parting words. He could see the world-famous Grand National course stretching away on his right. The huge stand—empty—seemed like a skeleton awaiting the advent of the flesh with which to cover its bones. But the afternoon was hot and close and the end of March a long way off. The doors of the somewhat dingy-looking hostelry that faced him were unfriendly towards a thirsty man, for they were, of course, shut. Thirst has to be regulated now in England. Anthony therefore proceeded straight to the house in Crossland Mansions numbered 17. There was nothing beyond its number to distinguish it from 18 or 16. He pressed an obtrusive bell, which was answered somewhat tardily by a slatternly-looking woman who had seen better nights.

"Good-afternoon!" said Anthony sweetly. "Am I correct in supposing that a Mr. Leslie Chadwick lives here?"

The woman grimaced a negative.

"You're not, young man, because he don't."

"I'm sorry to have troubled you, madam, but I was certainly informed on excellent authority that this was Mr. Chadwick's address."

He was met with the sourest of looks. The lady took no pains to conceal her real feelings.

"Seems to me," she declared, "that you're either a fool or a liar to tell me a thing like that."

Anthony raised his hat in gallant and chivalrous acceptance.

"You underrate me, madam, surely, which disturbs me. Why not call me both? Although I admit that I fail to understand which of my remarks is the direct cause of your discrimination."

For some reason or another, the woman appeared to relent suddenly. If a reason has to be forthcoming, let us put it down to Anthony's charm of manner, although it is a far cry from Pauline, Lady Fullgarney to Mrs. Owen of Crossland Mansions, Liverpool—as far perhaps as from the Colonel's lady to Judy O'Grady! Somewhat grudgingly she changed her attitude towards the young man with the pleasant grey eyes who was addressing her.

"You've made a mistake, haven't you?" she said. "That's all there is to it, isn't it? Aren't you referring to my young lady lodger, *Miss* Leslie Chadwick?"

For the moment Anthony was certainly taken aback. But he quickly recovered himself.

"I beg your pardon, madam, for my mistake. But I took the name Leslie to apply to a person of my own sex. You will forgive my carelessness, I am sure. I should have remembered the other possibility."

The woman grunted an unintelligible something.

"Is the lady at home?" pursued Anthony.

"No, she's not. What's she been up to this time?"

"Up to?" queried Mr. Bathurst, the personification of innocence.

"She'll find herself in nice trouble before she's finished," proceeded Mrs. Owen, arms akimbo, "the flighty bit, as I've told her more times than I can remember. Fair ruins my 'pillarcases,' she does, with her lipstick and such-like. 'Kuddle-proof,' they call it on the box—I like that!" She expressed herself scornfully. "'Kuddle-proof,'" she repeated, "did you ever hear such stuff and nonsense? They ought to have to wash them." Then she tacked from her course. "What is it this time?" she asked again. "Instalments due on the gramophone?"

Anthony protested. Miss Chadwick's fragile reputation would be safe in his hands.

"Don't alarm yourself, madam. There is no trouble on this occasion. I merely wanted a few words with the lady—that was why I called."

"Then you'll have to go down to the 'Gerunda'. She's an attendant there, and there's a matinée this afternoon, so she's on. She does the programmes for the stalls. Then the refreshments between the acts."

"Thank you. What's she like? How shall I recognise her?"

"Tall—she's a good-looker all right. Knows how to 'give the glad' with the best of 'em. Never takes Lady Leslie long to get off. Her hair's fair—this year." She added the last two words with just the right touch of feminine spite to give them emphasis.

"I am obliged to you," said Mr. Bathurst, as he raised his hat in acknowledgment and farewell. "I will do my best to find her. From your description it should be easy."

The door of 17, Crossland Mansions closed with a bang that shook the terrace and Mrs. Owen returned to her more serious afternoon task of slumber with nasal accompaniment.

As he walked away from the house, Anthony pondered over his next move and eventually came to a decision. He would take a risk that he felt convinced would ultimately prove to be no risk at all. He would waste no more time upon what he had definitely decided had been a vulgar intrigue upon the part of the dead man! Whittaker had doubtless met the girl in the theatre at Liverpool upon one of his excursions to that city and, during his association with her, had written to her as a man from the point of view of matrimonial safety. A letter addressed to 'Leslie Chadwick Esq.' would have occasioned no suspicions in the mind of either Miss Whittingham, his secretary, or Mrs. Whittaker herself, should either chance to see it. He determined to get back to Swallowcliffe Hall for the drama's final staging. Looking at his wrist-watch, he resolved to dine in Liverpool and then travel home via Holmedale. He might be in time to catch Coppinger and journey over with him. If not, it didn't matter very much, for he knew the carrier would be at his post at midnight with the others. Mr. Bathurst checked their names off mentally. "Neville, Peter Daventry, Richardson, Coppinger, and Colonel Fane. And possibly one other." Mr. Bathurst smiled to himself. "Possibly two others." He would dine where he had dined with Peter a few nights ago. But this time—alone! Afterwards there was a certain Inspector of Police whom he wished to interview.

CHAPTER XXIV
THE WINDOW OF THE BEDROOM

ANTHONY MADE his journey from Holmedale to Swallow-cliffe Hall alone, for Coppinger, in accordance with his promise already given, had gone on ahead. It was a quarter past ten when Mr. Bathurst made his destination and he entered the grounds of the Hall by the unusual method (at least for him) of climbing the imposing wall at the back of the house. The spikes had to be negotiated with the utmost care and agility, but what man has done man can do, and after all there is such a place as Oxford as well as Harvard.

All was intensely quiet and for the time of the year it was a comparatively dark night. The sky was well-clouded and overcast and what moon there was was well obscured, only a few beams struggling through the mass of clouds intermittently.

He made his way down the garden, past the tennis-pavilion from where they had watched the night before, and towards the house. His objective at the moment was Neville's bedroom, a room that interested him hugely. The window of this room was a matter of about fourteen feet from the ground and he had observed that there was a convenient pipe close to it, up which a moderately active man could climb. Mr. Bathurst, be it observed, was much more than a moderately active man. He kept within the shadows as he approached. It was as well that he did, for suddenly he brought himself to a full-stop and flattened himself full-length upon the grass. He could now see the window of Neville's room quite plainly and also the pipe beside it. To Mr. Bathurst's utter astonishment and amazement, a man was descending by way of the water-pipe, descending by the very method that Anthony had purposed ascending! The question was, which way was he coming? If, as Anthony shrewdly suspected, he intended making his exit over the wall at the end of the garden, it was a mammoth to a maggot that he would pass very close to Mr. Bathurst on his way there. It did not take the latter very long to make up his mind. He wriggled across the grass, during a period when the moon was thoroughly hidden, until he found himself in the lee of the side wall of the garden. By this time he could just hear the sound of approaching footsteps—the unknown climber of water-pipes was drawing near. Anthony held his breath, because to be discovered now might mean disaster and ruination to all his plans. The soft footsteps came nearer and nearer—the man was walking swiftly. Anthony pushed his long body into the friendly darkness of the wall and lay there motionless. Directly the man reached the strip of grass of the tennis-courts, Mr. Bathurst knew who he was. Once again Mr. Horace Garland-Isherwood of Philadelphia was indulging in what seemed to be his favourite occupation—taking exercise at nights in the grounds of Swallowcliffe Hall.

But Anthony's luck held. The stars in their courses and the saints in the calendar joined irresistible forces upon his behalf. The intruder passed on rapidly and almost silently, unobservant of the figure in the shadows. When he reached the wall at the end of the garden, he stopped and gave a low whistle. As far as Anthony's ears could tell him—he was determined not to show himself yet awhile—the entomologist from Philadelphia was waiting there at the garden's limit for somebody or other on the other side of the wall. As events subsequently transpired, this idea was accurate, for, wriggling over on to his other side so that he could look towards the wall at the end, Mr. Bathurst heard an answering whistle from an invisible person somewhere fairly near at hand and saw Mr. Garland-Isherwood hoist himself up very suddenly and climb to the wall-top. Once there, he quickly disappeared on the other side. No sooner had this happened than Anthony picked himself up from his neighbourhood of peach and nectarine and ran swiftly and silently towards the house. As he came near to the bedroom of his quest, a friendly figure came out of the comparative darkness and accosted him.

"Is that you, sir?"

It was Coppinger. Anthony could tell that at once from the voice.

"Yes, Coppinger," he said. "How long have you been here?"

"Been here about half-an-hour, sir. Your Mr. Daventry asked me to keep watch out here till he should stop me."

"Seen anybody yet?"

"No, sir," was the sturdy answer. "But I thought I heard footsteps just now. That's what made me come out and stop you. I wasn't sure who it was."

"Good!" said Anthony. "Where's Neville? Do you know?"

"I heard your Mr. Daventry tell the Colonel just after I arrived that Neville was in his bedroom."

"I see. Well, I'm going to countermand Mr. Daventry's order. But you can tell him as you go through the house what you're doing and why you're doing it. He'll understand. Tell him you've seen me. As soon as you've done what I want you to do, you can come back out here again as Mr. Daventry desires. Now for what I want you to do. Go upstairs to Neville's bedroom and tell him that Mr. Daventry wants him downstairs. See that he obeys the order. If it's necessary and you can manage it without incurring suspicion, wait until he does so. Understand me?"

Coppinger the dour touched his cap with an odd gesture of obedience.

"I get you, Mr. Bathurst. I'll get into the house now and do as you say."

"Right! I'll wait for you, then I shall know if it's all right. Tell Mr. Daventry to keep Neville downstairs for a time at least. Then he must send him upstairs again to rest until he's wanted. Impress that on him. Get along with you."

Coppinger turned on his heel and made his way with rapid strides through the kitchen garden towards the house. Anthony waited for his return with some impatience—it did not suit his book to be out there too long from more than one standpoint. At any moment now the gentleman with the butterfly net from Philadelphia might return to the scene of his former exploits and Anthony feared that he might not return alone. But things went smoothly—Coppinger did not try his patience unduly—for within the space of five minutes the indefatigable carrier was back. His usual imperturbability had not deserted him.

"I've seen Mr. Daventry, sir, and given him your instructions. Neville has come down from his room and is now with the other gentlemen in the library. As soon as I saw him there, sir, I came back to my post here. Mr. Daventry has also told him to try to get some sleep before midnight. I told him what you said with regard to that."

"Excellent, Coppinger. I shan't forget this, I assure you. When you see me again, I hope matters will have progressed considerably. Au 'voir for the present."

The carrier grinned as Anthony slipped away into the darkness. It was the nearest approach Coppinger's face had had to hilarity that Mr. Bathurst had witnessed since he had known him.

Once clear of his companion, Anthony ran swiftly round the house until he came to the pipe that ran up the wall beside Neville's bedroom window. Digging his toes into the brickwork, he caught hold of the pipe and ascended slowly hand by hand until he came abreast of the window-sill. It was the work of a moment to get one knee on to the sill itself and clutch the brick-coping with one hand. Steadying himself and suddenly letting go of the pipe, he obtained a kneeling position on the sill itself, pushed up the window and slipped into the empty room. Once inside, he listened carefully, but there was no sound to disturb him. For a moment he stood there, evidently in consideration of his next step. Decision came to him almost immediately. Mr. Bathurst crept deliberately under Neville's bed. The position was moderately uncomfortable, but he didn't anticipate that he would be forced to remain there for very long. He was just in time, for, within ten minutes, Neville entered and made preparations for the hour's rest that Peter Daventry had promised him.

CHAPTER XXV
MIDNIGHT OF AUGUST THE SIXTEENTH

WHEN, shortly before eleven o'clock on the night of August the sixteenth, Peter Daventry received Anthony's message via Coppinger, he found an exceeding measure of comfort therein, for, truth to tell, when he had been told to rely upon the initiative and resource that he himself possessed, he had appreciated the compliment that Mr. Bathurst had so generously accorded him, but at the same time had not looked forward to the occasion when these two qualities were to be displayed with any strong degree of passionate anticipation. Had he been told to tackle the members of the Silver Troika single-handed, he would have relished that task (however impossible it might prove to be in reality) far more agreeably than he was now looking forward to this conference in which he was about to take part and perhaps conduct. But Coppinger's story of Anthony being close at hand comforted and steadied him considerably, for he began to understand better what he himself was supposed and expected to do. His work was to play for 'keeps' until Anthony Bathurst considered it propitious to come out into the open and declare himself. Now that he saw his game in front of him, he naturally felt better able to play it.

A few minutes before midnight, therefore, he assembled his forces in the library—himself, Colonel Fane, Richardson, Coppinger and Neville. The last-mentioned had been instructed to report again in the library a few minutes prior to twelve o'clock and had done so. Neville always prided himself that his reliability was beyond question. Although he looked fit, it was plain that he was not free from anxiety. Peter, on the other hand, presented a calm and nonchalant exterior to his four companions. This was not, however, a faithful representation of his feelings, for inwardly he was nervous and disturbed. The uncertainty of the whole affair bothered him. It reminded him of having to play a part on the Stage, entirely ignorant of the lines, and of being prepared to 'wing' them whenever the necessity arose. If only his native shrewdness and natural resources would carry him through!

He went across the room and spoke to Colonel Fane. The latter gentleman listened gravely at first, but at length nodded a benign approval. At a sign from him, Richardson opened the French doors with their still shattered glass—evidence of the Silver Troika's first visit.

"I have Bathurst's orders," contributed Peter, "to tell you that none of us here is to use or show the old revolver unless circumstances absolutely demand it. Is that clear to everybody?"

Assent came from each.

"I understand that part of it all right, Daventry," put in the Colonel, "and that's all I do understand. But I tell you frankly that if I consider that demand does materialise, I shan't hesitate about protecting my interests with a little shooting practice. Take that from me, here and now. If Bathurst were so keen on arranging this meeting, why the devil isn't he here? That's the main point that strikes me about the whole thing." He glared at Peter as though responsibility for Anthony's campaign had now descended upon him.

He attempted to appear oblivious of Fane's stare, but before he could evolve a satisfactory reply to the question, a movement from Richardson abruptly checked him.

"I fancy they're coming, sir," said the chauffeur.

"Everybody keep cool," said Peter softly, "and keep his head. Leave the rest to me." His remark held an airy confidence which he himself was far from feeling.

Five seconds passed and then the forms of the five Russians could be seen. As previously, the members of the Silver Troika were led by the "President." Behind him came Schmidt and Verensky, behind them Krakar and Loronoff. There was no other with them, as Peter Daventry had half-expected, although he wouldn't have been able to have given a reason for this piece of anticipation had he been tackled. Perhaps Anthony had sown the seeds of the idea in his mind. The "President" seemed to have discovered an ill-fitting mantle of amiability, ephemeral though it might well prove to be. He bowed somewhat elaborately, but Peter observed that he kept his right hand within his pocket.

"Good-evening, English gentlemen!" he opened unctuously. "The comrades of the Silver Troika are here. They are pleased to attend what you have called the conference." He moved his mouth and cheeks in what—in anybody save a lipless person— would have been a mocking grin and, turning to the four supporters behind him, said: "Comrades, to your places! And remember what I have told you!"

Peter Daventry accepted his mood and manner and finessed with it.

"Take a seat, old dear," he urged, "and make yourself at home. How about a cushion and see the game in comfort?"

The "President" smilingly shook his head in refusal of the invitations.

"Ah, my old friend of the woodland walk, but not, I think, the man you pretended to be! You are kind. Perhaps it suits you to be, eh? Perhaps it fits with your book, as you say in this vile country. I am the dog on the top, eh? But *chacun à son goût*—I prefer to stand." There was a braggadocio and a strong hint of challenge in his tone.

But Peter kept a tight hand upon himself and upon his combative inclinations.

"As you please, Alfonso," he returned. "Your preference, of course, must be considered."

The "President" seemed to change his tactics.

"Which of you arranged the conference? Which of you wrote the letter that notified us of it? I would deal with him and no other. That is what I have come here for."

These questions produced the most awkward moment that Peter had as yet been called upon to face. He was by no means certain how the "President" would take the news of Anthony's absence. It appeared to him that his opponent had found his weakest suit. He sought safety therefore in evasion.

"He will be here very shortly. He has been—er—detained. A little business requiring his personal supervision. The personal touch, you know, and all that. But his absence need make no difference to the conference. He has authorised me to treat with you upon his behalf. I have full authority from him to settle the question that lies between us."

"So," said the "President," caressingly almost, softly certainly, "so! That is indeed good news. You refer, I suppose, to the English sneak-detective and eavesdropper, Bathurst? You act for him? I thought I missed his cunning face from our gathering to-night." Another of his leering smiles broke over his evil face.

"Have no fear, though, on that account. In no way do I regret the fact that we have no Bathurst with us. I give you my assurance that I shall shed no tears." His right hand never left his pocket, but Schmidt muttered something to him which caused him to turn his head and answer. He replied in Russian and to

Peter's attentive ear it sounded as though there were venom in his tone.

"Good!" thought Daventry to himself. "A little spot of civil war in the old Troika and we'll pull it off yet."

The thought had hardly materialised in his mind when the lipless horror was at him again. There was no silkiness in his tone now and the mantle of amiability that he had worn during the early part of the interview was definitely doffed and discarded.

"Time passes," he said coldly, "and I talk when I should act. 'Twas a trick I learned from a Tartar wanton, but she'll teach no man again—anything," he added in a kind of gloating bestiality and the meaning his voice held was obvious to all his audience. Then his tone rang with fierce intentness and he used the words that Colonel Fane, Neville and Richardson had heard him use before. "Where are they? What I have come for?" The "President" had come to the point.

Peter realised that the action of reply must be quick and decisive if he wished to hold his own and avoid an ugly situation, and even then he thought that delay would be a better word to use.

"It is with regard to that, Mr. President, that we have—er—convened this little pow-wow. You are aware that Major Whittaker is dead. That fact, you will admit, may be said to complicate matters somewhat. But since his—er—unfortunate decease, we, his friends and advisers, have realised that this matter of yours must be faced with the old shoulders squared and the old head back, so to speak, and can, on no account, be shelved. That is why we are all here to-night—all friendly and so on. You know what I mean—brother clasps the hand of brother, marching forward—"

Colonel Fane hastened to speak in support of Peter's statement.

"It is exactly as Mr. Daventry says. We feel that it is just to go into your demands very thoroughly. Now, in respect of these papers that you claim to—"

The "President's" voice, at the mention of the word "papers," came like the crack of a whip.

"By the Virgin," he cried, "have done! For I am not here for froth and frolic. By the Holy Ikon I am not. Talk not to me of 'papers,' 'documents' and 'minute-books.' I thought that farce was finished. I came for words, but by Saint Nicholas, those words may turn to blows with the speed that snow melts beneath the sun. For the last time, where are they?" There was no mistaking the venom now.

Fane spread out his hands helplessly as the four Russians advanced a step behind their leader. Peter half-rose in protest against the "President's" attitude. As he did so, the "President" pushed him back contemptuously into his seat.

"Be silent," he cried, "or I'll slit your throat!"

Then came Peter Daventry's greatest trial. He was forced to remember the orders that Anthony had given him. "Don't use your revolver unless things get very hot and then only out of sheer necessity." All very well for old Bathurst to talk like that, but when it came to being shoved back into your chair with the scantiest of ceremony by a filthy poisonous hound like this! If he did it again—

At this moment of reflection, Peter's attention was arrested and ultimately sent racing down another channel. The "President" had addressed Neville, who up to the moment had remained in the background and neither said nor done anything.

"*You* heard what I said, Comrade Neville. You should know that when I say a thing, I mean it! None indeed should know it better. *Where are they?* Tell me or I'll flay you alive and burn you afterwards. I came for Whittaker two nights ago, but Hell claimed him first. I shall not fail in the other half of my errand. Where are they, you traitor?"

Neville's face burnt with a spot of fire in each cheek.

"Traitor?" he echoed hoarsely. "What do you mean, you scum?"

"Oho!" exclaimed the "President" with what was doubtless intended to be ironical humour. "The cock crows, does it? But I fear only upon his own dunghill. Like most cocks!" His voice changed again. "What do I mean, you lily-livered swine? What I say, and nothing more. I called you 'traitor.' Why should you resent it? Can I find a name that fits you better? Tell me that." He pushed his face as near to Neville's as he could, his right hand still ominously hidden.

"Accusations are easy," defended Neville sullenly. "Proofs are more difficult. When have I played traitor, you lying—"

"Be careful," menaced the "President." "Don't tempt me from my chivalry and courtesy. I might forget my obligations as a guest. You betrayed your master days ago, you dog, and murdered him for aught I know."

Neville's mouth opened in amazement at the charge. "What?" he almost screamed. "I betrayed my master? In God's name, how?"

"Oho, you deny it, do you? You wrote to me—the letter was anonymous, I know, but I've no doubt that it came from you— telling me that the detective Bathurst was coming down to take a hand in the game, so I made my plans. How else could I have known of Bathurst's coming? I had him trailed from the moment he left London till when he landed in the docks at Liverpool. Only by low cunning did he succeed in getting through. Who else could have written me but you, you cur!"

Neville laughed contemptuously.

"You lie. No letter came from me. I'd sign on with Satan before I'd lend a helping hand to you. I was a British soldier once. We don't betray our masters. Find somebody else to pin your lies to."

The "President" fixed him with a baleful stare.

"It matters not, my friend. After all, it is of small consequence—the measure of your deceit. Give me the pretty toys, for you have them, my friend, you have them! Otherwise I shall be reluctantly compelled—"

Peter watched him, fascinated at the play of his nervously-quivering fingers. Neville shrank back and, as he did so, raised his hand as though in self-protection. Loronoff and Krakar moved a step forward, but, anticipating them from the advantage of the position that he held, the "President," quick as lightning, pulled his revolver from his pocket and with the butt end struck a smashing blow at Neville's head. Major Whittaker's servant, taken completely by surprise, fell heavily to the floor. The Russians gathered round him in a body. As they made their first move, a strange voice sounded in the opening of the doors leading on to the garden. For the moment, it electrified everybody.

"Say," said the stranger, "I just hate to butt in, but reach for a bit of sky, will you? That's the idea—all together."

CHAPTER XXVI
THE HIDING-PLACE

"THAT'S RIGHT," he continued. "That's real kind of you. Travers, take that bunch of filth over there, will you? O.K.? Good! Russell, see to the landed gentry. That's the idea."

Three men stood in the room, each holding a levelled revolver in either hand. The six weapons commanded the entire apartment, fore and aft. The man in charge of the situation was Horace Garland-Isherwood, but his voice and manner were not now those of the hunter of butterflies, for this identity was now completely shed. They were far more incisive and alert.

"Empty their pockets, Travers," he ordered crisply. "Reckon what they're carrying 'ud spoil the cut of any coat, and I always was sartorial. Say, don't move. I kind of prefer you motionless." He addressed the last remark to the red-lidded Krakar, who had shifted his feet a trifle as Travers approached him.

Mr. Garland-Isherwood went on:

"You see, if you did, my finger might tremble on the trigger-bo! And as I can hit the pip of a card at forty paces, I guess I'd drill one little hole in your carcass that would cool your brain, though I reckon there'd be too much dirt on you for you to feel much. That's the ticket, Travers. Put them all on the table there." Then he caught the eyes of Colonel Fane and Peter Daventry. "Guess I'm kinder real sorry to have to include real and genuine gentlemen like yourselves along with this outfit, but, you see, even if you aren't birds of a feather, I caught you all flockin' together, so to speak. But what I've got to do won't take me very long—at least, so I calculate."

Colonel Fane uttered an indignant protest.

"This is an outrage, sir, nothing more and nothing less. Who are you, I'd like to know? What right have you to enter here at all?"

Mr. Garland-Isherwood smiled an easy smile.

"Throw any shootin'-irons you've got with the others, will you? Thanks very much. It's real thoughtful of you."

Peter Daventry felt the throes of humiliation as he surrendered his revolver, but his perceptions were keen enough to understand that this gentleman meant every word that he said. Who in thunder was he—and where was Anthony Bathurst? These were the two questions that raged violently through his brain.

"We won't argue about my right to enter," proceeded Mr. Garland-Isherwood. "It wouldn't seem too amicable and I always like the boys round me to be amicable. Let's leave it that I'm here as a guest of all of you. For I'm here—it's a sure thing."

The "President," thwarted at the moment of his triumph, looked the picture of vindictive rage. He let go a torrent of Russian, apparently to Loronoff and Verensky, who were huddled next to him. Verensky replied, but Loronoff shook his head meaninglessly.

"Now that's real pretty," interjected the gentleman of the double-barrelled name. "I ain't criticisin' your elocution, but when I hear that I'm all for Esperanto. Would you five gentlemen from the gut of Hell mind getting into that corner?" He pushed his two revolvers in their faces. "Move," he cried, "or by the Hokey I'll ventilate you! That's better. Pretty little run you've got, Verensky."

The five Russians were now herded into one corner of the room to the left of the garden as they faced it. Neville, still unconscious, lay straight across the floor at the other end.

"Travers," cried the man in command of the situation, "look after this bunch of exotic beauty, will you, and I'll get to business." He indicated the members of the Silver Troika.

Peter Daventry, with Coppinger at his side, and Colonel Fane flanked by Richardson, the chauffeur, stood against the wall nearest to the prostrate body of the servant. The third of the invaders, Russell, as the principal had called him, held them at the revolver's point. But they almost forgot all that in the fascination of watching the performance of Horace Garland-Isherwood. The last-named gentleman caught the eye of Colonel Fane and smiled pleasantly.

"Guess what you're thinking, General, and you're quite right. I was always taught it was rude to contradict. I didn't cross from little old New York to catch butterflies. I was huntin' bigger game than that."

He replaced his two revolvers in the side pockets of his coat, took out a knife, and, stooping suddenly, ripped up the trouser that covered the prostrate Neville's right leg. The cloth was cut to the knee as cleanly as the wire cleaves cheese and the unconscious man's artificial leg was exposed to the sight of all. Then the gentleman from Philadelphia felt for the calf of the leg. Evidently he quickly found that particular part of it that he wanted, for after a short interval a smile spread over his face. Peter Daventry, watching spellbound, saw part of the leg fall away, as it were on a hinge, and disclose a small square cavity in the limb. Mr. Garland-Isherwood inserted his fingers triumphantly and drew out a wash-leather bag. He held it in the palm of his hand and for an almost imperceptible moment his face appeared to harden a little. The "President" and his four followers were open-mouthed and wide-eyed in amazement.

"I am very much afraid, Comrades of the Silver Troika," he declared, "that you're kind of going to get left right here and now. Henceforward you and I are strangers, for from now we part company. If one of you dies of 'Mat fever,' you all will, because it's catchin'. But I guess you'll all meet in Hell, which will be darned unfortunate for that place. You'll tend to lower the standard." He thrust the wash-leather bag into his pocket, together with his knife, and took out his two revolvers again. "Russell," he cried, "Travers, with me, boys, we're off!" The two men backed towards the French doors, still holding the threatening revolvers.

"Russell," said Garland-Isherwood again, "get the engine going and when you've done so, throw the ladder back this side. Travers will follow in a minute and do the same for me."

"Right, chief!" cried Russell.

He ran down the garden towards the wall, whilst the two other men stayed behind. Within a few minutes, Travers received a similar order regarding the ladder and followed Russell. Mr. Horace Garland-Isherwood, with his two revolvers commanding the position, listened for some little time with ears cocked for the slightest sound. Somehow he didn't seem quite as talkative as he had been. Eventually he backed towards the doors.

"Good-evening, gentlemen!" he said. "I'm goin' back to the shack where the Black-eyed Susans grow." Turning swiftly, he bolted down the garden.

Immediately he turned his back, the members of the Silver Troika seized their revolvers from the table where Travers had thrown them and rushed after him. But Mr. Garland-Isherwood, true to form, had made his preparations that night very thoroughly. A rope stretched across the garden brought forth, after it had done its work, a volume of blasphemous execration. By the time that Verensky, Krakar and Co. had picked themselves up, sorted themselves out and climbed the wall, their quarry was safely away.

It was about that time that Mr. Bathurst stepped through the doors into the room to find Peter, Coppinger and the Colonel assisting Neville to his feet. Consciousness had by now come back to him and, as he surveyed the torn trouser that revealed the secret of his artificial limb, his bitterness and chagrin were easy to behold.

"I don't know what extraordinary affair I'm taking part in, Neville," expostulated Colonel Fane, "but whatever it is, there's no doubt that Mr. Garland-Isherwood—not to put too fine a point upon it—has got away with the goods, and several people seem to have known more than appeared on the surface. Where on earth have you been, Bathurst?"

"Not far away, Colonel. I've seen and heard all that there was to see and hear, and perhaps a bit more besides."

"He's got away with the stuff right enough, Bathurst," put in Peter Daventry. "As he remarked just now, he didn't cross all the way from little old New York for butterflies."

"That's as may be," returned Mr. Bathurst. "But we're all tired and Neville has had a pretty bad knock, I'm afraid. We'll hear his story in the morning. When we've heard his, you'll hear mine. Each will probably prove interesting. At any rate, whatever happens, you can take it from me that Swallowcliffe Hall has seen the last of the Silver Troika." He stroked his chin. "All the same, I'm surprised at our butterfly friend crossing the herring-pond and going to all the trouble he did for a wash-leather bag. Still, there's no accounting for taste." He turned away and spoke in a low tone to Coppinger as Colonel Fane burst out impatiently:

"For Heaven's sake, don't be wilfully blind, Bathurst. A wash-leather bag you call it! What's in the bag? That's the point!"

"How true you always are, Colonel!" murmured Mr. Bathurst. "As you say, that *is* the point. But you see, there is nothing in the bag. What *was* in there, I took out about a couple of hours ago. Good-night, Colonel!"

Chapter XXVII
SOME OF THE TRUTH

"I think, Neville," said Mr. Bathurst, "that I can hear the wheels of a car. It should be Sir Roderick Hope. I asked him to be here by eleven o'clock this morning. By the way, is Miss Whittingham here?"

Neville, his head swathed in bandages, nodded an affirmative.

"Yes, sir. I understood from her that you sent for her last night, sir. There is a car, sir, you were quite right." Neville walked to the window. "As a matter of fact, sir, there are two cars. One is close behind the other."

"If the first car is carrying Sir Roderick, the second car contains Mrs. Whittaker, Mrs. Fane and Miss Pennington, Neville, or vice-versa. I think it only right that they should know the truth of the tragedy. With regard to Mrs. Whittaker, there can be no argument about it. Did Satterthwaite, the milkman, call this morning, do you know?"

Neville looked very surprised at the question.

"He did, sir! Why?"

"Did you actually see him?"

"Yes, sir. He was round at his usual time. I saw him talking to Mrs. Chamberlain."

He turned away and went out as Colonel Fane entered with the others.

"Well, Bathurst, the ladies are here, as you promised. Will you meet Sir Roderick?"

Anthony bowed to the three ladies as they entered. They seemed to have benefited by their short stay away from Swallowcliffe Hall.

"Well, Mrs. Whittaker," he said, "how are you? I've sent for you because I think I have accomplished the task that I set myself. I am going to ask you to listen this morning to a very strange story—a story that will cause you no small amount of pain, I am afraid, but one which I feel sure you would rather hear and know than be told about by perhaps irresponsible people on some future occasion. I am right in that opinion, am I not?"

Constance Whittaker's face was white and strained with grief and anxiety, but she replied with quiet dignity.

"You are quite right, Mr. Bathurst. I would much rather hear the truth at once than wait for it in a suspense that would be intolerable It would be only worse perhaps when I did hear it."

"I am glad that I did not misjudge you. Sit between Mrs. Fane and Miss Pennington, will you? If you will pardon me, I will join you in two minutes."

On his way back, he met Neville in the hall conducting Sir Roderick Hope to the room that he had just vacated.

"Good-morning, Sir Roderick! I felt that you wouldn't fail me. I was right then?"

"You were right, Bathurst," replied Sir Roderick with extreme gravity. "It took me very little time to discover that. I've got it here."

"Good! Give it to me, will you? Thanks."

Sir Roderick Hope passed something over to him that he took from his pocket. Anthony put it carefully away.

"I should like you to hear the whole story, Sir Roderick, if you can possibly spare the time. Can you? I assure you that you will find it interesting. Doubly so from the point of view of your profession."

"I should like to, Bathurst. Did you communicate with Sir Austin?"

"I wired to him as I told you I was going to when you were here the time before. I've had his reply."

"That's all right then. Carry on!"

"In here then, Sir Roderick, if you don't mind." Anthony opened the door of the library and they entered. He at once introduced the three ladies to the famous pathologist. That accomplished, Mr. Bathurst turned to Neville.

"Now, Neville," he said, "let's have your story. I think that should come first."

The man addressed grinned a little sheepishly and shame-facedly and glanced in the direction of the widow of his late master. He appeared to hesitate.

"Do as Mr. Bathurst says, Neville," said Mrs. Whittaker quietly. "Surely it will be best in the end."

"Thank you, madam," returned Neville, encouraged by the statement. "If I know that you understand, it will relieve my feelings considerably and help me in my story. It is not a long one. The job will be to start it—But you all know that the Major was on a secret mission in Russia early in 1918. Perhaps the most ticklish job he had was the rounding-up of one of the strongest secret societies in the whole of Russia at that time. You know their name, because you've heard it a good many times these last few days. They called themselves the Silver Troika.

But Major Whittaker tackled his job with his usual determination and steadily, one by one, they got snuffed out until only about half-a-dozen of them remained. Well, in July of that year came the assassination of the Tsar and his family. I don't know the details of what actually occurred. I don't think there's a soul living that knows the whole truth of that matter, except perhaps those directly responsible, but there's little doubt that the Silver Troika crowd had a lot to do with it. Krakar is supposed to have been in the cellar itself. One of their last half-dozen or so, however—his name was Mikaelovitch—fell into our hands. By 'our hands' I mean the Major's crowd that was working for the Allies. I am sorry to say that the Major let him go. I didn't know for a long time what had actually happened or why he escaped, but after the Major's recall, which came soon after, he told me. Mikaelovitch was supposed to have escaped through a woman, but he didn't. He offered Major Whittaker a bribe, and although it goes against the grain for me to publish the fact, the Major fell for it. But I had a soft spot in my heart for the Major and I think he had for me—we'd been together for so long. I resolved to stand by him if trouble came. I say 'if' trouble came. We both knew that it was bound to. The day that Mikaelovitch's perfidy came out to what was left of the Silver Troika, we knew that the 'President' and his crowd would move Heaven and earth to find us. That was, of course, the reason why the Major came to live up here. But Fortune was kind to us. Mikaelovitch fell foul of the Russian authorities and went to prison, where he died two months ago. Before he died, he told the truth of his escape."

Neville paused and at once Mrs. Whittaker put a question to him, despite the fact that Colonel Fane did his best to prevent her. The agitation on the Colonel's face at the news of his friend's turpitude was pitiable to behold. There was no doubt that he felt the position very keenly—more keenly probably than anybody present.

"Tell me, Neville," intervened Mrs. Whittaker, "how did Mikaelovitch bribe my husband?"

Neville looked straight into her eyes.

"After the murder of the Tsar, the Silver Troika had feathered their nests with the best of them until Mikaelovitch betrayed their secret to your husband. The bribe that was offered to Major Whittaker was the Troika's hoard. It was several magnificent specimens from what was left of—"

A familiar voice—familiar now where it had been strange before—sounded in the doorway. It finished Neville's sentence for him.

"The Crown Jools of the Romanoffs." The speaker was Mr. Horace Garland-Isherwood. Before any of the astonished company could find words, wherewith to check him, he proceeded. "And once again, ladies and gentlemen, my sincere and heartfelt apologies for being perhaps just a little—shall we say *de trop*? I just hate buttin' in, as I told you before, but—well, there you are, I'm always doin' it and needs must when ol' man Satan does a bit of shovin'."

"I don't think I have the pleasure of knowing your real name, sir," cut in Anthony, "for I feel certain that the name under which you introduced yourself to us before was a much less distinguished one."

"Now that's real kind of you to put it like that. I am Henry K. Lovell of Pinkerton's, representing the gentleman named here, for Mikaelovitch's story reached him very quickly."

He fished in his pocket and handed over a card upon which a name was printed. Anthony read it with uplifted eyebrows and passed it on to Sir Roderick Hope and Colonel Fane, who each received it with surprise, for the name was the name of one of the most august of the Romanoffs, now exiled in the 'Land of the Free.'

"I'm getting all the kick that's coming to me," proceeded Mr. Lovell engagingly. "Guess I know when to throw my hand in, and I guess, too, that that old time has duly arrived. I don't know who you are, sir—that's a pleasure that lies just round the corner—but you're no he-doll, and whoever you are, shake! Henry K. Lovell's proud to join fins with you." He held his hand out to Anthony.

The latter accepted it, pleasure and excitement dawning in his eyes.

"My name is Bathurst—Anthony Bathurst," he returned to the American. "I think I rather expected you this morning."

Lovell received the information with delight.

"You don't say? Gee, that's better than a tonic, I'm convalescent already. Say, I'm sittin' up sippin' the Sarsaparilla. Henry K. Lovell has taken himself to task very seriously, I give you his word. You bested me last night, Mr. Bathurst—in a way that is! But don't think I didn't know it. Directly I touched the cute little bag, I came over kind of catacomb cold. I was darned sure it was empty from the feel of the blamed thing. But what was a man to do? I played 'Poker-face.' I figured it out that if I could get the Troika bunch chasing my men Travers and Russell, they might chase 'em back all the way to Pinkerton's. Maybe they're well on the way now, calculating that Henry K. Lovell's with 'em—and the Jools. But he's not—neither are they." He chuckled.

"I thought you would come back, Mr. Lovell," said Anthony smilingly, "and I don't think that I can be said fairly to have bested you. It's very sporting of you to suggest it. Let us say rather that I was able to complete what you so successfully began. That, I think, is a truer description of what has happened."

"Waal," said Lovell, "that's darned good of you. I've heard of you often, but I'm real exhilarated to run alongside."

"Shall we ask Neville to resume his story?" suggested Mr. Bathurst. "For there is still a little for him to explain and there is also the question of Major Whittaker's death to be cleared up. I owe a thorough explanation of that to more than one person present. If I had—"

The door opened and Peter Daventry entered with Coppinger. Between them walked Richardson, the Major's chauffeur, and Satterthwaite, the milkman.

"Good-morning, gentlemen!" said Mr. Bathurst. "I now have the last of my essential witnesses. When Neville has finished his story, that fact will enable me to outline to you some of the details of a very strange affair. What's the matter, Colonel?"

"It's frightfully hot in here, Bathurst. I'll open another window."

"By all means."

Colonel Fane rose and did so.

Chapter XXVIII
THE REST OF THE TRUTH

THE REQUEST roused a reminiscence in Anthony's brain. Just before Whittaker died, Colonel Fane had made a similar request and Richardson, the chauffeur, had risen to put it into execution. It struck Mr. Bathurst, as he remembered it, as an extraordinary coincidence, one of those coincidences with which one meets sometimes in life's adventure. They are contradictory. At one moment they appear meaningless—at the succeeding one they seem eminently purposeful.

"Leave the door half-open, Colonel," suggested Anthony. "It certainly is stuffy in here. That will be an improvement as well. Now, Neville, will you kindly continue?"

The old soldier pushed his fingers through his hair. "There's not a lot more for me to say, Mr. Bathurst. My late master had originally, I believe, seventeen of the most magnificent of the Crown Jewels, including one of the finest pigeon-blood rubies you ever clapped eyes on and five emeralds among the best in the world."

"You'll excuse me, I'm sure, Mr. Neville." The interruption came from Lovell of Pinkerton's. "There were nineteen all told—it's nineteen I've been trailin'. Two's a lot when it's twins."

Neville accepted the correction.

"Maybe you're right, sir. I was never sure of the number that there were in the first place. The Major, you see, realised on several of them before we returned to England. He bought this house, furnished it lavishly, as you might say, and was able to gratify his slightest whim." He turned to Mrs. Whittaker. "Your pardon, ma'am, for putting it like that, but you know what I mean, don't you? You won't misunderstand me?"

Mrs. Whittaker bowed her head in reply.

"I understand everything perfectly, Neville, but all the same, it's very hard for me to realise—for a time at least."

"I'm sorry, ma'am. I suppose it is." He looked at her doubtfully, but seemed to gain a little in reassurance as he saw Mrs. Fane and Miss Pennington bend over her and speak to her. He went on: "Well, the Major and I talked things over and we put our heads together, so to speak, against the day when the Silver Troika would get busy, for we each thought it was a sure thing that they would, as I said just now. The question, of course, was a cunning hiding-place—we knew it would have to be cunning to defeat those murdering devils. Our plan was to stick to the jewels and deny that we ever had them. Now the best hiding-place for anything is on one's person, if it can possibly be done, because you've always got it with you. But it's not easy, as anyone can see that thinks it over. One day the Major cottoned on to an idea. He was watching me walking towards him one morning when the notion struck him of using my artificial leg as the hiding-place we required. He made me have a compartment fitted into the back of the calf, which worked on a spring hinge, and he made me swear that, if anything happened to him at the hands of the Silver Troika, I would fight like a tiger to keep the jewels for Mrs. Whittaker here. I have done so, sir. When the summons came a fortnight ago or so, we decided what to do. But all the same, I'd like to know how both of you gentlemen saw through the secret of the hiding-place, because it was known only to the Major and me. It beats me, that does."

"That was sure slick-easy," put in Henry K. Lovell. He smiled. "I was pretty sure you had 'em somewhere, being what may be termed the late Major's pet confederate. You see, I learned of the Major's death from the message you sent the Troika. I may as well tell you I had the audacity to read that."

"Yes, we saw you," said Anthony quietly.

"You did? Now that was real smart of you." He smiled again. "But you shouldn't have sneezed, you know," he added whimsically. "It's too noisy and explosive for a real slap-up sentinel."

"Touché," conceded Anthony smilingly, not troubling to explain Richardson's *faux pas.* "Go on!"

Lovell continued.

"Waal, I knew if I watched Mr. Neville here long enough, he'd give me the information I was sure thirstin' for. It was only a question of time. He did—last night. I had a seat in the orchestral stalls—outside his bedroom window. I saw him testin' his leg mechanism. It was a sure cinch to guess what for."

Anthony attacked again.

"I watched you climb down the water-pipe," he contributed lightly. "You short-headed me—no more. I went up after you, because I had the same idea. I meant to make Master Neville show me his hand—if I had to look over his shoulder for it. I meant to go further than that even. I got into his room and hid under his bed. When my opportunity came, I took it and the Crown Jewels of the Romanoffs." He swung round on Neville. "There you are, Neville. Now you know. You showed me the hiding-place yourself."

Neville made no reply, but the ubiquitous and irrepressible Lovell of Pinkerton's rubbed his hands with delight.

"Gee, but you're sure a hell of a feller, Mr. Bathurst. Say, I'm right proud to be paired with you and little old New York'll think more of you than ever before when Henry K. Lovell's done talking. I'll swear I'll tell the world."

Anthony smiled at his enthusiasm.

"Having satisfied Neville," he proceeded, "I will come to the important matter of Major Whittaker's death. And if it be of any little satisfaction for you to know this, Mrs. Whittaker, I want to tell you that the Major did not meet his death at the hands of the Silver Troika. Therein lay the real reason of my failure to save him after getting through to his assistance. I was beaten by the unknown quantity existent in the case, a quantity for which I could not possibly have been expected to look. There was yet another dark chapter in Major Whittaker's life of which we were all ignorant. What it was exactly, I don't know now. I will admit that quite frankly. I have only the glimmering of an idea."

"Mr. Bathurst"—Mrs. Whittaker half-rose from her chair and there was a note of imploring appeal in her voice easily recognisable by everybody present—"if you are not sure of your facts, as you hint to us, must you—is there any need for you to—"

She paused, at a loss for words to express her protest adequately, and all of them who listened looked at Anthony to see what the effect was that she had produced upon him. He shook his head in undoubted sympathy with her.

"I am sorry, Mrs. Whittaker, and you must know that I appreciate how you feel. That enables me to extend to you a full measure of sympathy. But although, as I said a moment ago, I have only the glimmering of an idea, that glimmering is sufficiently strong and steady for me to follow it faithfully until it leads me to the truth. It will be a lighthouse to me as I follow it—certainly not a will-o'-the-wisp. You see the difference?"

"Very well, Mr. Bathurst," she conceded. "If it must be, it must be, I suppose."

"Very well," continued Anthony, "I will now return to the night that Major Whittaker died. With regard to the incidents that led up to his death, I am able to speak with certainty, for I was with him—close to him—for some time before his collapse. I had therefore ample opportunity to observe everything that went on round about him. Major Whittaker's death was not encompassed by the Silver Troika—I deliberately repeat the statement that I made just now. It was brought about by an agency, the existence of which even he could scarcely have suspected. It took me a considerable time to see the truth, and even then I was materially assisted by those who should have hindered me, who should have done their best to prevent me seeing it. I refer to the criminals themselves, for there are, I feel sure, two people implicated. They made the usual mistake—the mistake that is invariably made in matters of this kind. They showed their hand unmistakably for one brief instant perhaps and from that moment I have been on their track. This morning Sir Roderick Hope confirmed my suspicions and I am able to say that my case is complete. Perhaps it would be better for me to say almost complete, for I do not know how long it will be—"

There came a tap at the door.

"Come in!" cried Mr. Bathurst.

All stared wonderingly to see the nature of the unwelcome interruption. Miss Whittingham entered. She made the usual apologies for such an entrance, crossed to Anthony and said something to him in the lowest of voices. The company saw him nod approvingly and his face flush a little. They heard him mutter something under his breath—after she had walked away from him again and made her exit—and to Peter Daventry's quick ears the word that Mr. Bathurst used sounded very much like "Good!" But whatever it was, it was soon lost, for the speaker took up the threads again.

"I was about to say, when Miss Whittingham disturbed me, that I do not know—"

Once again he was destined not to complete his sentence, for there came a second tap at the door. This time Mr. Bathurst rose, walked to the door and opened it. The maid Fothergill stood there with a telegram upon a salver.

"Yes?" said Anthony. "What is it?"

"A telegram, sir," replied the maid, "for somebody here, sir. I know he's here—I saw him come in."

"Deliver it then by all means," said Anthony with evident impatience, "and please be as quick as you can about it."

Fothergill tripped across the room and handed the telegram to Coppinger, at the same time pointing to the name on the envelope.

"Excuse me, gentlemen," he said, as he opened the buff envelope. "I'm afraid this is bad news." He read the message in a tense silence. Then he looked at Anthony standing at Colonel Fane's side and spoke almost carelessly. "I am sorry, sir, but I am called away at once. Will you excuse me?"

"Certainly, Coppinger, and many thanks for your help."

The carrier followed Fothergill quickly across the room and out of the door. As it closed behind them, there came a piercing scream and a torrent of oaths, to be followed by the noise of a falling body and of yet another scream. The occupants of the library were momentarily spellbound, Anthony Bathurst standing in the middle of the room with the gleam of excitement in his eyes. Suddenly the door opened. A man in the uniform of an Inspector of Police stood on the threshold. He looked round the room until he caught Anthony's eye.

"All right, Mr. Bathurst," he said. "Everything according to plan."

"Good!" said Anthony. He then turned to the others. "Ladies and gentlemen, this is Inspector Webster from Holmedale police-station. He has just arrested the murderer of the late Major Whittaker and also a lady who will be charged with being an accessory before the fact. You knew them as Coppinger and Fothergill, but I rather fancy that they will prove to be a Mr. and Mrs. Forrester." He picked up the telegram that its reader had crumpled up and let fall upon the floor. He smoothed it out. "At any rate," he added, "the gentleman in question certainly answers to the name."

CHAPTER XXIX
MR. BATHURST SUMS UP

"SIT DOWN, Colonel," said Mr. Bathurst, "next to Mr. Lovell. You, Neville, take that chair at the side of Mr. Daventry, You, Satterthwaite, stay there, will you? I've heard from Inspector Webster—about half-an-hour ago. Our man has confessed, which will ease matters considerably from the point of view of the prosecution. It was murder for revenge, so I understand from the Inspector. The murderer claims to have avenged his brother, who served under the late Major Whittaker in France. According to his story, Whittaker shot his brother down in cold blood for not advancing in the face of very heavy German fire in the spring of 1917. At the time the regiment seethed with the story, for the man was very popular with everybody. The news was carried home to the elder Forrester by two regimental chums of his brother, who swore to him that young Forrester had been already hit and was in a semi-dazed condition at the time when the Major shot him down like a dog. Forrester—it was his only brother, so he says, and the loss hastened the end of both his father and mother—vowed that he would avenge his brother if it took him fifty years of his life and every penny of his money. He traced his enemy up here and took a small business in Holmedale in order to be close to him. That was about a year ago. A few months after he came, he deliberately began to chum up with Neville here. Neville has already told me that, haven't you, Neville?"

"Quite true, Mr. Bathurst," confirmed Neville. "He used to make a point of talking to me whenever the opportunity came."

"Exactly. And when Mrs. Whittaker had a vacancy arise among the maids here, he recommended Fothergill to you and you passed the recommendation along to Mrs. Whittaker. About seven months ago, I think. Anyhow, it doesn't matter. Fothergill arrived. What actually occurred was Mrs. Forrester arrived. It may be a shock for you, Satterthwaite, but I'm afraid it's the truth."

Satterthwaite made no reply.

"An old game that," put in Henry K. Lovell, "and usually as easy as fallin' off a log. Surprisin' how they fall for it. You got chirrupin' after somebody else's Sheba, Mr. Satterthwaite."

"That is so," admitted Anthony. "But Mrs. Whittaker was satisfied with the new maid—that was all that counted. From that moment onwards, Forrester started his campaign of revenge in deadly earnest. He was extremely like his dead brother physically and when he put on khaki the resemblance became even more pronounced. He determined to play with his quarry as a cat tortures a mouse. He commenced to haunt him in more ways than one. He confesses to writing to him anonymously, accusing him of murdering young Forrester, as a start-off. Then, having prepared the Major's mind, as it were, for further assaults, he appeared to him—you can see the idea—'back from the grave.' We have heard from Mrs. Chamberlain, the cook, that the Major on one occasion was very rattled at the apparition of this young fellow of his own regiment whose life he had taken all those years before and whom he had such cause to remember. The whisper with which the regiment had buzzed was, after all this time, assuming more definite and larger proportions. But Forrester was content to bide his time. He had determined to kill Whittaker without the slightest suspicion falling upon him, when suddenly the time came when he was forced to act. The Silver Troika appeared, bitter enemies of *his* enemy. If he didn't kill the Major soon, there would be no Major to kill."

"Just a minute, Bathurst." It was Colonel Fane who spoke. "How did he know of the Silver Troika?"

"From Neville, Colonel. Neville was indiscreet and will, I am sure, be the first to admit it. When my aid was requested, Neville—acting for Mrs. Whittaker—roped in Forrester to help to get me here and told him some of the story at least. Because of that leakage of information, I was trailed from the moment I set foot in Liverpool."

"But what I can't understand," insisted Peter Daventry, "is this. How did the Troika know you'd come by water? That beats me properly. How could they possibly—"

"I explain your point in this way, Daventry. Forrester didn't want the President and Co. to kill his man for him, but he didn't mind them giving him hell in other ways. He put the Troika wise (as Mr. Lovell here would have it) to the fact that I was coming down to Swallowcliffe Hall. The 'President' thought the letter had come from Neville, but he was wrong. I was watched by another Russian agent from the day that I received Mrs. Whittaker's appeal, followed down to North fleet, from where I started, the name of my boat noted, the information forwarded on, and as a result the deputation met me when I put my foot on shore. Quite a simple matter, wasn't it?"

"You've hit it, Mr. Bathurst," contributed Lovell.

"That's a sure thing."

"But it helped me, that did," acknowledged Anthony, "for the very reason that it proved to me conclusively that there was somebody—supposedly on the Major's side—who very obviously wasn't. So you see I started in the happy condition of being forewarned, and you know what that means." He smiled and turned to Neville. "If it interests you, I suspected *you* at first, Neville, and my suspicions grew when I knew you didn't mind deceiving me."

Neville reddened at the accusation.

"How do you mean, sir? I don't know that I—"

"Come, come, Neville! What about the mythical papers, minute-books, for which the Silver Troika hungered! How long do you think I believed that? I had to force your hand and theirs to discover only part of the truth. When you lied to me, I—"

"Lied to you, Mr. Bathurst?"

"I set a trap for you, Neville, and you blundered into it. The night upon which you were supposed to have watched for the Troika before my arrival, you saw, according to the Major's concocted story, the 'President' and Loronoff on the courts. I varied that tale to you purposely, substituting the name of Verensky for that of Loronoff. You fell into the trap badly. You claimed to have seen Verensky, because you didn't know what the Major had told me—it was all the same to you. You also denied all knowledge of the Forrester incident on the night of the storm—of which you must have known."

The man flushed again and nodded.

"I remember you asking me about the night I was supposed to have watched, sir, now you mention it. But you see I didn't know quite what to do—or say."

Mr. Bathurst went on.

"I might even have been inclined to have suspected the bona-fides of the whole thing. But I saw enough from my bedroom window to convince me that the Troika were after something, and I also had my experience with them in Little Knype Wood upon which to reflect. Then something happened that directed my attention away from Neville. *You* entered the picture, Satterthwaite."

The milkman shifted his feet uneasily.

"I never reckoned I'd get—"

Anthony interrupted him.

"I don't mean when you got the bang on the head. I will come to that later. I refer to an occasion before that. I overheard the fragment of a conversation between you and one of the maids. But at the time I didn't know it was you. I couldn't see the man—I could only just hear his voice. But the girl to whom he was talking was warning him against an absent third person. 'He'll stick at nothing' was one of the phrases she used in connection with him but no doubt you regarded him as no more than an ordinary rival for the lady's attentions. I had occasion several times afterwards to remember it, for I was able to identify you as the man I heard talking. When Colonel Fane recognised you as Major Whittaker's milkman after you had been attacked, my mind went back to an oddly-familiar noise that I had heard when you left the girl to whom you were talking on this first occasion. The noise was the jangling together of milk-cans! I had heard it from a fair distance and had been unable to identify it properly. After you came Mr. Lovell here. For a long time I couldn't place him in the affair at all. But I was able to satisfy myself eventually that he was antagonistic to the Silver Troika. On the assumption, that is, that he who was not for them was against them." He turned towards Peter Daventry. "You remember how Mr. Lovell cleared when he heard the Troika people approaching, don't you?"

Lovell grinned, showing his even, white teeth.

"That's true, Mr. Bathurst. I beat it good and hard."

Anthony smiled in companionship.

"Well, I determined to wait to assess you properly, which I did. That brings me to the Major's death. You all remember it—there is no need for me to recapitulate what happened. But the chief point on to which I froze was this. There were undoubted rage and disappointment in the 'President's' face and eyes when he first discovered that Whittaker was dead. I felt certain of it! It was a position that I tried hard to abandon, but my reason told me all the time that it was impossible for me to do so. *Another agency had committed the crime!* Not only were the questions now who and why, but very much more so even—how? I attempted to revive in my mind everything the dead man had done, for my thoughts were turning now to poison. I considered almost every possibility, even to that cigarette of yours, Colonel Fane, that he had smoked just previously. I knew that he had been writing before his death. Was it possible that the poison had been conveyed to him in any way out of this? Whilst I was questing here and there—backwards and forwards, as it were—the murderers betrayed themselves! They stole one of the three letters that Whittaker had written! When I considered this I felt certain that I was on the track. The maid who is no doubt Mrs. Forrester saw me take them from the desk that night and entered my bedroom to get the important one. It was vital for them to have it, because their secret was in it and, moreover, it must not be delivered to the people to whom it had been addressed. Happily, I was able to remember that address. Here is the letter in question, gentlemen. Its envelope is our chief concern." He produced what Sir Roderick Hope had handed to him. "Do you see this gummed flap?" said Mr. Bathurst, indicating it as he spoke. "This envelope—already addressed to the firm where the dead Forrester had been employed before he joined up—was sent by the murderer to the Major enclosed with a letter that purported to come from the firm. See how it has been folded? It asked, I should say, for particulars of the man's death, judging by the Major's reply. This practically made certain that Whittaker would answer the letter himself, for the gummed flap, gentlemen, had been skilfully treated with aconitine, one-sixteenth of a grain of which has been known to cause death. Forrester incidentally has had an extensive training in chemistry. He tells Webster he was a dispenser at one of the London hospitals. When the Major licked the poisoned flap of the envelope that he was almost certain to use, the younger Forrester's death was avenged! Diabolically clever, wasn't it? When Sir Roderick Hope confirmed my suspicions in this direction, I began to move, and the move I made next was the obvious one. It was to call upon the people, the address of whom had been on the envelope."

Lovell nodded agreement.

"Sure! That was bound to bring you out somewhere, and you had to find out where!"

"That's what I thought, Mr. Lovell, but in the meantime something else had happened that meant a great deal. I refer to the attack on Satterthwaite in the Hall grounds, which I naturally connected at once with the threat that I had previously overheard. Luckily I was able to pick up two definite clues that arose out of it. The first was a lady's glove, dropped close to where the injured man lay. It all fitted, you see! Was this the something at which he wouldn't stick, as I had heard predicted? Now the glove that I had found was very small—certainly under average size. The maid with the smallest hands was Fothergill! I determined to watch her carefully. The second clue was the blow which had been inflicted upon Satterthwaite—there was no doubt that it had been made by a heavy, blunt instrument. Like a flash, it came home to me. Coppinger had been armed with a truncheon for our watch upon the Silver Troika—I had seen it in his pocket. Had he been on his way home and found Satterthwaite paying attentions to Fothergill and attacked him? Was the carrier the man the maid had mentioned? As I toyed with the idea, I found it gradually grow in attractiveness. Again, who was he? Neville, I found, knew nothing real about him and he seemed to turn up in most places connected with the conundrum. I found myself saying, 'Is he a Forrester link?' You see to where I'm leading?"

The Colonel indicated that he did by a movement of the head.

"Yes, I see. You were still keen on that then?"

"Well, it needed to touch somewhere, didn't it? At Thornton and Jackson's, the firm to whom the fatal letter had been addressed, I ran into my first real Forrester. He had been employed there before the war. I was getting warm with a vengeance. I knew I was at last getting the threads into my hands. On my way home, after arranging for our friend to be out, I made a burglarious entry into his unpretentious premises. A search gave me something for which I had hoped, but had hardly been optimistic enough to expect to find. He had kept his weapon—to gloat over his success possibly. This!" Anthony touched the envelope again. "I don't know what he wrote to the Major that purported to come from the dead soldier's employers, but here is Whittaker's reply."

They listened attentively as Mr. Bathurst read it.

> "Swallowcliffe Hall,
> Near Buttercross, LANCS.
> August 14th.

Sirs,

In reply to yours of the 12th inst. relative to the death upon active service of your late servant, Pte. T. Forrester of the Northshire Regiment, I beg to inform you that he was killed by gunfire during a counterattack upon a German trench. There is no truth in the rumour to which you refer and I cannot understand it cropping up all these years after. With regard to the memorial you suggest, I shall be pleased to subscribe upon receiving further particulars.

> Faithfully yours,
> GUY S. WHITTAKER, (Major.)"

"Whittaker answered it, you see, and went to his death. Now, I said to myself again, who is our friend? It didn't matter very much. As I knew I could get him whenever I liked, for he was secure, as he thought, in the fortress of his own cunning, I made up my mind to get the Silver Troika business settled first, which we did, as you are all aware. I also arranged for the man I wanted to meet you, Daventry, on the morning after. He was unsuspecting and curiosity and exultant appreciation of his triumph brought him over. Vanity's a big trait in the temperament of most murderers, you know. But I undertook a little experiment. If it came off, it settled everything—if it failed, nothing was lost by it. I had a telegram sent to our man, addressed to him here as Forrester. The message was, 'Get away at once. All is known. Thornton and Jackson.' I arranged with Miss Whittingham that this should be handed in to Fothergill by the telegraph-boy, and to Fothergill only. If he were a Forrester, as I suspected, she would scent danger at once and deliver it to him by hook or by crook. You remember that this was exactly what she did do and

Webster and his man were quick to complete matters. I had put the case to the Inspector in Holmedale the night before, and if certain things occurred, he knew how to act."

Henry K. Lovell rose and stretched himself.

"Good for you, Mr. Bathurst! But there's still one more little matter for you and me to settle. And that's a sure thing. Otherwise I'm still hangin' round like a bimbo. Where's the jools for the Grand Duke? That's what's gettin' my goat. Where do we stand, you and I?"

Mr Bathurst's eyes twinkled.

"I've spoken to Mrs. Whittaker, Mr. Lovell, and the Crown Jewels of the Romanoffs—or what is left of them—are at present at her bank. I have given them to her and suggested that she lodged them there. But only temporarily! She will be pleased to interview you to-morrow with regard to the matter. I can assure you, from what she has told me, that she has no desire to retain the jewels in her possession. So you will not return empty-handed to the Grand Duke, after all."

Lovell let loose his finest smile and held out his hand. "Put it there, Mr. Bathurst! If ever you come to little old New York, whatever you do, be sure you—"

"Look out for the Silver Troika, Mr. Lovell." Anthony smiled a warning. "As *you'll* have to, without a doubt."

Lovell smiled back and his eyelid drooped in the direction of Peter Daventry.

"Waal," he observed, "that isn't quite what I meant, but there's one thing! If you met any of 'em, it would be a sure difficult job not to recognise them, now wouldn't it? They ain't no Goldylocks."

THE END